SHAMELESS SEDUCTRESS . . .

April slipped between the sheets and lay her head on Peter's shoulder. Slowly, her soft white hand caressed his hairy chest, moving down over his hard, flat stomach. She put her mouth over his nipple and began tickling it with her tongue.

Despite all his determination, Peter felt himself start to respond, but he'd be damned if he'd do anything to encourage her, he kept telling himself.

She began to nibble at his earlobes, then her tongue licked the side of his neck, moved over his broad, muscled shoulders and back to the pouting nipples on his chest. His whole body was drawn taut as her lips continued downward. She eased away the sheet and when she reached his navel she paused long enough to get out of her filmy nightdress.

He couldn't help himself, he found. A deep, almost tearful sigh escaped his lips as her creamy, smooth breasts brushed his groin. His rigidity jutted up between them as he pinched shut his eyes and surrendered to his own lust.

Moving as if under the control of some other's will, he began to writhe and moan under the hot sensations her mouth was producing. He tried desperately to unleash the torrid lava that bubbled deep down inside him and have it done and over with. Her lips were tormenting his flesh and he never wanted the delicious torment to end yet, he found himself contradicting: part of him wanted to be away; the other part wanted to stay forever. . . .

Also by Jessica Stuart:

THE MOONSONG CHRONICLES
DAUGHTERS OF MOONSONG

SINS OF MOONSONG

Jessica Stuart

PINNACLE BOOKS   NEW YORK

This is a work of fiction. All the characters and events portrayed in this book are fictional, and any resemblance to real people or incidents is purely coincidental.

SINS OF MOONSONG

Copyright © 1982 by Ben All, Inc.

An original Pinnacle Books edition, published for the first time anywhere.

First printing, February 1982

ISBN: 0-523-41169-3

Cover illustration by Norm Eastman

Printed in the United States of America

PINNACLE BOOKS, INC.
1430 Broadway
New York, New York 10018

SINS OF MOONSONG

Part One

San Francisco—1891

Prologue

Lydia Moonsong stretched on tiptoe, trying to see Peter MacNair among the crowd of passengers waiting for the gangplank to be lowered.

There—yes, there he was! She waved, but could not tell if he had seen her. Well, surely he wouldn't have sent her the cablegram telling her of his arriving home if he had not intended for her to meet him.

It was odd, receiving the other cablegram, the one from April, the very same day Peter was to arrive from China. It had come only a short while before she'd left the house. Lydia took her daughter's cable from her pocket and read it again: "Coming home. Stop. Will advise when. Stop" was all it said, except for her name.

David was dead; Peter's cable had told her that. April was coming home, but not with Peter. What did it all mean, she wondered for perhaps the hundredth time? She hoped Peter could explain some of it to her.

Someone touched her elbow and Lydia turned, meaning to excuse herself. "Raymond!" she cried, surprised to find the husband April had abandoned in Paris standing beside her. "But I thought you were in Europe."

"I just arrived back," Raymond said, taking her arm in a proprietary manner. "Mrs. Clary, your secretary, told me you were here. Expecting a shipment?"

"I—no, I was looking for someone—a friend," she said, glancing back toward the ship. The gangplank was down and the passengers were beginning to file off; there was no sign, however, of Peter.

"I'll wait with you," Raymond said. "I've been so eager to see you that I couldn't stand to wait around for you to return to the office. Is your friend coming?"

Lydia scanned the crowds, but Peter seemed to have disappeared. Perhaps . . . but then she caught a glimpse of Lorna MacNair and a tall man with sandy hair—Peter—embracing her.

She felt a raging deep inside her but forced it back. She gave Raymond a helpless smile. "No, I suppose she isn't on this ship after all," Lydia said as the last of the passengers trickled ashore. She shrugged. "But then she did say there was a possibility she would have to catch a later one."

Raymond gave her a peculiar look, but didn't argue. He took her arm instead and began to lead her through the crowd toward where he had a carriage waiting.

In the distance, Peter caught a glimpse of Lydia leaving with the Frenchman. He turned his wife carefully away so that Lorna would not see them as they got into the carriage. It had been the merest bad luck that his secretary had taken it upon herself to inform Lorna of his arrival.

4

The merest luck too, he supposed, that he had seen that Lydia was with the Frenchman before he'd dashed down the gangplank and seized her in his arms as he had been burning to do. A pretty kettle of fish that would have been—her with her latest suitor on her arm, and Lorna there to watch the entire debacle.

"The carriage is this way," Lorna was saying. "Heavens, what a mob . . . do you see someone you know?"

Peter watched as Lydia's carriage disappeared away from the dock. He gave his head a shake and started resolutely in the direction Lorna had indicated. "No, no one," he said.

As they settled themselves in the brougham Lorna studied her husband for a moment. "You are looking very tired, Peter." She put her hand on his arm.

Peter tactfully reached for his handkerchief, moving from beneath her touch. "I am feeling very tired," he said, ignoring her angry frown.

"I must admit, Peter, that I am completely at a loss to understand why you did not tell me you were arriving home today. And why isn't David with you?" She saw his expression darken, as it often did when he wanted to shut her out. "I know we aren't exactly the ideal married couple, Peter, but David is my son and I am still your wife; I feel entitled to some courtesy, after all. You could at least have written during all the time you've been in China."

Her presence, the very sound of her voice, irritated him. He twisted the handkerchief angrily. She had to be told about David and he decided now would be as good a time as any. Peter leaned

5

his head back against the seat and closed his eyes. "David isn't coming home," he said simply.

"What? What do you mean, David isn't coming home?"

Peter let out a sigh. He turned and looked at her. "I'm sorry, Lorna. David is dead."

He watched the color drain from her face. "Dead?" she breathed as though not understanding the meaning of the word. She kept staring at him, not believing what he'd said.

"He was caught taking something from the palace, the penalty for which is death." He would never tell her the horrible way he'd been put to death.

Lorna sat quite still, staring at him. Then a long, low, agonizing moan came from the depths of her being as she collapsed against the side of the carriage. She sat, not crying, just moaning the terrible, torturing pain that was gripping her heart.

"David was trying to help me," Peter admitted softly as he bowed his head under the weight of his guilt. He fumbled with the handkerchief in his hand, looking at it as though it were some odd object. "He knew about the financial trouble the company is in and he thought he would be able to help by taking one of the Empress's scents, which we could then duplicate."

Lorna suddenly stiffened, her eyes blazing. "Just as that odious Lydia Moonsong did! Damn you both to hell!" she shouted. "I'll kill that evil woman with my bare hands. I'll kill her, I tell you, if it is the very last thing I ever do. . . . I swear I will."

Peter closed his eyes, trying to let the sound of the carriage wheels drown out his wife's voice.

6

Lorna seethed. "It was that horrible woman who put the idea into your head before you left to find David. I know you saw her."

"Stop it, Lorna. Lydia had nothing to do with what happened. David wanted to help when he learned of the company being near bankruptcy. It was his concern for you and me and the children that led him to do what he did."

"And you said nothing to dissuade him?" she accused.

He passed his fingers across his brow. It was true, he hadn't tried to prevent David, but then would Lorna herself have done any differently? She was too accustomed to money to ever be without it, at whatever risk. "I tried to point out the dangers, of course. There was nothing more I could do."

Lorna turned on him. She started to argue, but a terrible sobbing poured out of her as she collapsed against him.

The feel of her was uncomfortable, yet he put a consoling arm about her shoulders. The long weeks overland and at sea had taken the sharp edge off David's death, dulling it to a gnawing ache. As he held his wife and pined over his loss, he suddenly thought of Lydia again. He had to see her.

"I must go to the office," Peter told Lorna as the carriage pulled up the curved drive of their Nob Hill mansion.

She clutched his arm. "Peter, please."

He saw the need in her eyes, the pleading, but tactfully eased himself away. "We're almost broke, Lorna. I've made some contacts on my way from China. I can't allow them to get cold." He felt her grip tighten. "I'll be back as soon as I can get away, I promise."

"Forget the company for today, Peter. While you were away I made some arrangements for money."

"I told you I didn't want you to go to your family," he said sternly. "I got us into this mess and I will get us out."

She let herself go limp and removed her hand. Her tears filled her eyes. Her voice went hard. "You are going to HER, aren't you?"

Peter started to get out of the carriage, saying nothing.

As he helped her down she said it again. "You are going to Lydia. I can see it in your face."

He gave her a granite-like look. "I will be home as soon as I can." He got back into the carriage and rode off down the drive, leaving Lorna standing alone staring after him.

Lydia was alone in her office when Peter walked in. The moment he got close to her, inhaled her haunting aroma, and saw her exquisite beauty, the old weakness grew inside him, making him tremble with desire. He looked at her and found himself once more in that shabby Chinese village, rescuing a shy sixteen-year-old girl from the amorous fumblings of a young lout in a bamboo grove.

"Thank you for coming to meet the ship," Peter said. Anger tugged at the corners of his mouth. "I didn't expect you to invite the Frenchman as part of my welcoming committee."

Lydia put aside the accounts she'd been studying. "Nor did I expect to have to share your home-coming with your wife."

"That was accidental. My secretary told her."

Lydia found herself smiling. "We should do something about our efficient secretaries. That is precisely how Raymond happened to join me on the dock." She came around the desk. The grief of David's death was etched on Peter's handsome face, but she could neither think of anything to say nor know whether she should say anything at all.

"A drink?" she asked, motioning toward the liquor cabinet in the corner of her beautifully appointed office.

Peter shook his head and kept gazing deep into her eyes.

A moment later she found herself in his arms, crying over his loss. "Your cable . . . David . . ."

"He is dead, Lydia. Executed. You know the Chinese."

"Oh, dear God. If only they would have listened to us. Ke Loo . . ."

"It wasn't Ke Loo," Peter said. He told her of his meeting with David and how David failed to do what Lydia had once succeeded in doing. "The Empress was quick to punish him."

Lydia began to shake, suddenly remembering the night she and April had fled the Dragon's palace and had seen the head of the concubine who'd helped them escape, impaled on a pole in the courtyard.

As if reading her mind Peter said, "I buried David intact in the American legation cemetery."

"Peter," Lydia wept, groping for some words to comfort him, knowing there were none.

9

He let her cry for the both of them, then tilted her face up to his. "We've lost them, Lydia. Your daughter and my son. We've lost them. I don't think April will ever return now."

Lydia sniffed back her tears and frowned up at him. "But I received a cable from her just today. It said she is coming home and would let me know when to expect her." She fumbled in her pocket and handed him the message.

Peter read it and shook his head. "I don't understand. David told me April had been restored to her royal station as Ke Loo's daughter . . . a Manchu princess. David was going to try and force April to leave with him, but . . ." He sighed. "I wouldn't put too much hope in that cable, Lydia, unless April is coming on orders of the Empress—and we know what that means. No, dear, I'm afraid we've both lost. April is where and what she has always wanted to be. I think it would be best if we just tried to forget."

"April can't remain in China, Peter. We both know that. She has as much of my blood in her veins as she does Prince Ke Loo's. The Dowager Empress will never forget that, regardless of how many privileges and honors she grants the girl." She forced back the tears. "I know her well, Peter. Believe me when I say that April is more *me* than she wants to accept." She looked at the cable. "No. April will come home. Maybe not tomorrow, but she'll come home."

Chapter 1

CHINA—THREE YEARS LATER

Something was wrong. The signal had not come, which meant that the Empress's soldiers were still watching the escape route. If the way·had been unguarded she and little Adam would have been on their way to Shanghai harbor an hour ago, April told herself.

She heaved a sigh, and in the darkened room rose from the windowseat and lifted Adam onto her lap. "I'm sorry, darling," April said as she hugged her three-year-old son. "We won't be leaving tonight either."

The little boy yawned and put his arms about her neck. "Why won't the soldiers let us leave, Mama?"

"Because the great Empress wants us to stay with her in the palace."

"Will they cut off our heads then?"

A shudder ran through her body as April remembered what had happened to Adam's father. One day she would have her revenge on all those responsible for David's execution, including the Dragon Empress herself. She remembered the vow of vengeance she'd made that gray day four

11

years ago when she had stood over David's grave. She had sought refuge in the American legation, never imagining her refuge would wind up being her prison. Her need to escape to America and make her mother and David's father suffer for what they'd caused was as great now as before—greater. The years had only increased her bitterness.

Moving through the dark room she'd come to know so well, she carried Adam to the trundle bed in the alcove, undressed him, and tucked him snugly beneath the covers. Slowly, and with a sinking heart, she unpacked the small portmanteau.

"Four years," she said as she went back to the window and looked out at the deserted compound surrounded by the high Tartar wall. The moon was high and full and deep yellow in the black sky, adding to the eeriness of the night. It had been a similar night four years before when she'd climbed the bare apricot tree that leaned over the garden wall of the Imperial Palace and went to swear vengeance over her husband's grave.

But her plans for vengeance had had to be postponed. The weather had turned treacherous and she'd found herself pregnant with David's child. To complicate matters she'd left her travel documents in the palace. The American minister had told her it would take months to obtain new ones—if they *could* be obtained at all.

"You say you lost your travel papers?" the minister had said.

"Yes." It was a lie. She'd forgotten them in her hurry to escape the Forbidden City and there was no possible way of going back for them without again becoming the Empress's prisoner.

The minister then looked uncomfortable. "To be perfectly candid, my dear, there is no way of disguising the fact that you are . . . err . . . Chinese," he'd said. "Your father is Prince Ke Loo, I understand. Surely you are familiar with the problems in Washington and the Chinese Exclusion Act."

"But my mother is an American. I lived in America. Mother is very prominent in San Francisco society. She owns a very large cosmetic enterprise. Surely you could cable her and she would verify whatever needs verification."

The minister shrugged and began shuffling through the stack of papers on his desk. "The Oriental Exclusion Act is enforced most strictly. The odds are very much against your petition, I fear."

It took a year before her application was officially and decidedly denied, and by then her situation was further complicated by the birth of her son. She knew they'd never bothered to contact her mother because she herself had written her mother and her letters had gone unanswered, which Lydia would never have done. The legation was filled with ambitious politicians who didn't want to make waves with their superiors in Washington, D. C., and April was positive her letters home were never put into the dispatch pouch. China was a subject Washington did not want to be reminded of. A revolution was brewing and both sides preferred to pretend to ignore it.

What she thought were wasted years only resulted in a deeper need for revenge. The delays

13

only multiplied her vengefulness until it became an obsession. She spent her days constantly dreaming of the glorious satisfaction that awaited her in America. First she would avenge herself on David's father, the man who'd induced his own son to steal from the Forbidden City. Making Peter MacNair suffer would make Lydia suffer, for as much as her mother protested, she was desperately in love with Peter MacNair.

"You'll never have him, Mother," April swore as she leaned her forehead against the windowpane. "You will both pay dearly for killing my husband."

A sudden wind whipped across the compound, setting the lanterns swinging. Her eyes began to sting as she thought of David lying in the cold grave just beyond the rise. April gave her head a hard shake. She would never again think about the execution, the ax severing David's young, handsome head from his body.

You must never look back, she told herself, as she pulled her thoughts away from that horrible scene and turned from the window. She'd cried the last of her tears; now she wanted only to punish those who'd killed her only love, a love that she would never replace.

The baby moved restlessly, kicking aside the covers. April retucked him in and kissed his tousled head. His forehead felt warm to the touch. She smiled down at him. He looked so like his father and other than the need for retribution, little Adam was her only reason to keep herself alive.

She paced the room, wondering for the thousandth time when she could get away, reminding herself that if Edward Wells hadn't been appointed as an embassy official last year, she'd never have been given any hope of leaving China.

She heard the quick, careful footsteps on the stairs and hurried to light the lamp on the table. A moment later, Eddie tapped on her door.

"They're thicker than gnats," he said breathlessly as he came into the room, taking her in his arms. He kissed her. "I'm sorry, darling, but the Empress's men would have overtaken us before we'd gone more than a mile. Our scouts reported that there are three of them to every one of us."

"Oh, Eddie," April moaned dejectedly as she leaned against him. "Will I ever be allowed to escape?"

"Of course you will." He tilted her face up to his. "I arranged for the falsified travel papers for you and Adam, didn't I?" He smiled. "You don't think for a minute I'm going to let that old Dragon Empress catch you after all the trouble I've gone through?"

"Oh, Eddie," she said, hugging him. "It's just that the time drags so. And since the Empress knows where I am, she will never let me leave China."

"Don't talk like that. They'll tire of guarding the road. New skirmishes with those Boxers are breaking out more frequently. One day the old witch will have to send her soldiers off to put down an uprising and we'll be free as birds."

"I feel so guilty about your staying to help me now that your tour of duty is finished."

"My job in Washington will always be there. Father will see to that. I've explained that I've been delayed. He bought the lie just as easily as he bought all my others." She knew he was refer-

15

ring to having official entry papers issued naming himself, Edward Wells, as Adam's father.

April felt no guilt at having seduced him when he first arrived at the legation. She would have seduced Satan if it meant settling her score with Peter and Lydia. As he embraced her she felt his need for her. "Stay," she whispered.

"I shouldn't," he answered, glancing toward the door.

She knew he did not want her to send him away—not yet. "Please," she urged, placing her leg between his thighs. "Adam is sound asleep. You can stay with me for just a little while."

April knew he didn't love her anymore than she loved him. Eddie Wells was a rake, a wastrel, the only son of a prominent politician who indulged his son anything. The liaison that had developed between herself and Eddie was almost like a game they both got pleasure in playing.

"April," he murmured, as he moved her toward the bed, at the same time they were struggling out of their clothes.

She enjoyed being in his arms because it reminded her of all those pleasurable hours in David's arms. It was heavenly to close her eyes and pretend that David's hands caressed her breasts and stroked her thighs as his mouth ravaged hers.

His flesh was warm and exciting. April pulled him closer, giving herself to her fantasies as he kissed her ears, her throat, her breasts. She let him part her thighs and reveled in the exquisite sensations of penetration. She kept her eyes tightly shut and her ears deaf to all sounds. She gave herself up to the sheer physical pleasure of the act as she moved up to meet his thrusts. The rhythm of their

16

sex act increased as he moved more urgently, yet with a strange tenderness that was so reminiscent of David's lovemaking.

April gave herself over to the passion that was building higher and higher from deep inside her. She strangled the cries of ecstasy that she'd so freely vented with David; with Eddie such cries had no meaning.

He groaned as he pushed himself completely into the heat of her body and felt the flood of his passion burst out in jolting gushes of molten passion. He moaned, gasped her name, and then fell, spent and content, on top of her.

April cradled him like a child, stroking the smooth, taut muscles of his back until she felt him relax. The frightening tensions of the last several hours, the disappointment of a foiled escape were forgotten for the moment. There would be other nights. She only hoped that they would not all end like this one, as had so many earlier ones.

Eddie stirred. "Now I surely must leave you. It will be dawn in a couple of minutes." He got up and started putting on his clothes. "Get some sleep, pet. Just have patience. I made you a promise that I'd get you out of this infernal country and I will." He leaned over and pecked her mouth. "We made a bargain, you and I. You've been keeping your part magnificently and I swear to you that I will keep mine—or die in the attempt."

He meant it. She could tell by his voice. Scoundrel that he was, he was an honorable scoundrel, she knew, with all the romantic ideals of a teen-aged boy, which Eddie had forgotten to shed.

He paused before the mirror to tie his tie. "One

thing I can't understand, though; never could." He glanced over at her lovely face with its almond eyes and skin of pink porcelain. "You are a Chinese princess and look every bit the part. It beats me why you want to chuck away all that royalty stuff and go back to San Francisco, where Orientals are not exactly the favorite citizens."

She knew what he meant because she remembered only too well how badly she'd been treated when she lived there with her mother.

"I told you," April said. "I have a debt that needs to be paid. Besides, the Dowager Empress would only make me a prisoner, perhaps even kill me if I'm taken back inside the walls of the Forbidden City. She and my father are not particularly close."

She snuggled deeper into the covers and watched him slick back his hair with her brushes. He was a good-looking man and a very accomplished lover. She felt a stirring below her waist. The lovemaking had been too brief, but that was always the way with Eddie Wells—the one important way in which he differed greatly from David.

"But you're nevertheless a princess," he insisted with his practical American way of thinking. "A member of her family."

"In China, royal family members are the most susceptible to the High Executioner's hatchet."

He stooped and kissed her again, briefly. She had to smile to herself as she thought that "briefly" was a very appropriate word to describe him.

"The next contingent of Marines leaves in a week," he said. "If the road is clear we'll try again

to hide you and Adam in one of their caissons."
He blew her a kiss and was gone.

Left alone, April heard Adam move uncomfortably and mutter something in his sleep. She
slipped out of bed, pulling a robe about herself,
and went to his trundle bed. Again he'd kicked off
the covers and again April tucked him in. As her
hand brushed his little arm she frowned. It felt
warm. She placed her hand on his forehead. She
couldn't decide whether or not he was running a
temperature, but to be safe she'd have the doctor
look at him in the morning. It might well be just
the excitement that was making him flushed and
feverish.

As she started back to her own bed, a glint of
moonlight reflected on the silver box she'd removed earlier from her portmanteau and had left
lying atop the bureau. Unconsciously she lifted its
lid and sorted through the collection of exquisite
jewels and packets of money she'd taken when
she'd fled the palace. As she picked up the sap-
phire ring the old Empress had given her she bit
down on her lower lip to stop its quivering.

"You too, you old devil," April swore, remembering the Empress's stony face as she sat stolid
and unmoved while David was dragged to the
block. The woman she'd once revered above all
the gods would also feel the sting of her revenge
one day, April vowed. If it meant the giving of her
own life to accomplish it, the three of them—
Peter, Lydia, and the Dragon Empress Tz'u Hsi—
would suffer as they had made her suffer, April
swore.

She took up the long strands of pearls she'd

19

braided into her raven, waist-length hair that night in Paris when she and David planned their flight to China, to what they believed to be the security of her father's royal house. It all seemed so long, long ago and yet, as she gazed at her reflection in the mirror, she was pleased to see that the agonies and terrors she'd undergone had left no scars on her lovely young face. Her dark almond eyes were just as lustrous; her flawless complexion still exquisitely delicate. She'd be twenty-four in the spring. She smiled at herself, glad to see she still looked like a young girl.

Her youth and her beauty were the only weapons she had with which to fight them, she decided, as she replaced the jewels, lowered the lid, and replaced the box in the top drawer. It would take most of what she had to pay for her protection to the harbor in Shanghai and once there for passage on a ship bound for San Francisco. Once in America she would be a princess no longer. She'd be despised and demeaned as she'd been once before. She hated the city and the people in it, but that was where her enemies were and that was where she had to go. Afterward—and time being on her side—she would come back and somehow wreak her vengeance on the Dragon woman who thought herself invincible and eternal.

Again she would have to seek her father's help, April told herself. Perhaps by then he would have lost the incestuous interest he'd expressed in her. She'd learned early that in China a woman was a woman, nothing more; and being a woman was a mere commodity any man could bid for, regardless of kinship. A shudder ran through her as she thought of the way Prince Ke Loo, her father, had coveted her with his eyes. Again she gave her head a hard shake and went back toward the window.

Outside the legation compound was beginning to stir under the growing light of dawn. In the years she'd lived here she noticed the gradual dwindling of the presence of foreigners. Eddie said it was the ever growing threat of the Chinese rebels who called themselves Boxers. April couldn't understand why the Occidentals feared these Boxers, an unorganized ragtag of Chinese peasantry who wanted change, but did not know what kind. It took any peasant forever to accomplish anything so she could not see what everyone feared. There was no immediate danger.

The light in the sky heightened. April unlatched the casement window to relieve the closeness of the small room. There was a winter chill in the air and the sky was already beginning to turn slate gray. Winter was getting nearer and Peking would again be a deserted city when the royal parties retreated into the recesses of the Forbidden City, and peasants stayed sheltered in their hovels, having no need to bend under the yokes of their lords. Winter in China was a time for quiet and boredom, a time when the people, like the earth itself, turned hard and cold and slept.

"I pray I'll never see another winter here for some time to come," she said as she closed the window against the cold morning.

She went over and checked Adam's temperature again. It seemed higher. She scooped him up and carried him to her bed, then crawled in beside him, cuddling him protectively in her arms.

21

Chapter 2

The following morning April thought Adam's temperature felt still higher. It could well have been nothing more than excitement, but rather than take chances she went to find the doctor. She found Eddie instead at the bottom of the stairs leading to the doctor's quarters.

"Doctor Lemming had to go out on an emergency," Eddie told her. "Are you feeling unwell, April?"

"It's Adam. He's feverish, I'm afraid. It may be nothing, but I want to be on the safe side."

"I understand." He thought for a moment, then snapped his fingers. "There's a Chinese chap who arrived here in the compound late yesterday. He lists himself as a doctor on his travel papers. Shall I find him and send him up to your rooms?"

"I'd very much appreciate it, Eddie. Thank you."

The Chinese man who entered her rooms a while later was stocky and short, dressed in western clothes. His black hair was slicked back and he wore a wide, flat moustache. He seemed to have no neck; his round, Oriental face rested heavily on a high celluloid collar and string tie. He was carrying a small black satchel.

He bowed low. "I am Sun Yat-sen. Your child is not well, I am told," he said in almost flawless English.

"He appears to be running a temperature," April answered in Chinese, feeling the man would be more comfortable in his own language.

The man bowed again. "With your permission, Princess, I would prefer if we spoke in English. I want to perfect my knowledge of the language as much as I can before I arrive on those shores."

April stared at him. Her mind had stopped on the word *Princess*. "You know me?" she asked.

"Permit me," Sun Yat-sen said, ignoring her for a moment. He laid his hand on Adam's forehead. "I know your father, Princess, Prince Ke Loo." He took a thermometer from his case and put it under Adam's tongue, muttering childlike instructions and at the same time checking the boy's pulse.

April frowned as she watched him. It seemed incongruous that this very Western-type Oriental would be acquainted with her father. "You lived in Kalgan then, I assume?"

"No, Princess. I was born of humble parents in the Chungshan district of Kwangtung province. I met your father through mutual . . . shall we say, *friends*?"

"Has my father been ill?" April persisted, trying to make a connection between these two men of unequal stations.

Sun Yat-sen shook his head slowly. "I do not practice medicine anymore. I was coming to visit you, Princess, when I met up with Mr. Wells and his concern for your son's fever."

23

He felt the glands at the sides of Adam's neck and nodded approvingly. He glanced at April, then concentrated on the boy again. "Your father told me of your beauty. He is a man who is sometimes prone to exaggeration; I am glad in this instance he spoke truthfully."

April returned his bow. "Then I presume you have come with a message from my father?" She suddenly felt wary.

He nodded and took the thermometer from Adam's mouth, holding it up to the light from the window. "The boy is running a slight temperature, but not one of any significance. Some aspirin powder should bring it to normal."

"Thank you, I feel much relieved." She reached for her money purse.

Sun Yat-sen held up both hands and gave her what she construed to be an angry look, though he was smiling. He replaced the thermometer in the case.

An uneasiness gripped her, a sense of apprehension, as if the man had come bearing terrible news. She lifted Adam and carried him to the deep chair near the window. "You said you have a message for me from my father?"

He came closer and leaned toward her. In a low, conspiratorial voice he said, "Your father is in great danger, Princess. The Empress suspects Prince Ke Loo is plotting to overthrow the throne. She intends making you a hostage in the summer palace. Ke Loo requests that you come to him in Kalgan where he can keep you safe from the dragon's claws."

April watched him with suspicion as she let Adam squirm out of her lap. "I have no intention

24

of being made a prisoner in either palace, doctor."
She did not trust this man. It was highly possible
that he was but another agent of the Empress's
who'd come to trick her.

"The Empress, as you know, is having you
closely watched."

"I am only too well aware of that," April said.
She thought for a moment. "You know then that
my efforts to leave here have thus far been unsuc-
cessful. If the Americans can't get me safely past
the Empress's soldiers and spies, how do you propose to manage it?"

He smiled a secret, sly smile. "They are Americans. I am an Oriental and know secrets."

She definitely did not trust him. "I am going to
America," she said firmly.

He only smiled and bowed. "I, too, go to America, but unlike you, Princess, the Empress has no
plans to prevent my leaving. If she knew my mission she would most assuredly make certain I
never left China."

"Mission?"

His eyes narrowed as he smiled his enigmatic
smile. "Your father's ambitions are not far from
my own. We have that in common."

April looked surprised. "You are helping my father to unseat the Empress?"

He nodded gravely. "I go first to Hawaii to begin organizing sympathizers to our movement and
to seek financial assistance. I plan on touring the
United States, Europe, Japan—anywhere where I
can find an ear and a pocketbook that shows interest in a better China."

Her royal bearing would not permit her to believe him. It wasn't possible for her to accept such

25

a common man as a trusted respresentative of Prince Ke Loo's. Her father was of too high a noble station to put himself in league with so ordinary a fellow. Furthermore, there was something in the way he looked at her that told her he did not approve of her any more than she approved of him. She'd seen that haughty look of contempt before on men who'd made the mistake of showing their displeasure toward their betters.

"I again ask you to reconsider your leaving China, Princess," he said. "Go to your father in Kalgan. Everything can be safely arranged for you."

"No!" She said it a little too sharply and saw his face darken.

"I can only remind you that it would be most unfortunate if you fell into the hands of the Empress."

"I am already a prisoner here and would be in no better circumstances with either my father or the Empress. I have every intention of reaching Shanghai harbor and boarding a ship bound for America."

When she thought of it, it seemed her entire life had been spent in one form of prison or another, both here in China and when she had lived with her mother and then with her husband in San Francisco. She hadn't thought of Raymond, her legal husband, for a long, long time. After she and David ran off she had stopped thinking of Raymond completely. He'd been a miserable mistake into which she'd been forced. She despised him, though she did, all too often, long to see their daughter. Caroline would be almost seven now.

Sun Yat-sen brought her back to the moment. "Your father will be most disappointed in your decision to leave."

She wanted suddenly to be alone with her thoughts, and the way Sun Yat-sen was watching her made her annoyed. Again she reached for her money purse and handed him two yuan. "I insist you take this for your trouble, Dr. Sun." When he backed away and bowed again she stiffened her back. "I said I insist!"

The disdain that flooded his expression was impossible to hide. April cautioned herself again that there was something to fear in this man. When he reached out, she dropped the money into his palm. "Thank you for coming, Doctor. Now, please excuse me." She turned, picked up Adam again, who had been playing quietly with a set of wooden animals, and walked into the alcove. She did not turn until she heard the door close behind the doctor.

She let out the breath she found she'd been holding. A minute later there was a tap on the door. She was certain the man had come back. Angrily she went toward the door and yanked it open, still holding Adam tight in her arms.

Eddie Wells's eyebrows went up. "You look mad enough to bite a snake. Is anything the matter, honey?"

She let her shoulders sag. "I'm sorry, Eddie. Come in. I thought the doctor had come back."

"He angered you, obviously." He glanced at Adam. "The boy's all right, isn't he?"

"Perfectly all right. It's just that the man upset me." She told him of the message from her father.

27

"There is something very suspicious about this Dr. Sun. He looked at me as if he were sneering at me. I neither like nor trust him."

"You won't have to bother much about him after this afternoon. He's arranged for bearers to take him to Tsingtao. From there he takes a packet across the Yellow Sea to Korea and, according to his declared itinerary, he expects to cross into Japan."

"He told me he is going to Hawaii. From the route you describe he is in a rather large hurry to leave China. I suspected him of being a spy for the Empress; obviously, I was wrong. He seems too anxious to leave here."

"Well, as long as little Adam is hale and hearty that's all that matters. I think my plan for getting us to Shanghai with the Marine contingent is going to work."

"I hope so, Eddie," she said without much enthusiasm. There had been too many disappointments for her to become overly optimistic about another prospect.

"Trust me," he said gaily. "Now." He tilted her face up to his. "How would you like to go to a party tonight?"

Her heart leapt. "A party?" Her eyes went bright with excitement. "Where?"

"The British Ministry. Claude MacDonald has finally asked to be sent home. The gang decided on the spur of the moment to give him and his Lady a proper send off. It's been rather hastily thrown together, but I was expressly asked to bring you."

April had always liked the old Scotsman who headed the British legation, though almost fifteen years ago when she'd first laid eyes on Claude MacDonald she'd been frightened of his fierce moustache and flint-gray eyes.

"I'd love it," she gushed. She looked at little Adam. "But perhaps I shouldn't. Adam's fever may get worse."

"I'll have the housekeeper sit with him. And we'll be just across the compound if anything should happen."

April hesitated. "Yes, I suppose he'll be all right and it has been oh-so-long since I've been to a proper party."

"Wear something that will knock their eyes out. I want every woman there to be pea-green with envy."

April cocked an eye. "I needn't remind you that those ladies do not approve of your attentions to me. I am not deaf to gossip, you know."

"Who cares? They object because there isn't a one of them who wouldn't pay the devil for your youth and beauty."

"But not for my Chinese blood," she chided.

"Even that, if they came out looking like you." He grew serious. "You're the most exquisite creature I have ever seen, April. Are you certain you won't change your mind and come with me all the way to Washington?"

"We've spoken of this before, Eddie." She put Adam aside. "We would both be in each other's way once we got to America."

"I know," he admitted good-naturedly, "but I'd love to put my old dad in a tizzy by bringing you home with me."

April laughed. "You'd give him a heart attack."

Eddie shrugged.

29

"You're horrible." She patted his chest. "Now get out of here. If you want me to be ravishing, I will have to sort through my wardrobe for just the right dress. And for a woman, that may take the remainder of the day."

She chose the yellow silk with the elaborately embroidered chrysanthemums that cascaded from her shoulder to the hem of the train. She braided the strands of pearls into her shimmering black hair, and was not displeased with her efforts when she looked at her reflection in the full-length glass.

"Fantastic," Eddie gushed when she came down the stairs. He offered her his arm and leaned close. "Maybe we should have the party in my room," he said with a wicked wink.

"If you behave yourself, that might be agreeable but not until later. I'm in the mood for laughing and dancing."

They started toward the British legation, ignoring the coolness of the night. They didn't have far to go to reach it, a rambling building set in seven acres and housing the chancery as well. The legation district as a whole was a world within a world, which never failed to impress April, though she longed to be away from it. There was a large orange moon, white rimmed; April pulled her silk shawl about her shoulders and snuggled against Eddie.

"I know we are something of a scandal here," she said as they walked along.

"The sad part of it all is that they will have nothing to gossip about once you and I are out of here next week."

30

"You think our chances of escape are that good this time?"

"Good? They are better than they ever were. I've started thinking the way these slanty-eyed devils—" He glanced at her and stammered, remembering she herself was Oriental. "—These Chinese think," he said catching his slip. "We'll not be detected by the Empress's men this time."

"When do we leave?"

"Tuesday next."

They entered the grounds of the British legation where a cluster of dancers on the tennis court danced to the music of a Chinese band playing western tunes. Paper lanterns swayed unevenly in the tree branches, champagne corks popped, glasses clinked. Everyone was smiling, talking, laughing.

Eddie escorted April up the steps and across the wide Victorian veranda. Sir Claude MacDonald, the British minister, greeted them warmly and even embraced April, causing several of the ladies to frown in disapproval.

"April, my dear girl. I'm so pleased you could come on such short notice. Of course," he added with a laugh, "I'm surprised anyone of us came on such short notice. The boys did a bang-up job, don't you think?" He didn't wait for her to answer. Sir Claude never waited for anyone. "You look enchanting; positively enchanting," he said, offering his arm. "Come along and let me get you some refreshments. Mr. Wells can well look after himself."

The crowd in the room parted, making an aisle for them. April saw the deprecative looks that she

31

preferred to interpret as envy. She held herself aloof, unbending, reminding them all that she was of royal blood, that they were nothing.

"I remember the first time I saw you, my girl, dressed like some ragged peasant."

"A disguise," April was quick to remind him.

"An American chap, I believe it was, who rescued you and your mother from an opium den or some such place. Wasn't that it?"

"We were hiding from the Empress." She looked up at him. "I always seem to be hiding from Her Imperial Highness."

"Your mother?" Sir Claude asked. "She's well?"

"We have both been rather remiss about corresponding. Last I heard she was in excellent health and her enterprises were thriving."

"As beautiful as ever, I suspect. Beauty like hers and yours, my dear, always withstand the ravages of time." He handed her a cup of punch. "A perfume factory, isn't that your mother's occupation now?"

"Empress Cosmetics, Products Fit for Royalty," April proclaimed grandly, then laughed. "She has made a handsome fortune from what she refers to as her misadventures in China."

Sir Claude rubbed the line of his jaw. "Yes, there was a bit of gossip about the bad blood between her and the old Dragon Empress."

"Mother builds dynasties on bad blood," April said, her voice bitter and hard. She saw him look surprised at her caustic remark and smiled sweetly. "I'd like for you to ask me to dance, if that is permitted."

The old man laughed. "Like you, my dear, I was never very fond of conventions. Just like our

Scottish lassies, you've got grit and spunk. I like that in a lass." He took the punch cup from her hand. "If you are in a mood to dance with an old codger like me, then dance we shall, my girl."

Eddie strolled through the crowd, watching them move off. Again an aisle opened up for him, as if the others feared contamination from this brash American who obviously preferred Chinese women to decent Occidentals like himself.

"Ah, Edward," one of his friends from the American legation said, slapping Eddie on the back. "You've got more guts than I'll ever have." He moved his eyes toward April as she let Sir Claude embrace her and begin to dance. "Look at the other men lifting up their noses and all the time we both know they'd give their eyeballs to bed her. What does that delicate little blossom see in the likes of you?"

Eddie grinned. "Because we are both delicate little blossoms from the same tree, Phillip." He lifted his cup. "You just never took the time to learn what a sweet, innocent fellow I really am."

His friend rolled his eyes. They both started to laugh.

Chapter 3

The cold rain started early Tuesday morning, just after dawn. April bundled Adam into his quilted coat and pulled the cap flaps down over his ears. The boy's eyes were bright with anticipation; his unmistakably American face looked eager and a bit defiant.

She glanced around. The room was suddenly a friend she was seeing for the last time, a friend who'd been true in its fashion, a friend she felt she shouldn't leave. Perhaps she shouldn't go.

She gave an impatient shrug as she finished packing Adam into his cocoon of clothes, reminding herself that she'd seen too much of these rooms. Besides, there was no time to stop and think, or worry about the dangers that might be waiting outside, or the fact that tomorrow might well never come for her.

With a swift sweep of her hand she gathered up her essentials. Adam first, and then the cloth bag of jewels and money, which she slipped into the lining of her coat.

Eddie had exacted his final payment last night and had told her to meet him at the storehouse

34

next to the Marine barracks at seven o'clock. It was almost seven now. She picked up her reticule and without hesitating walked out, closing the door firmly behind her. This time she would make good her escape. She knew it.

"Are we going with the soldiers like Uncle Eddie said?" Adam asked, holding tight to April as they made their way out of the legation building.

"Yes, darling. Then when we reach the sea a ship is going to take us across the water to your grandmother's big house in San Francisco."

"Will she let us stay?"

"Of course she will." At least I hope so, April said to herself, remembering the hard feelings that had existed when she abandoned everyone in Paris.

Under the command of a young lieutenant, a contingent of Marines, about twenty, were lining up in front of the arsenal when April noticed Eddie motioning to her from the doorway to the storehouse.

He hurried her inside where a soldier was hitching a team of horses to a canvas-covered caisson, attached to which was a small cannon.

"Inside with the both of you," Eddie said cheerily. "I've thrown in some blankets and pillows to make the ride as comfortable as possible, but don't expect luxury."

"A munitions wagon?" April asked, hesitantly.

"A decoy. There aren't any weapons or ammunition inside. The Marines are picking up a load in Shanghai. The cannon is just for effect. If the Chinese decide to harass us, seeing the cannon might give them pause to reconsider."

He took Adam out of her arms and lifted him

into the wagon. As he helped April in he said, "The caisson hasn't any springs so I hope you two don't get too knocked about."

"Just so we get away." She hugged him. "I'll be only too happy to arrive black and bruised."

"I'll be riding alongside," Eddie said as he pulled on his slicker and motioned to the soldier that they were ready to move out.

April settled herself and Adam in a mound of blankets and pillows as the wagon started off. Through the flap she watched the Marines in their ponchos step out briskly, seemingly ignorant of the icy rain that slashed at their faces.

When they started through the Tartar wall, passing the red stone lions that flanked the gateway, Eddie motioned to the open canvas flap. "Better close yourselves in until we are through the city. We wouldn't want the old witch's spies getting a look at you."

April did as he asked, but deep down she had a feeling that the Empress already knew what the caisson was carrying. She only hoped the contingent of Marines and the cannon would discourage any attempt to interfere with the journey.

With the canvas closed tightly, the inside of the wagon grew hot and breathless. April listened as the rain increased to a steady downpour. As uncomfortable as she was, she was glad for the shelter.

Outside she heard the noise of the city, the chattering merchants, the clip-clop of the wooden sandals on the cobblestones. Though they were moving at a snail's pace, she and Adam were shaken and jolted from side to side. Every now

36

and then the caisson gave a terrific jerk as the wheels hit a rock or sank into a pothole.

By the time they left Peking, April was certain she would never be able to survive the trip. Once they reached a safe distance, she told herself, they would get out and walk.

Unfortunately, they never reached a safe distance. Sometime after noon, as they passed through a small bedraggled village, the lieutenant called a halt to eat and rest.

Eddie climbed into the wagon and handed April a knapsack of rations. "Strictly Marine fare. Hardly food for a princess." He grinned. He tied back the flap and allowed a breeze to waft into the dank interior. "The rain stopped," he commented.

The fresh air felt heavenly. Just as April was about to ask if he thought they were safely away there was a commotion outside. A small army of Imperial guards pulled their circle around the contingent several yards tighter.

Too late, Eddie started to draw the canvas flaps closed.

"We want the woman and boy," April heard a Chinese officer say to the Marine lieutenant.

"This is an official United States government party. You have no right to interfere or demand anything of us."

It was as if the Chinese officer had not heard. "We will take the woman and the boy. The Empress commands it."

Eddie jumped down from the wagon. "Command all you like," he said coldly. "Any rough stuff and your Empress will get a taste of American retribution."

"Please, no trouble." It was a girl's voice April heard as she crawled to the back of the wagon and looked out.

April saw the familiar face of her stepsister, Mei Fei, who sat astride a milk-white mare. Her hand rested on her officer's arm, restraining him as he reached for the hilt of his sword.

"Mei Fei!" April gasped. It had been almost four years since she had seen the girl, but there was no mistake that it was she. Though she was no more than thirteen or so, she had already blossomed into a lovely woman and looked equally as regal.

When she saw April the girl smiled broadly and spurred her animal toward the caisson. "April!" she called. "How wonderful to see you again."

April's pleasure at seeing her stepsister faded when she realized why Mei Fei was here. "It is so good to see you again, Mei Fei. I only wish we were meeting under different circumstances." She saw Mei Fei look crestfallen. "I assume you are here on orders from the Empress."

"Yes," Mei Fei admitted sadly.

"And if I refuse to come back with you?"

Eddie interrupted. "What do you mean IF? You are not going anywhere but with me to America."

The Chinese officer drew his sword. The Marines quickly reached for their weapons. A second later a new wave of Imperial soldiers came out from the stand of trees on either side of the roadway. There were at least a hundred of them, April saw, all with drawn swords and murderous looks.

The young Marine lieutenant unsnapped the holster of his side arm. "I will remind you again, sir, that this is an official United States government party. We will not be interfered with."

They were hopelessly outnumbered and April knew the young lieutenant's courage would only mean his death; in his eyes she saw that he, too, knew it.

"Wait!" April called as the lieutenant drew his pistol and backed toward where Eddie and his men had grouped beside the caisson. "There will be no slaughter on my account."

"We are taking you to Shanghai," Eddie said. "Get back inside, April."

"You are not taking me anywhere if I refuse to go. Be sensible, Eddie. There are ten to our one. You may kill a few, but they will kill all of you."

"They wouldn't dare," Eddie answered, keeping his eyes fixed on the Chinese officer.

"They would, believe me. I know my people," April assured him.

"We're Americans."

"That makes no difference to them. They'd kill their own relations if the Empress commanded it."

"That's insane."

"I'll prove it." She motioned at Mei Fei. "This girl is my stepsister, the daughter of Prince Ke Loo, heir to the throne of China," she said to him. To Mei Fei she said in English, "If I refuse to return with you to the palace and manage to escape these soldiers, what is your punishment for returning to the Empress empty-handed?"

Mei Fei shifted uncomfortably. She shrugged, finding she could not look at April.

"Tell the gentleman, Mei Fei," she insisted.

"My head would be forfeited."

"I thought as much," April said. She looked at Eddie. "There, you see? And Mei Fei is the Dowager Empress's favorite."

Eddie gaped. "She'd cut off the girl's head?" he asked with a shudder.

"As she cut off my husband's, and he, too, was a favorite for a while, having killed a man who had attempted to assassinate the Empress. That was the reward she paid him—the executioner's block. Don't you see, Eddie, that my people aren't like you? We are taught to obey the Empress regardless of what she demands, even if it means giving up our own lives. Even if you and the Marines managed to annihilate every single one of these men, they would consider it an honor to die for the Empress."

"Well, we may just give them that honor," the young lieutenant said.

"No." April climbed out of the wagon. "Come along, darling." She lifted Adam down after asking him to hand her her reticule. To Mei Fei she asked, "You brought a horse for me?"

Mei Fei motioned toward the stand of trees.

"We will go with you, sister."

The horse was brought forward.

Eddie grabbed her arm. "You are not going back! For God's sake, April, you've been waiting years for this chance."

"These men's deaths would always be on my conscience, Eddie. And I could never permit Mei Fei's sacrifice." She forced a smile. "Don't make trouble, Eddie. Go with the Marines to Shanghai." She kissed him lightly on the mouth. "I will be all right. I should have known all along that I would never be allowed to leave China without the Empress's permission. Take heart. I haven't given up. I am only returning to the Forbidden City to obtain my cousin's permission, and believe me, I will get it. Thank you for everything. Perhaps we will meet again in America."

"You're sure you want to do this, April?"

"I'm sure," she said. "Go along. I'll be fine." She smiled. She wasn't too sure about her last remark.

Eddie helped April to mount the horse, then handed up little Adam. "I hate like the devil to see you go back, April."

"I hate like the devil to be going back, but it is just only another delay. Perhaps this is what I should have done years ago."

"Take care of yourself, love."

"You too."

The Chinese officer gave a command and the small army started back toward Peking with Mei Fei riding beside April and Adam. As they reached the bend in the road April turned back in time to see the Marines regroup and to see Eddie still standing in the middle of the road. When he saw her turn he waved until she was out of sight.

April looked over at Mei Fei's sad face and gave her a bright smile. "Your head is much too lovely to fall victim to the ax blade, dear sister. Do not be sad for my sake. There is much unfinished business between me and my cousin, the Empress. It is only right that it be settled before I leave."

"It is David's child?" Mei Fei asked, looking at little Adam. "Foolish me, of course it is David's. He looks exactly like him. The amah said she thought you were with child when you ran from the palace." They rode in silence for a while. "Wu

41

Lien will be pleased to see you, April. He is, of course, with the Empress."

Wu Lien, she thought as she said his name to herself. "I am not so certain I will be pleased to see him. He was responsible for David's arrest and execution—all the while pretending to be his friend," she said bitterly, as if speaking to herself.

"He did it because he loves you, April."

"Loves me!" She tightened her hands on the reins. "I detest and despise him. Given any chance I will see that he gets repaid for what he did to Adam's father," she said, hugging the child.

"You must never let him know that, April."

"Oh, have no fears, little sister. I am an old hand at playing court politics. I know Wu Lien has the Empress's ear. I will not give him any excuse to chop off my head and exhibit it on a pole under the Dowager's balcony. In fact, once I reach the palace he would be well advised to make certain *his* head doesn't get hoisted up on that pole."

"Wu Lien has designs on making you his bride."

April laughed. "Never. I have had husbands enough . . . one dead in China, one very much alive in America, if he hasn't divorced me for deserting him and our child." She sighed. "And I would do it all again for David." There was a stinging behind her eyes. She quickly stiffened herself; then laid her cheek on little Adam's tousled head. "I would have done anything in the world for your father, little one."

She smiled as she realized the child had fallen fast asleep, heedless of any danger. As unaccustomed as she was to riding horseback, it was hard for her to understand how Adam could possibly fall asleep, even though the horse's pace was very slow.

Mei Fei began chattering on about palace gossip, talking about people April had long since forgotten existed.

"And our father," Mei Fei whispered, "is in serious trouble. It is better for us to be under the Empress's protection than with him in Kalgan."

April remembered Sun Yat-sen's message and mentioned it to Mei Fei.

"Ah, yes. That was the man who escaped before the Empress could learn who was in league with Prince Ke Loo."

"Then Dr. Sun told the truth."

"I do not know all of what happened, only that Prince Ke Loo has opposed the Empress and she vows to destroy him. Unfortunately, many are in sympathy with Prince Ke Loo, especially the people in the northern provinces who—" She leaned closer. "—Who wish to be rid of what they call the Empress's tyranny. It has a great deal to do with the foot-binding of female infants. Many are complaining, saying if the women of the royal families do not bind their feet, why must the peasants?" Mei Fei shook her head, looking shocked. "I do not know what is happening of late. The people are so outspoken. Of course, the Boxers are behind all the unrest, Wu Lien tells us. They are inflaming the peasants with their talk of freeing China from Western influences, all of which they say the Empress condones. A terrible time is coming, April. I feel it as surely as I feel the mare beneath me."

April had stopped listening. She was working on a plan to reach America with the Empress's blessing. The need to avenge herself on David's father and then on Lydia was paramount in her mind. She'd need the Dowager Empress's help and she had a good notion as to how she would go about getting it. Afterward, she would come back and have her revenge on Her Imperial Highness—and she knew exactly how she intending going about that also, thanks to Dr. Sun.

You will be avenged, David, she vowed to herself. *If it takes my lifetime, I will see to it that all those responsible for taking you from me will pay dearly for what they did.*

Chapter 4

The party for Empress Cosmetics in the main ball-room of the San Francisco Hotel was lavish. A huge cake dominated the buffet table, the number "9" sculptured in yellow frosting. Almost everyone in the city's social register was there, dressed in the finest, wearing jewelry that lay most of the year in private vaults.

Lydia mingled easily with the guests, all the while keeping an eye on the doorway. She had not seen Peter MacNair for several months and hoped he would come to her anniversary party tonight. Secretly, she prayed he would come alone. His wife, Lorna, made it only too clear how much she hated Lydia. The scene Lorna made at the Hearsts' party a few years ago was still vivid in everyone's mind. Why Lorna had openly accused her for causing David's death was incomprehensible, but Lorna MacNair made it known to everyone there that Lydia Moonsong made her fortune as a result of a theft and had encouraged her son to duplicate her crime.

"My son David was murdered because of this

woman's example," Lorna had charged. "And one day I will get even, I swear it."

It had caused a scandal, but she was accustomed to scandal by this time, Lydia told herself. First was that sordid business with Walter Hanover, the man who bankrupted her and then blackmailed her out of fifty percent of her now thriving Empress Cosmetics empire. Peter MacNair had bought Walter off and still held a right to half her fortune, though he never claimed it, even when his own cosmetic firm was on the verge of collapse.

When she glanced toward the door again Raymond Andrieux touched her arm. "Who are you waiting for? Peter MacNair, I suspect."

Raymond was still the same handsome Frenchman she'd hired as her *nez* years and years before, the only man with the unique talent of duplicating the scent she'd taken from the Dowager Empress when she and April fled China. Without Raymond there would never have been an Empress Cosmetics empire, let alone a ninth anniversary. Without Raymond and the exclusive Moonsong Perfume he'd duplicated, Empress Cosmetics would cease to exist.

Lydia ignored him and smiled at a passing guest.

"You did invite Mr. MacNair, didn't you?" Raymond persisted.

"I invited Mr. *and* Mrs. MacNair, naturally. They are very prominent San Franciscans."

"Even though the woman almost had you ostracized from the upper crust with her nasty tongue."

46

"Lorna MacNair may say whatever she pleases. That's why they call this a free country."

"And you are far too rich and far too powerful a businesswoman to be ignored." Raymond laughed and leaned closer. "Just don't forget, dear Lydia, that I am the one responsible for all your money and your success."

"I believe I pay you handsomely for your talent, Raymond. There is nothing you lack. I see to that, do I not?"

"I lack a wife," he reminded her, giving her a knowing look.

"You have a wife. I need not remind you that you are still legally married to my daughter."

"Yes. It's about time I did something about that. April never intends coming back from China, I'm beginning to realize."

That was another scandal the newspapers had had a field day with. "The Continuing Moonsong Chronicles," the gossip columns headlined when April abandoned her husband and children and ran off to China with David MacNair. What additional fun the gossips would have had if they knew that the young son April had abandoned, Marcus, was really Lydia's child and that Peter MacNair was the father. Even Peter didn't know, and Raymond was never told the name of the child's father when Lydia bore him in Paris and gave him up to April and Raymond.

"I don't agree with you," Lydia said. "Why did April send me that cablegram saying she was coming home?"

"That was ages ago. Knowing my dear wife," he said with a touch of sarcasm, "she took up with another young buck, or maybe that prince who fathered her married her off to a royal relative."

It was all possible, of course, Lydia had to admit to herself, recalling how headstrong and independent April had always been. She had never lived by the rules, but Lydia blamed herself for all of April's faults and fantasies. She'd done everything for April, much of it shameful to recall.

"I am sure a good lawyer would arrange to dissolve my marriage to April," Raymond said. "What was the name of the legal firm that got you legally unbound from that Oriental prince of yours?"

She told him. "And I'll remind you how long it took for that matter to be settled without publicity."

"Then I'd better start proceedings tomorrow." He smiled into her eyes. "Then I may just propose to you."

"Really, Raymond. Don't you think we have been smeared enough by the scandalmongers?" His tone had been flippant, but she knew he was being serious. Too often he'd pressured her to go to bed with him and, traitorous as it was to admit, he was the only man other than Peter MacNair who aroused her sexually.

"Who cares about scandalmongers? I should have married you in the first place. April and I were all wrong for each other."

True as it was, though, Raymond found he could never close his eyes without being reminded of April's beauty. But having married an half-Oriental girl, he soon learned how bigoted Americans were. He found himself snubbed by society. The Chinese were the subject only of abuse and scorn in San Francisco. Being a native from Paris, he hadn't known that until it was too late. Everyone came to the wedding because of Lydia's financial bribes.

Secretly, he hated America. Having been born and raised in France he'd never learned what the word *prejudice* meant because he'd only known Frenchmen. One day he'd return . . . go back where he belonged, where people were light and gay and had fun. Here all they did was work and build things. With a sigh he told himself that it wouldn't be long now before he would be in a position to move the main operation of Empress Cosmetics to its Paris branch. If April came back, he'd take her there to live, if she didn't, he'd take Lydia.

Raymond said, "You would marry me, wouldn't you, Lydia? I mean, when I'm free of April, of course."

Lydia glanced toward the door and her heart gave a little tug when she saw Peter MacNair standing there. "I'd have to think on it, Raymond," she said, not really having heard exactly what he'd said. Peter MacNair always made the world stop for her.

Raymond grabbed her arm. "You will never marry Peter MacNair, if that is what you're plotting. He'd never divorce Lorna, she'd see to that. She isn't like you, Lydia; the scandal would kill her."

She wrenched herself free. "I am not planning on marrying anyone at the moment, Raymond," she said as she turned and started toward Peter. She flashed him a broad smile and held out both hands to him.

"Congratulations, Lydia," he said, his face lighting up when he saw her coming toward him. He eyed her admiringly. "Both on your ninth anniversary and the fact that you are the most ravishing woman in San Francisco."

"Only in San Francisco?" Lydia chided.

"The country! The world!"

The years hadn't touched her. She was just as beautiful as she was the first day he met her, almost twenty-five years ago.

She linked her arm in his and started through the clutter of guests, all smiles and nods. "Your wife isn't coming?" Lydia asked, trying to sound casual and yet be heard by those standing near.

"You knew she wouldn't," he answered in a normal voice, not caring who was listening. "She is much too smart to try and embarrass you at your own party with all your friends gathered around you." He smiled. "I am not supposed to be here either."

"Why not? Rightfully, half of all I have is yours, Peter, and the other half I have only because you gave me the idea."

In a quieter voice he said, "I will never file claim to anything of yours, except you yourself, Lydia." She didn't believe him. As much as she loved him, she knew him too well to ever believe him. She had been hurt too much by trusting him. Still, his flattery continued to please her, though she looked up at him disapprovingly.

"Does it still anger you when I speak of how much I love you?" he asked.

"No," she said meekly. Her heart was pounding in spite of what she was telling it to do.

"Then you don't hate me any more?"

"I don't hate you, Peter." She never thought she

50

would hear herself say those words. The old scars had practically disappeared and the years had gradually made her see that Peter's betraying her into the hands of that Manchu prince Ke Loo had been his way of saving her life. Still, though she didn't hate him, she didn't trust him either.

She felt the pressure of his hand on her arm. The touch of him disconcerted her as it had always done. She spoke what she was thinking. "I don't trust you anymore than I ever did, Peter," she reminded him as she moved slightly away.

He laughed, which didn't surprise her.

"And if you say you will never file claim to the fifty percent of Empress Cosmetics, why don't you give me those documents, or at least sell them to me."

"Maybe I will."

"You won't. I know you too well, Peter Mac-Nair. You were always a man who kept an ace in the hole."

They were interrupted by a guest who wanted to congratulate her and offer her some business. When they were alone again Lydia said, "I never did understand why you didn't come to me for help when your company was ruined by that lawsuit."

"Come to you? A woman?" Peter laughed again. "You really don't know me after all."

"How is your new company progressing?" What she really wanted to ask was where he'd gotten the money that was financing the new MacNair Products, Incorporated.

"Very well indeed. Naturally, we are not in your league yet. We have nothing to equal Moonsong Perfume. But I haven't given up hopes of one day developing a scent far superior to Moonsong."

Lydia smiled. "I wish you luck. It will take a unique fragrance to usurp Moonsong's position as the most coveted and most expensive perfume in the country—if not the world."

"Which you only achieved by stealing away my *nez.*"

"Raymond was never really yours, Peter. You may have found him in Paris, but I know you brought him here solely for the purpose of stealing Moonsong away from me."

It was true, of course, Peter reminded himself as he gave Lydia a sly grin. Lydia had taken the perfume from the Forbidden City but had had no way of reproducing it. He'd never learned how she found out about Raymond Andrieux or how he found out about Moonsong and Lydia's dilemma, but knowing Lydia's ways, he had a good idea of how she'd seduced Raymond to join her ranks.

"Now you are stuck with him," Peter said, motioning to where Raymond was standing in a circle of beautiful women.

"I don't consider myself *stuck with him,* as you put it. Raymond is a loyal and talented man."

"Talented, yes, but I wouldn't lean too heavily on his loyalty if I were you. Given the least provocation, I am certain Monsieur Andrieux would walk out on you in a second and then where would you be without your precious Moonsong?"

What he said was true, Lydia told herself. There was no way of stockpiling an exotic perfume. Large quantities deteriorated quickly, which was why smaller batches had to be developed and each had to be concocted individually by a *nez*—a "nose." Men like Raymond were so called because of their rare talent of being able to smell a scent and tell its composition. The could identify not only flowers from which the scent was made, but also how many flowers, their variety, even where and when they were grown. This was why Moonsong was so expensive and so much in demand by the women who could afford it. Without Raymond to duplicate the exact scent each time, there would be no Moonsong Perfume.

Defensively Lydia answered, "Moonsong is not the only product I sell. My chemists are constantly coming up with excellent creams and powders and lotions. If Raymond decides to move on, I am sure I will survive without Moonsong."

"Unless, of course, he decides to go into competition. He could easily reproduce all your products and sell them at a lower price."

"And I would have him in a law court before he had a chance to dress and shave."

Peter chuckled. "I'll let you have your Raymond and your Moonsong," he said as he took her hand. "All I want is you, Lydia."

She felt herself go warm all over as their eyes met and held. She recognized still that hard, calculating look that had always made her both weak and wary. "Me and Moonsong," she said, trying to sound flippant. "And, if I remember correctly, Moonsong always came before me. I may have forgiven you for what you did to me in China, Peter, but you will never convince me that you want me solely for myself."

"But I do. To hell with Moonsong." His eyes

shifted slightly when he said that. "I have a whole new concept about cosmetic sales," he said. "I'm putting out a new line and you will never guess what I'm calling it."

"I can't imagine."

"Lady Lydia," he announced.

Lydia's eyes widened and her pleasant smile disappeared. "Good God, Peter, no."

"Why not?"

"What will Lorna say? What will everyone say? There has been too much gossip about the Moonsongs as it is, what with me and April and your David."

A deadness came into his eyes for a second when she mentioned his son's name.

"I'm sorry," she said.

"It's all right. David's death is something I've tried to put out of my mind. It was something that happened . . . that's all. I've stopped blaming myself, or you, or anyone."

"You blamed me?"

"In the beginning," he admitted, then quickly added, "I blamed everyone, mostly myself. I tried to stop him. If I'd never told him how you'd acquired Moonsong, he would never have gotten the crazy notion to do the same thing." He turned away for a moment, afraid she would see how much he hurt. When he turned back he shrugged. "We both must forget David."

"Then you must not call your new label Lady Lydia. It will just rake up all the old stories."

"The containers are already in production. Besides, I don't want to change the name. I think Lady Lydia is an excellent label for a cosmetic line."

"Lady Lorna would be just as good."

He smiled sweetly. "Not so far as I am concerned." After a pause he said, "Anyway, it isn't going to be an over-the-counter item or even a mail-order item."

Lydia looked quizzical.

"I intend selling house-to-house, starting in the east." He grinned. "The way the Bible boys do it, letting the ladies test and decide in the privacy of their own home."

"An interesting idea, Peter, but I can't help feeling there is something a bit seedy about it. However, if you had female salespeople—women selling to women—it might be a unique and successful concept."

"Women selling door-to-door." He laughed. "You have to be joking. It's bad enough that some ladies are going into the business world without encouraging them to take sales jobs away from veterans who know their customers and their territories."

Lydia was not convinced. "Regardless, I still think ladies would be more apt to buy from another lady than from a man."

He winked and whispered, "Ladies underpinnings are sold by men and their sales are booming."

Secretly Lydia was pleased Peter did not like her suggestion; she filed it away in the back of her mind, deciding to keep an eye on Peter's new concept for selling. If it showed any degree of success she'd train ladies to do the same work, knowing it would be a greater success.

"I'm sinking all my capital into the project," Peter admitted.

"I'd make some tests first."

"You always were too cautious."

"And you always too reckless."

"I suppose that is what attracts us to each other. Opposites and all that." He looked lovingly down into her beautiful face. He took a step nearer and put his lips close to her ear. "Right now I'd like to tear every stitch of clothing from your gorgeous body and have you right here on the floor in front of everyone."

Lydia's cheeks flamed as she put her hand against his chest and averted her face. "Peter," she breathed.

"I don't give a damn who sees us. I want you more than I want my own life."

"Don't, Peter." Her heart was fluttering and the heat in the lower part of her body was building.

"And you want me. I know you do," he accused.

"Peter, no," she breathed, not trusting her voice. But she was not speaking the truth. She wanted to feel the hard nakedness of him overpowering her, pressing heavily atop her own vulnerability. She wanted to writhe and twist and moan under his onslaught. Only too easily did she recall how he'd entered her, made her seethe with desire and wanton passion as he took her forcefully, manfully, pounding into her unmercifully, knowing her need matched his own.

"Lydia," he sighed. "Isn't there somewhere we can be alone? It's been too long," he reminded her.

"You mustn't talk like this, Peter. People are looking at us."

"Let them." He reached for her hand but she snatched it away. "I adore you. And I promise that as soon as MacNair Cosmetics is completely on its feet again I intend divorcing Lorna so we can marry."

"Divorce! Oh, Peter, no. You can't. I've just finished reminding you of all the scandal we've already caused. My quiet, legal dissolution of my Chinese marriage, discreetly as it was handled, is still gossiped about in some circles. You know how everyone feels about out-and-out divorce. It would ruin not only our reputations but our businesses as well. There is too much working against me now, Peter. I'd never permit you to divorce Lorna for my sake."

He looked crestfallen. "You don't love me anymore, is that what you are trying to say?"

"I will not be named co-respondent in any divorce action," she said, avoiding his question. "Your wife despises me as it is. I wouldn't want your children to despise me as well." She saw his hurt. "Dear Peter. I am more than flattered that you'd even consider such a drastic notion. However, if you won't be sensible then I must be."

Peter's broad shoulders sagged. "You make it all seem so hopeless."

"Let us allow things to go on the way they are, Peter. Time has a way of solving even the worst of situations."

She noticed the sensual curve of his lips as he smiled gently. A passionate glint lit his expression. "On one condition," he said.

"And what is that?" She knew what he would ask and only stood there trembling with anticipation.

"I must have you tonight. I must," he said urgently.

"Yes," she breathed. She glanced around. "I've been neglecting my guests. Stay late, Peter. You can drive me home." She gave his hand a little squeeze and moved off across the room. She caught Raymond's eye and motioned him to her. "I believe it's time we cut the cake."

She could feel Peter watching her. All she wanted was for the party to be over so she could be in his arms.

Chapter 5

"We seem to have spent a lot of time riding in carriages," Peter said as he held her hand in his, listening to the clip-clop of the horses' hooves on the cobblestones. "I remember that mad dash to the waterfront the first time April and David tried to elope."

"And the night I fled from Walter Hanover when he tried to blackmail me into marrying him."

"That carriage ride didn't end the way I had hoped."

Lydia laughed. "Truthfully, I wanted to ask you in, but you were so certain I couldn't resist you that I had to show you I could."

"And denied both of us one of the few pleasures we've had together."

Inside the mansion they were too consumed with their own needs to bother with preliminaries. Peter looked around the handsome drawing room and nodded toward the archway that he knew led to Lydia's downstairs sitting and bed rooms. "You haven't lived in a one-level Chinese house in years and yet you still persist on sleeping on the ground floor."

"The children and their nurse have the run of the upper floors. It gives us both the privacy we all enjoy."

"Children," he mused, then shook his head. "I never could understand how April could abandon Caroline and Marcus. They should be pretty big by now."

"Caroline is six. Marcus is five, but believes himself to be quite the big man, always bossing Caroline about. A lot like his father," she said.

Peter nodded, thinking she was referring to Raymond.

Lydia smiled, knowing she referred to Peter himself. She wondered if one day she'd tell Peter of their son, then thought of what she'd told him at the party, that time solved everything.

"A nightcap?" she asked.

"I don't need anything to stimulate me," he answered, taking her in his arms. He lifted her easily and carried her through the sitting room into her sleeping chamber beyond.

"Peter," she moaned after his lips left hers. She clung to him with brazen abandon. "It has been a long time, hasn't it?"

He didn't answer but kissed her again more passionately. "Let's get out of these clothes."

"You make me feel so shameless," she said as she let him undress her.

"You are shameless," he said, smiling. "Much as you don't want to be."

Lydia found herself naked before him as Peter scrambled to get out of his evening clothes. She liked to watch him undress, moving with the gracefulness of a performer, enticingly sexual, provocatively sensual.

Moments later they lay together, their bodies molded to one another, losing themselves in their love, their ardent need for physical release. The hard impatience of his shaft pressed against her thigh as his kisses seared her lips, then her throat, her breasts.

Eagerly she allowed his knees to part her creamy, warm thighs, exposing her vulnerability. His hands moved deliciously over her nakedness, sending shivers through her entire body.

"Peter," she moaned as he poised over her, adjusting his position. She reached down and wrapped her fingers around his hardness, reveling in the smooth, satiny feeling of his lust.

He stayed poised, thrilled by her touch, then moved forward as she guided him into her. As he penetrated the wet warmth of her being his mouth covered hers, silencing her moans of ecstasy.

Peter moved slowly, gently, luring her into agonizing rapture, making her body heave and thrash as she arched upward to meet his slow, then more forceful thrusts. His hands caressed her. His mouth scorched her skin as his attack became more urgent, almost brutal.

"Peter," she moaned under his mouth.

"I adore you."

She felt his movements become quicker, more violent, and she welcomed the harshness of his attack, wanting it to hurt so she would always remember.

Lydia let her hands slip down his back and felt the tensing and untensing of his muscles, the exciting curve of his buttocks as she urged him on.

Her movements matched his as they began building toward a mutual climax. A hot, searing flame engulfed her loins as Peter brought her to complete fulfillment.

They floated in soft, limitless space until their breathing began to return to normal. Lydia's entire body was weak and limp as Peter raised himself and rolled onto his back. Then he took her lovingly in his arms and kissed her passionately.

"I'm going to divorce Lorna," he said. "I don't care about scandal or gossip or anything else in this world except you."

She gave him a coy look. "Except me and Moonsong," she corrected, smiling.

He shrugged. "If that's what you want to think then there is nothing I can do to change your mind."

"Don't you see, Peter? If we ever did marry I would really never be convinced that you wanted me for myself."

"Then my only alternative is to make MacNair Products such a huge success that it will overshadow all other cosmetics, including your precious Moonsong Perfume."

"If that happens, then Lorna will take you for everything you have and you'll still need Moonsong."

"You're impossible," he answered with an annoyed twist of his mouth. He glanced at the clock on the night stand. "Good Lord. I had no idea it was this late. I have to go." He leaned over and kissed her again. "My only desire in this whole world is to be able to stay with you all night, every night for the rest of our lives."

She put her arms around him and idly toyed

with the shaggy hair at the back of his neck. "You made me very happy this evening, Peter. Thank you."

"Lunch with me tomorrow. I'll call for you at your office at twelve-thirty."

"I can't. Leon is coming down from school. I promised I'd take him to lunch."

"Oh, yes, Prince Ke Loo's boy."

"MY boy," Lydia insisted. "He wants nothing to do with his father. In fact, he's even Americanized his name from Li Ahn to Leon. I swear I'm not imagining it, but the longer he remains here the more Occidental he looks. His eyes seem to have lost the slight slant they once had and even lightened in color." She gave a little laugh. "I know that's impossible but I swear its true."

"I haven't seen the lad in several years. He should be quite a young man now."

"Nineteen and very much a man, he wants everyone to think."

"It's strange that he has adapted so well, especially with the prejudice many Americans have against Orientals."

"He had a terrible life with Prince Ke Loo. Do you know they used to bleed him when he was a child in order to drain him of any trace of my blood in his veins?"

"Good God, no wonder he's so opposed to his father."

"And as far as prejudice is concerned, you above everyone else should know that where money is concerned prejudices don't exist."

He kissed her quickly. "I must go." He got up and started to dress. "Perhaps I could join you and Leon tomorrow. I'd like to get to know the boy.

Perhaps introduce him to my son, Efrem. The two are about the same age."

"Heaven forbid, Peter. What are you thinking? Your wife would throw a tantrum that would be heard across the state. You know how she despises anything connected with me—including my products, I understand."

He laughed. "She'd die before she'd wear any Empress Cosmetic product, even though all her friends think her foolish. I must hand it to you, Lydia—for a silly little girl of missionary parents you certainly made something of yourself."

"Perhaps I've made too much of myself," she answered wistfully. "The price was high."

He leaned down and kissed her mouth as she pulled the sheet over her naked body. "Dinner tomorrow night?" Seeing her hesitation he added, "Lorna is going to visit friends in Sacramento for a few days. There's no chance of her causing a scene."

Lydia thought for a moment. "Very well," she said.

"Good. I'll call for you at seven-thirty."

He was fifteen minutes early. "My place was like a morgue," he explained. "I got restless. I hope you don't mind."

"Of course not."

He looked around. "For some reason I thought I'd find you in the bosom of your family, as the expression goes. You know—little tots on your lap, your son sitting dutifully at your side."

She chuckled. "Leon is off somewhere with friends from school and the little ones are already asleep upstairs with their amah." She made a face

64

and corrected herself. "Their *nurse*. After all these years it is one of the few Oriental expressions I can't stop using."

He winked suggestively. "Then we have the downstairs all to ourselves again tonight."

She saw his eyes move toward the bedroom. "Behave yourself, Peter MacNair. You are taking me to dinner." She moved toward the liquor cart. "Would you care for a cocktail?"

"Yes, thank you."

Minutes later they settled themselves side by side on the Victorian settee, she with a cassis and he with a scotch over ice.

He said, "Did I tell you you look ravishing as usual."

She smiled demurely. "Thank you, kind sir."

The doorbell rang.

Lydia looked annoyed. "Who could that be? I'm not expecting anyone. Excuse me, Peter. The servants are off. I'll see who it is."

When she opened the door Raymond removed his hat and smiled. "I was in the neighborhood and wondered if you were free for dinner."

"As it so happens, I am not free," Lydia said, frowning.

"Entertaining?" He nodded to Peter's carriage tied to the hitching post.

"You always were inquisitive, Raymond. One day that nose of yours will get you into trouble."

"MacNair's carriage, isn't it?"

Lydia gave him a defiant look. "Yes, it is."

"Good," he said forcing down his anger. He pushed past her. "I'll join you for a drink."

"Raymond, please," she called after him as he went directly toward the drawing room.

Peter was refreshing his scotch when Raymond walked in. "Good evening, Raymond," Peter said pleasantly.

Raymond glanced at the scotch decanter in Peter's hand. "You certainly are making yourself free enough in this house."

Peter merely widened his grin. "It's Lydia's liquor and I'm sure she doesn't object to my helping myself to it."

"But *I* do."

"Raymond!" Lydia snapped, standing nervously in the doorway. "Peter is a guest of mine."

He turned on her. "Well, I strongly object to your asking him here. If I recall, you've always expressed an intense dislike for the man." He saw Lydia glance anxiously at Peter and saw Peter frown.

She said, "You are being purposefully rude, Raymond. I'd appreciate it if you would kindly leave."

Raymond did not move. "Now don't tell me this is a business meeting between two competitors?"

"Think what you like," Peter said smugly as he sat down and put his feet out in front of him, crossing his ankles.

Raymond glowered. "I don't want you seeing Lydia."

"That again is for Lydia to say." He looked around Raymond. "Lydia?"

She came forward and put her hand on Raymond's arm. "Please, Raymond, don't make a scene."

He knocked her hand away. "You seem to forget how much you need me, Lydia. Now tell this gentleman . . ." He slurred the word. ". . . . to get the devil out of this house." He threw Peter a furious look. "I am surprised Lydia hasn't told you that she and I are to be married."

"Raymond!" She looked helplessly at Peter and saw his shock. "That isn't true." To Raymond she said, "You are being overly presumptuous, Raymond. I will remind you that you are still my daughter's husband and I would never agree to marrying you even if you *were* free."

"You sang a different tune just last evening at the party before this loser showed up."

Peter jumped to his feet, clenching his hands into fists.

"Raymond!" Lydia cried. "I never accepted your proposal and you know it."

He whirled on her, ignoring Peter's outrage. "You'll accept me. I said I'd get myself free of April and you will marry me."

It was all so ridiculous, Lydia suddenly realized. Here stood two men who claimed they wanted to marry her and neither of them was in a position to do so. She suddenly began to wonder if they really meant what they said or if they were simply toying with her, knowing they need never live up to their proposals. She would be making a fool of herself by believing either one of them.

"Raymond, kindly leave." To Peter she said, "Would you fetch my wrap and evening bag from the sitting room, please. They are on the divan."

Peter hesitated, then did as she asked, leaving them alone for a moment.

When he was out of ear shot she glowered at Raymond. "How dare you come here and make a scene! I highly object to your proprietary manner. I am not planning on marrying you or anyone else.

Peter MacNair asked me to dinner. I accepted purely because I am interested in finding out all I can about his new line." The lie came easily, but then she reminded herself that she had had a lot of practice over the years.

She saw the doubt in his face. "Just keep in mind, Lydia, that you are nothing without me. So if I act proprietarily toward you I heartily believe that I have that right. Empress Cosmetics would be bankrupt in six months if I decided to pull out. Just keep that in mind, Lydia, my dear." He chucked her under the chin. She expected him to try and kiss her and drew back. "Have a pleasant evening," he said with a vicious smile. "Say good night to our competition for me." He turned and left, his angry footsteps echoing across the marble foyer. When the front door slammed shut she let out her breath and then turned when she sensed Peter behind her.

"I'm afraid you will have serious trouble with that Frenchman," he said. He laid her wrap and bag on a chair and freshened his drink.

"I've been handling Raymond for years. He's just another spoiled little boy who must have everything his way."

"And you give it to him."

"Yes," she said bluntly. "I have more than enough for myself and for my family. Raymond is welcome to the rest."

"Men who are given a free hand get very greedy as time passes. Be careful, Lydia, and don't give him too much or he will wind up wanting it all."

She knew there was truth in what he said, but she saw no way out of her situation. Raymond wasn't really a bad sort—wild and impetuous like so many men, but of all the men she'd known Raymond was the only one who'd made her forget Peter for a time. It was wrong for her to have gone to bed with Raymond; at the time, however, she'd had no other choice. He had demanded it and to her surprise she hadn't found it unexciting. He was an expert at pleasing a woman, but then he was a Frenchman.

She chuckled softly. "He already wants it all, Peter. Marrying me gives him everything."

He stared at her, his mouth slightly open. "You aren't considering marrying him, are you?"

"No, of course not."

"Then you'd better do something about him before he takes you over completely. He's already acting as if he were the boss and you the employee."

Lydia toyed with a stray lock that had come unpinned. She went toward the mirror, keeping her eyes fixed on Peter in the glass. "I know only one way I can be rid of Raymond's influence."

"What's that?"

She pinned the curl and turned around. "If you and I consolidated our companies." She saw him frown. Quickly she said, "I'm convinced, Peter, that the two of us could make Empress Cosmetics a success without Raymond's talented nose."

"Empress Cosmetics?" Peter sneered. "Why not MacNair Cosmetics?"

"Because my company has the better reputation, if you want a perfectly blunt answer."

"*Me* become secondary to *you*?"

"We'd be equal partners with neither of us holding more than a fifty-percent stock interest.

I've been thinking of that new venture you are planning with the Lady Lorna . . ."

"Lady Lydia," he was quick to correct.

"I think that is a big mistake. And another mistake you are making is that you're insisting on having the product sold by men. Women would be far more successful."

"Women?" He put back his head and laughed.

"Don't scoff at the idea, Peter. I've thought it through and I believe between us we could really build our cosmetic companies into one of the largest empires in the country." She touched his arm. "Come in with me, Peter. Let's work together."

He thought for a moment, then put down his glass. "No, I want to make a success of my venture by doing it my way."

"You're being stubborn."

"I'm being sensible. Besides, my enterprise isn't being financed with my money. I have a backer who must be taken into consideration."

"Who?"

"I don't want to say."

"Who's backing you, Peter?" she insisted, looking at him with suspicion.

"That is none of your business, if you'll excuse my being rude."

He was looking uncomfortable, which strengthened Lydia's suspicions. "It's Lorna's money, isn't it?"

Peter glared at her. "I said my money affairs are of no concern of yours."

"It is Lorna's money. I can read it in your face."

"All right, so what if it is."

Lydia felt herself beginning to crumble. None of his promises of love and marriage meant any-

70

thing. He was all tied up snug and tight to his wife, and he'd taken the money Lorna had offered. "How could you, Peter. If you wanted to marry me and love me as you claim, why didn't you come to me for the money?"

"Because Lorna is my wife. There's a difference."

"She's still a woman."

"She's my wife, damn it."

"A wife you told me just last evening that you are only too anxious to be rid of. What kind of a man are you, Peter? It's all too obvious to me now that you prefer Lorna's money to me. You will never leave her; I can see that now. You are nothing but a hypocrite," she spat. "You've been leaning on that woman and her rich family too long to be able to do without the crutch."

"You're dead wrong," he said angrily. "All right, I'm using Lorna's money. So what?"

"She has a hold on you, Peter, one you will never be able to break. I see that now. I was a fool to think you might have changed. You're still the same selfish, self-centered, male peacock I met twenty-four years ago. You used Lorna then. You used me. You'll use anyone if it benefits you. You're a monster." She felt the tears threatening and hurriedly averted her face.

He came to her and tried to take her in his arms.

"Don't touch me. Please leave. I think I've made a big enough fool of myself for one night."

Peter grabbed her and shook her until the stray curl slipped from the pin again, taking several others with it. "You listen to me, Lydia."

She wrenched herself free, knowing she was

71

helpless when he physically overpowered her. "Get out of my house."

"No. I am not leaving here until we have had this settled." He pulled her forcefully into his arms and kissed her hard on the mouth.

Lydia fought against him and when he released her she slapped his face. "Get out! Go back to Lorna where you obviously belong. I never want to see you again."

Chapter 6

The distant Chinese mountains were cold and foreboding as April stood in the little private garden and watched the barren branches of the apricot trees move in the wind. She clutched her heavy cape tighter about herself and wondered why the Empress hadn't sent for her. She'd been here over a week and still there was no summons from the royal chamber.

April was aware of the flurry of activity throughout the palace as the royal entourage prepared for its annual trek to the winter palace, a mere seven miles away, but the change from one palace to another occupied everyone's time with the Dowager Empress supervising every detail. If April had a choice she would much prefer to remain here in the great palace with its innumerable halls, chambers, twisting corridors, its terraces and towers so expertly placed as to capture the most scenic views and the brillance of the summer sun.

Three quarters of the palace grounds were covered by a huge lake along whose shores an exquisitely painted, sheltered gallery wound its way through trees and arbors, connecting a scattering of small palace buildings. On the lake's north shore stood the Empress's two-story marble boat with its lacelike trim and multicolored glass windows.

White marble balustrades, emerald fountains, the Seventeen-Arch Bridge connecting the mainland with the Island of the Dragon Kind, were all architectural marvels, so perfect in design and symmetry that April often wept over their beauty.

This was the China she adored, not that horrible courtyard inside the Forbidden City with its executions block, or the unfortunate peasant women hobbling about on their bound feet; not the poverty and cruelties to which the less fortunate were subjected. At first April had reveled in being a royal princess, fawned and fussed over like a rare porcelain vase. The pampering paled as April saw the true nature of her once-revered Empress—her barbarism, her sadism, the ease with which she beheaded ministers, concubines, friends and enemies alike, a cruelty that seemed to be expected of all members of the royal Manchu family.

As a child-princess, April had never questioned anything her Empress did. As she grew older she had wondered why the Empress treated her subjects so vilely until it was explained that the Manchus did not consider themselves Chinese; they were Manchurians whose destiny was to unite the *Ch'in* and the other smaller states into one supreme empire. The Manchus, she'd been taught, were above every other human that lived on the earth.

Turning her back to a sudden cold gust of air, April returned to planning how she would escape China and continue her quest for vengeance. She knew she could decide nothing until after she had had an audience with the Dowager Empress.

The old dragon was only a woman, after all, April reminded herself, with a woman's foibles and hidden weaknesses. They were partly the same blood. April felt assured that once she'd learned what the Empress demanded—and she had a good idea of what that would be—she would formulate her plan more fully.

The biting cold whipped through her heavy cloak, sending it billowing behind her. April turned toward the stairs leading back into her tiny palace—her prison, she thought, as she went toward it.

Mei Fei was seated on a low silk couch, working on the intricate design of a gold tapestry when April entered the day chamber with its brazier of glowing coals. April went over and warmed her hands over the white-hot coals. "The weather gets colder and still we stay here," she said.

"The Empress decrees it," Mei Fei said without looking up. "When we are to leave she will tell us." She laid aside her needle and studied April for a moment. "Are you very angry with me for forcing you to return here?"

April smiled patiently. "No, Mei Fei. I suppose way down deep I always knew the Empress would never allow Adam and me to leave China unless she chose to permit it. I was silly to even dream I'd be able to run away without her permission."

"I had little choice in what I did," Mei Fei said. She glanced down at the magnificent jade and pearl ring on her finger and began turning it, feeling suddenly ashamed.

"You did what you had to do, dear sister. Don't

75

blame yourself. I too have done many things I would prefer to forget. I would have felt very bad indeed if I'd learned you'd sacrificed your life on Adam's and my behalf." April went to her and sat on the silk couch. She put her hand on Mei Fei's. "You had no choice but to do what you had to do." She felt Mei Fei's ring under her hand. "How perfect," April exclaimed as she raised Mei Fei's hand and admired the ring.

When she smiled into Mei Fei's face she saw the blush on her stepsister's cheeks. "You are embarrassed." Her smiled broadened. "A gift from a young admirer?"

Mei Fei lowered her eyes and began turning the ring again. "No."

April continued to admire it. "But it is exquisite. I don't recall seeing you wearing it before today."

"It is a gift from the Empress."

April frowned. "You had an audience with the Empress?"

"This morning. She summoned me to the royal chambers to . . ." She faltered, unable to look at April.

"To thank you for obeying her." She glanced at the ring. "And to repay you for your loyalty."

Mei Fei's eyes clouded with tears as she nodded.

April smiled again and took both Mei Fei's hands into hers. She glanced at them, then studied them more closely. They were lovely hands, long, very slender, as if carved of ivory. The nails were exquisitely painted. April thought she had never seen any hands so beautiful as Mei Fei's lanquid and elegant hands that reflected the pure breeding of centuries. Though she and Mei Fei were from the same royal bloodline there was something unique about Mei Fei's imperial hands. They were so perfect; April squeezed them slightly and ran her fingertips over them to assure herself that they were indeed real flesh and blood.

She said, "Do not be ashamed, Mei Fei. Hands such as yours deserve just such a ring. It would be lacklustre on anyone else's finger. It suits you. It is as though it were a part of you when you were born."

The idea of being born with so large a ring on her finger made Mei Fei giggle.

"Did the Empress say when she would see me?" April asked.

Mei Fei stifled her giggling and resumed her embroidering. "She only asked if you and your son were comfortable. She asked many questions about little Adam, even the wish to have him brought to her. This is unusual, is it not? The Empress rarely tolerates Westerners, especially Western children."

"Adam's father, as you know, murdered the man who attempted to assassinate the Empress. I suppose she merely is curious about what the boy looks like, whether he shows any of his Manchu mother's features." She stood, wanting to shake off the threatening reminders of the fate Adam's father had suffered at the hands of the same woman who'd told him of her debt to him. "Speaking of Adam, it is time he was put to bed for his nap. I don't like leaving him alone too long with the amah. He is not accustomed to our ways or to my being away from him. He is a quiet little thing, but seems to enjoy adventure. He thinks all

77

of this business is great fun. Unfortunately, he is too trusting of strangers. I believe if I did not look after him all the time he'd wander off on his own or with anyone who promised him a game." She went toward the door, pausing as she laid her hand on the latch. "The ring is very lovely, Mei Fei. Never be ashamed of how it was earned. You deserve it."

"Thank you for understanding," Mei Fei said as she glanced down at the ring. Again she began twisting it on her finger. "Still, somehow I feel it is a terrible omen, as though the ring were accursed."

"Nonsense."

"I can't rid myself of the feeling. Had the Empress not ordered me never to remove it after she put it on my finger, I would put it away out of sight, but she said if she ever saw me without the ring she would know I had been disloyal to her."

"Then you must learn to be comfortable with it, my sister, for you could never be disloyal to your Empress."

April returned Mei Fei's innocent smile, and went toward her private chambers where she'd left Adam in the care of the amah.

The rooms were empty.

"Adam! Ling Sao!" April hurried from room to room, looking in the alcoves, behind the peacock screens, the ivory grills. They were nowhere to be found.

"Adam! Ling Sao!" she called again and again as she went into the maze of winding corridors that connected the four separate apartments of the wing, each reserved to be occupied during each of the seasons of the year, though the winter suite was used only if on a whim of the Empress decided not to leave the summer palace, which was rare. The summer, spring, and winter suites were as empty as the autumn suite they now occupied.

Two fat, balding eunuchs bowed low when April accosted them just outside the doorway that led toward the Empress's royal chambers. The doorway was flanked by two palace guards.

"My son," she demanded of the eunuchs. "Where is he?"

"I am sorry, Princess. I do not know." The other shook his head and shrugged his shoulders. She could tell by their faces that they were lying. They wore malicious grins behind their blank expressions.

"I demand to see my cousin, the Empress."

"That is not for you to demand," one of the eunuchs reminded her.

"Your Western child is more than likely in one of the courtyards playing," the other said. "Certainly he is somewhere safe. I see no cause for your obvious concern."

What he said was ludicrous. There was no such thing as being safe anyplace where the Empress held reign. She'd learned that lesson only too well. These two grinning pawns knew it as well, she reminded herself.

April tried to brush past the eunuchs and push her way through the golden doors, but the palace guards threatened her with their spears.

"I am your princess," she reminded them. "I will see my cousin."

The guards stood firm.

One of the eunuchs continued grinning and

79

said, "You know we would be beheaded if we disobeyed our Empress. No one passes through these doors without a royal summons."

April clenched her hands and glowered at them, but she knew there was nothing she could say to dissuade them from their duty. She whirled in a flurry of silk and brocade and went back to where she'd left Mei Fei.

"She's taken Adam," April announced.

Mei Fei's eyes widened. "I am sure she has not."

"Adam is gone. Where else would Ling Sao have taken him without telling me? I left them comfortable in my apartment when I went for my stroll in the garden. No one is there now, not even the other servants. It is as if the rooms were picked clean of anyone who could see or speak." She began to pace. "Something is definitely wrong." She slammed a fist in her palm. "I swear if that old woman harms Adam in any way, I'll kill her!"

"April!" Mei Fei looked around quickly. "You must never make such a threat. The walls all have ways of hearing."

"I don't care. She had reason to kill David because he was caught stealing; I can understand that though I don't forgive her what she did. As for Adam, he represents no threat, he has done nothing to anger her."

Mei Fei tried to calm her. "As I told you, she asked questions about Adam. If he was indeed taken to her I am sure it is only to satisfy her curiosity."

The girl's innocence annoyed her. "You don't know what I've learned these past years." April thought for a moment that perhaps she should begin enlightening Mei Fei, but when she looked at her and saw the same trusting, innocent face, the same imperious tilt of the head that would have matched her own not too many years ago, she knew anything she said against the Empress would be wasted.

"You are worried and upset, April. Calm yourself. I am sure Adam is in no danger from anyone. He is well liked by the palace staff despite his Western features. Come," she said as she again laid aside her needlework and linked her arm in April's. "Go with me into the plum garden and help me decide on a branch design for my tapestry. Your talent for design is so much superior to mine and it will help settle your troubled thoughts."

Reluctantly, April let herself be helped into her heavy cloak and led outside into the cold air of approaching winter. The yew dragon sculptured out of hedge looked dark and gloomy in the afternoon light. Overhead the sky was gray and cheerless, giving the long sloping lawns, the terraces, and the pergola a dismal, melancholy complexion.

April found she could not concentrate on the various barren branches on which Mei Fei asked her opinion. She wanted to be away from this place. Even her hated San Francisco was a welcome thought just so long as Adam could be with her. She cursed herself for not having sent Adam along to America in Eddie Wells's care. He would have delivered him to the Moonsong mansion and Adam would be safe. But her selfishness hadn't allowed her to even consider being without her son, or Adam's possible peril if imprisoned by the Empress as they were. At the time she'd thought only of herself. The Dowager Empress had wanted Mei Fei to bring her to the summer palace. Adam would be in safe hands right now if she had not been so indulgent of her own wants and desires.

Not hearing any of Mei Fei's prattle, April started to think back. She supposed she had always been concerned only about her own happiness, her own comforts. She had done what she wanted to do and in every instance she'd been made to pay for her self-interest. It had caused the alienation of her mother, the separation from her daughter Caroline, the death of her husband.

Another part of her argued with her reasoning. She'd been forced to marry a man she found she despised. Her mother had forced her to pass as her maid because she was ashamed to admit to the society of San Francisco that she had an Oriental daughter. David had been her life, her love; she hadn't forced him to fly with her to China. It wasn't her fault that his father had induced him to steal, to commit a crime everyone knew was punishable by death, regardless of rank and station.

If only Adam was safe. The prayer repeated itself over and over as she directed it to every god of influence that she could remember.

Mei Fei tugged at her sleeve. "Here," she said pointing to a particularly graceful plum tree branch. "I could utilize the shape and perch a nightingale on it, its beak open in song."

April was forced out of her thoughts. She studied the branch without seeing it. "Yes," she said, "I believe it will do very nicely."

Mei Fei happily clapped her hands. "I'll fetch my sketching papers and ink sticks and will try and capture the curves and angles." She hurried away.

Finding herself alone again, this time April did not relish the solitude. The high walls of the secluded garden seemed higher. There was a strange, ominous smell in the air, like the threatening approach of some horrible disaster. Somewhere Adam was being held away from her. April strangled back her frustration.

Mei Fei returned and began sketching, having to struggle to keep the rice papers from flapping in the wind. April glanced up at the sky.

"Something terrible is going to happen," April predicted.

"A hard winter that will freeze the ground and kill the livestock, and then a terrible drought," Mei Fei said rather nonchalantly as she continued to sketch.

April gaped at her. "What are you saying?"

Mei Fei tilted her head and studied the branch. "It is common gossip in the palace. The royal advisers all say the Westerners will soon cause a terrible drought, or a plague, or the complete destruction of China. It is what the gods tell them." She glanced at her sister and saw she'd captured her attention. "You know of the growing discontent with the foreigners. Each year they increase their influence and move farther and farther over our land."

"That isn't true," April argued. "I lived in the legation compound. The Westerners grow fewer and fewer each year."

"But not their influence." She sighed. "I am only a stupid girl who believes what she is told and this is what I am told."

83

"By whom?"

"Wu Lien. He said the Empress's advisers caution her against the Western intervention that she permits. They say if she persists on tolerating the outsiders that the Boxers will rise up against not only the foreigners, but also against the Empress herself."

The notion she'd earlier toyed with flitted back into her head. After dealing with her mother and Peter MacNair, she'd encourage the Boxers in some way—through her father, possibly. They would accomplish what April herself wanted to accomplish—the killing of the Dragon Empress.

Her notion fell away when again she thought of her son. "What is it she wants of Adam? I know he is with her. Why did she summon him without me?"

"The boy is safe. No harm will come to him."

"Not yet," April said. "In time, however, I fear both Adam's and my lives will be in danger if we stay here."

Just then Ling Sao, the amah, appeared at the top of the stairs that led down to the garden. April rushed at her with her eyes blazing in rage. "Where is the boy?" she demanded.

Ling Sao cringed from April's fists. "I am sorry, Princess, but the Empress commanded his presence. We were taken immediately. You were not to be told, nor would you have been allowed to accompany the boy into the royal presence. This was her command."

"Where is my son?"

"I was excused. The boy remained."

April raised her fist to strike Ling Sao, and the amah cowered and fell to her knees. "He will not be harmed, Princess," she said, clutching April's cloak. "The Empress seemed pleased with him."

"She will terrify him."

The amah continued to kneel. "The child was not in the least frightened, Princess. He appeared to enjoy the adventure. He was quite in awe of the uniforms of the guards and the glitter of the golden rooms. He babbled happily all the time. Please do not upset yourself. The boy is in no danger, Princess."

April turned away. Somehow, she was disappointed that Adam had gone so eagerly and was so amused. Of course, the amah might be lying. It was more satisfying to think that the child was petrified without his mother.

"When is he to be returned to me?" April asked.

"That I do not know. Soon, I would think. The Imperial One is anxious to move to the winter quarters in the Forbidden City. A child in her charge would only delay and inconvenience her."

The heavy grilled doors of the palace opened. One of the two fat, balding eunuchs she'd accosted earlier stood with his arms folded across his ample chest.

"You will come," he announced to April. He turned and started back into the palace.

April hurried after him. She'd been summoned at last.

Chapter 7

She went quickly, not paying any attention to the lavishness through which she was being ushered. Rows of columns of green marble and jade supported the vaulted ceilings with their red beams inlaid with gold and silver. The ceilings themselves were of gold leaf and elaborately decorated with dragons and *foo* dogs.

At last they came to the double golden doors that led to the Empress's quarters. The guards swung wide the doors and stood stiffly, heads bowed, eyes fixed firmly on the marble floor. Those summoned before the Empress were never to be looked upon, even if they be the lowest of human beings. They were to be in the presence of the immortal guardian of the empire and were, therefore, considered sacred—even if they were going to meet their death.

April mounted the double flight of stairs that had red gilded balustrades. Another set of doors opened and she found herself in a small room of unimaginable beauty. The floor was covered with yellow velvet, trimmed with a gold fringe that stretched from wall to wall. Teak and bronze and ivory were scattered everywhere in all sizes of tables and urns and consoles. Under a gold canopy was placed the thousand-jeweled imperial throne in designs of dragons and clouds. Seated on a cushion of gold was Tz'u Hsi, Dowager Empress of all China.

The "Old Buddah," as she was sometimes lovingly called, was a small, square woman sitting straight and stiff, arrayed in an elaborate yellow dragon robe, sable hat, and high Manchu shoes, looking inscrutable and defiant. Yards of gray pearls hung from about her neck and her nails were encased in intricately carved silver sheaths.

April made her obeisance, prostrating herself before the imperious figure, fighting back the urge to show her defiance.

"You may rise, cousin," the old woman said. Her voice was as cold and as hard as her flinty black eyes.

"Where is my son?" April demanded, unable to control her impatience.

The Empress held up her hand. "I said you may rise. I did not give you permission to speak."

April ignored her. "I want my son!"

"Silence!"

April saw the look that came over the Dowager's face and recognized it only too well. It was the way she looked when pleased with an execution, or contemplating one. April reminded herself she had best control her anxiety. Bringing about her own death would accomplish nothing.

"I can identify with your motherly concern, cousin," the old woman said. "I, too, had a son." Her eyes narrowed. "I hope for your sake that your son does not suffer the same fate as mine."

April knew the story. At age seventeen, Ts'u Hsi had been a concubine of the emperor, the first woman of the Yehe clan to be taken into the royal harem in over two hundred years. She was quick to firmly establish her position in the imperial household by bearing the emperor his only son. And when the emperor died, Tz'u Hsi had her five-year-old child put upon the throne, naming herself regent and giving her subjects their first glimpse of her iron will, as well as of her gift for politics and rule. T'ung Chih, her son, died at the age of nineteen. Despite all challengers to the throne, the Dowager Empress held tight to her reins and continued her domination of nobles and commoners alike.

"We share the same hope," April said, hating the sight of the old witch.

The Empress chose to ignore April's defiance in disobeying her command for silence. "You annoy me, Princess. You are too strong-willed for your own good."

"I am of your blood. I cannot be held responsible for being much like your royal self." She thought she saw a flicker of amusement in the craggy old face.

"Do not waste your slyness on me, cousin. I admit you are a challenge to me—all clever, ambitious women are—which is why I tolerate them so seldom. Men I can see through as plainly as I do a pane of clear glass. Do not be deceived, however. I am old, true enough, but I am also immortal and all-knowing. I could crush you like a bug if I so chose so to do. Be advised not to toy with me."

April bowed, trying again to check her defiance and hide her hatred of the old woman.

"Your boy is safe . . . for the time being," the Empress added ominously.

April opened her mouth to speak, but the old woman silenced her with a look.

"He will be returned to your apartment. Of course, there are conditions."

A cold hand tightened around April's heart. "What conditions?" she asked, keeping her voice even.

"First. You are never to see Prince Ke Loo again. Your father is a traitor and will be put to death as soon as I can have that devil brought here to me."

Again April bowed. "That is a condition I can easily meet, Imperial One. Like you, I have no love or concern for Prince Ke Loo, my father."

"The second condition may not be so well to your liking, cousin. Once before you promised to do my bidding and you disobeyed me."

April frowned.

"Before your child was born, when you lived contentedly with me, you made me a vow that you did not keep."

"If my vow was broken it was no doubt because I was prevented from keeping it."

"No one prevented you. You disobeyed me, or else took me for a forgetful fool."

"Never, Imperial One."

The Empress switched her sleeves in a gesture of anger and aggravation. "You were to correspond with your American mother and with your traitorous brother, Li Ahn. You refused."

"I did not refuse, cousin," April said sweetly. "I had just recently married. I allowed my husband to occupy too much of my thoughts. The corre-

89

spondence was never attended to because I was mindless of everything but my love for him."

The old woman's eyes glinted. "Your husband was a thief. I trust you have put him well out of your mind."

"I do not know his name," April lied. "Nor what he looked like. I did not even call my son after his father, as is the Western custom."

"You say you do not recall what your husband looked like. Why then do you keep a reminder of him constantly by your side? Your child is the image of that American criminal."

"I keep the child as an instrument with which I avenge myself on the criminal's family, as well as upon my American mother."

The Empress studied her for a moment. April did not let her own steady gaze falter. "I see," the old woman said, letting her expression soften. "The similarity of your husband's and your mother's crimes occurred to me, of course. But avenging yourself on the woman in America is not the punishment I wish for her."

"I have not forgotten what you asked of me, cousin. I had no intention of forsaking my solemn promise. It was my only reason for wanting to get to America."

The old woman eyed her suspiciously. "And your brother, Li Ahn?"

"Again I wanted to find him. As you know, Royal One, I have been here in Peking for too many years. I know not where my brother is. My mother sent him off to a school. I was not told where, nor can I find out."

The Empress looked disgusted and flew into a rage. "I should have you and the rest of your family put to death. Your father has bred nothing but copies of himself . . . all traitors, all dissidents and usurpers. Li Ahn refused to carry out my orders. He deserted his Empress, his country. He will die under the blade of the same ax that beheads his father—and you, as well, if you think you can trick me."

April waited for the burst of anger to subside. Calmly she asked, "What is it you want of me, Empress? I will not disappoint you again."

Still angry, the Empress rasped, "I want you to have your brother and that American woman returned here to me for the punishment they both deserve."

A crafty gleam fluttered across April's face. "I will be only too happy to do so, Empress; however, I cannot fulfill either vow without returning to America, where I can locate them."

"You will correspond."

"But you yourself told me a long time ago that your agents in America are dwindling. Can you trust them to carry out your orders?" She saw the old woman hesitate and pushed her advantage. "It was my intention from the very start to return to America with my son, to taunt his grandparents with their grandson's existence, a grandson they will never be able to have. Then with clever and convincing threats and guile, I would induce my mother and Li Ahn to return with me to China." She gave the old woman a smug smile. "I know my mother's weaknesses. She loves her children too well, which, as you know, is sometimes unwise. I will connive to convince her to come back here with me, and Li Ahn has always done what I've asked." She took a daring step closer. "I originally fled the palace and sought sanctuary in the American legation so that no one would suspect me of working on your behalf, cousin. My plans always had your interest at their heart."

The old woman kept watching her, searching for a hint of lies, a glimmer of deception. She found none.

"I could not communicate my plot to you, for as you know the palace walls have many different ears. Prince Ke Loo's ears are ears you know well."

"Prince Ke Loo," the Dowager said in disgust as her mind suddenly shifted. She thought of the traitor and of the threatening pack that sought to unseat her. "He is in league with those filthy peasants," she charged. "I will crush them all." She pounded the flat of her hand on the arms of her golden throne.

After a moment she let herself relax, folding her hands calmly in her lap. She sat quite still for a long time, watching April all the while. When she moved it was with the trace of a smile on her lips. "Very well, cousin. I will agree to your departure."

Inside her breast April's heart leapt but she was clever to hide even the slightest clue of her happiness. "You will not regret the decision, cousin."

"I had better not."

With a wave of the Empress's hand, April was dismissed.

"My son?" April asked, refusing to move as the Empress nodded for her eunuchs to carry her from the throne room.

"I said he will be returned to you."

"When?"

"Tomorrow."

"I cannot accomplish my venture without him," April said, fearful that the old woman was planning on keeping Adam as a hostage. "Adam is absolutely imperative to my plan."

"You said yourself, Princess, that mothers are unfortunately sometimes too attached to their children. I trust you do not deceive yourself."

"Adam is the carrot I will dangle on the stick." She tried to make herself sound as evil as the old woman herself.

"You will have your carrot, Princess."

The eunuchs carefully lifted the Empress, placed her on an elaborate golden chaise, and carried her from the room.

I've won, April said to herself as she tried not to show her joy by running back to her chambers. But once out of earshot of guards and eunuchs she found she could contain herself no longer.

"You old fool! I'll have my revenge on you as well," April vowed as she tried to quiet the wild beating of her heart.

Back in the antechamber of the throne room, Tz'u Hsi summoned her chamberlain. "The Princess April," she ordered. "You are certain you saw the commoner Sun Yat-sen visit her rooms at the legation?"

"Yes, Your Highness."

"Do you believe she too is a party to Ke Loo's plot?"

Her chamberlain hesitated. "From all we could uncover, the girl is not in league with them. It is unfortunate Sun Yat-sen escaped before we could capture him."

"That is no one's fault. It is difficult for any

93

Manchu to believe a prince of the family would conspire with a common peasant." She thought for a moment. "Ke Loo's other daughter?"

"Mei Fei?"

"Yes." She thought for a moment. "Are the sisters friendly?"

"Very much so, I am informed."

"Good. I want the Princess April to be allowed to leave. There will be no attendants, no soldiers. It is to look as though she and her son are escaping." She ran a long nail across the back of her hand. "Now, is Wu Lien in residence still?"

"He is in the palace in the Forbidden City, Royal One, preparing for your arrival."

"Have him brought here to me. I have arrangements to make and a reminder to be given to the Princess April that I trust will insure her loyalty to me."

Chapter 8

Wu Lien was different from what April remembered. It had been so long since they had found shelter in that poor scraggly village near Paoting where David had shot the man who was about to stab Wu Lien. Now, seeing Wu Lien after so long, it was hard for her to believe that Wu Lien had betrayed him after David had saved his life.

"You are more lovely than ever," Wu Lien said as he came toward her.

He was shorter than she recalled, but still strong and handsome, though it was a cruel handsomeness. Once she'd almost loved this young Manchu; now she despised him with every fiber of her being. Reminding herself of his esteemed position with the Empress, however, April forced a smile and played the hypocrite she had to be. "You are looking extremely well, Wu Lien."

He thanked her and seated himself beside her in the window seat. "I was surprised that you gave your permission to receive me."

"You performed a duty that was expected of you. A man cannot be blamed for doing his sworn duty." She hated the nearness of him, the very sound of his voice.

"Then you have forgiven me for betraying David?"

She raised her eyes and held his gaze. "My husband committed a crime. As a loyal subject to the Empress, you had no choice but to do what you did."

When he took her hand a shiver of disgust ran through her and it was with the most supreme effort of will that she did not pull away.

He said, "I love you, April. I betrayed David because I had to have you for myself."

A terrible nausea suddenly seized her. She swayed slightly, sensing the blood drain from her face. Wu Lien steadied her. "Are you all right, my darling?"

April passed a hand across her brow and forced down the bile that was churning about in her stomach. After David's execution her Oriental mind had almost accepted Wu Lien's betrayal, knowing how rigid was his sense of duty. Now she hated him all the more. He'd killed out of selfishness, nothing more. It had been his lust that had wielded the ax, not a noble sense of allegiance.

"You were to marry Mei Fei," April managed to say as she sat there wanting to drive a dagger into his chest.

"The Empress decided that it would not be a wise choice of wife for me because of Prince Ke Loo's treason."

"Mei Fei is not Prince Ke Loo's only daughter," April reminded him, finding it impossible to look into his face for fear he would see her loathing.

"I know the Empress would never permit me to

96

marry you, April, but there are other ways in which I could show my love for you."

"I leave for America shortly."

"Then we must make the most of our days and nights." He took her into his arms. The feel of him repulsed her. Tactfully, she stood up and walked toward the door leading to the terrace.

Purposely changing the subject she said, "Tell me of this business between my father and the Empress. What proof does the Dowager have that Prince Ke Loo has betrayed her?"

"You have heard of The Society of the Righteous and Harmonious Fists?"

"Yes, those whom some call the Boxers."

"They have become most troublesome of late and the Empress's informants discovered that the movement emerged first in the north, near Kalgan, your father's home. Everyone thought they were merely peasants restless with the times and the economic distress and political uncertainty of China under the Empress's rule. It was reported that they were opposed to foreign intervention, both the interference of Westerners in the country's trade and the attempts of the Occidental missionaries to turn the people against our ancestral ways and religion. Their original targets were the missionaries and their Chinese converts."

"Why did the Empress decide my father was involved?"

"Her Highness always suspected Ke Loo of having a covetous eye on her throne and had him watched carefully. It was found that he was secretly turning the Boxers against the Empress, telling them that the missionaries and Westerners were here only because she invited them and that she was in league with them."

"And why hasn't she had Ke Loo's head before this?"

"Must I remind you that your father is high lord for the entire north? His death would cause an out-and-out rebellion. The Empress's army is not yet strong enough to put down such an insurrection. But soon—she is biding her time until she can carry out her own scheme to turn the Boxers in her favor."

"How does she intend doing that?"

"By declaring war on all foreign powers." He smiled. "That way she will gain the Boxers' support and ensure her throne."

"But what of the foreign powers? A war would crush China."

His smile widened. "There will be no war. The Empress will let the Boxers kill and pillage. On the other side, she will tell the foreign powers she is helpless to stop her rioting peasants and cannot be held responsible. One will destroy the other and whatever the outcome, the Empress will retain her throne."

"And Ke Loo?"

"When Old Buddah has the loyalty of the Boxers, Ke Loo will quietly disappear . . . a body without a head."

Knowing the evil machinations of the Empress's mind, April grew suspicious. "Does she really plan on allowing me to return to America? I, after all, am a member of Ke Loo's family. Am I not in danger of execution?"

He laughed. "You are the instrument that she is using to bring Ke Loo's male heir back to China for his punishment. Succeed in that and you will be safe from all harm."

"You know of my mission?"

"It has been confided to me, no one else."

"You've risen high, Wu Lien."

"I was rewarded for my loyalties, nothing more."

Her loathing of him grew.

"My son?" April asked, forcing herself to sound natural. "Have you seen him? He still has not been returned to me."

"He is a handsome child, as was my friend, his father."

"Two-faced snake," April said under her breath.

"He is to be brought to you this afternoon."

April brightened. "Today? Are you certain, Wu Lien?"

He nodded. "I heard the Empress herself give the order that your amah come for him at four o'clock, after he awakens from his rest. The physicians . . ."

"Physicians?" April cried. "Adam has been ill?"

"No, not ill. They were merely attending him."

She thought suddenly of the terrible story of Li Ahn's—how the physicians had bled him, drawing off all traces of his mother's American blood. "They've bled him?" she gasped.

"No." He put his hands on her shoulders. April turned away. "He has not been bled. He is being formally accepted into the Manchu dynasty. A harmless ceremony."

April did not understand.

"Having been a female child, you would not know of such ceremonies. All sons of a royal Manchu house must undergo the initiation."

"Her Highness looks upon Adam as royal?"

"His mother is a Princess, is she not?" he said with a sly grin.

He was making an excuse, lying through his teeth. The Empress would never accept Adam into her family. As she looked at him she wondered why she had never recognized this oily quality in Wu Lien before today. He was a loathsome, despicable creature with a snake's heart and ice in his veins. There were too many of his kind in the palaces of China and, she supposed, all the palaces in the world.

When he moved to embrace her April flattened her hands against his chest. "It would not be right for me to give myself to you, Wu Lien." With a coy look she added, "As you said yourself, I am a princess and therefore above your station."

A mask of fury slowly moved down over his face as April moved out of his arms. Wu Lien refused to be denied. "Mei Fei is a Princess and she was considered good enough to be my bride."

Haughtily, April reminded him, "Mei Fei is a bastard. Everyone knows that." His growing rage was giving her pleasure, but she was careful to conceal it.

"And you?" he spat. "Your mother was an American."

She felt smug. "She was received and acknowledged by the Empress. It is on the court records for everyone to see. I am not called *Princess* for nothing, Wu Lien, a title not given to Mei Fei."

Wu Lien stood seething with anger. Of a sudden he turned sharply and stormed from the room. When the door clanged behind him April threw herself across the divan and smothered her laughter in the silken pillows.

She lay there for a long time, watching the shadows lengthen, counting the minutes, listening for the amah's footsteps coming down the corridor. At last the door opened and the amah came in with Adam in her arms. April let the tears flow freely as she took him to her, smoothing his hair and planting kisses of love on his small, lovely face. Everything suddenly seemed right in the world and for the first time in a long time April felt genuinely happy

"Well," she said as she found the courage to hold him away from her, "I hear you were at a very great ceremony." She prayed Adam would prove Wu Lien the liar she was certain he was.

The boy looked blank. April saw a dullness in his eyes but quickly discounted it when she reminded herself that he had obviously just awakened from his afternoon nap. Still, she'd never seen that vacant expression before. It was as though he were looking at her but not seeing her.

"Did the great Empress speak with you?"

Adam slowly shook his head but said nothing.

"I was told you had to undergo a ceremony. Did you make any mistakes? Did you have to say words?"

Again he looked blank. "I slept a very long time," he said finally.

April quickly looked up at the amah who shrugged and walked away.

With a listless move Adam reached into the pocket of his little robe and pulled out a toy soldier. "Tsao Kun gave it to me," he said in a drowsy voice.

"Tsao Kun, the royal physician?"

"He said it is a royal soldier, just as I will be one day because I am Manchu. What is Manchu, Mama?" His speech was thick and heavy-sounding.

"A royal name," she answered, studying him intently, sensing that something was wrong. "Your grandfather is a Prince of the Manchu dynasty. I am a Princess."

She saw he didn't understand what she was talking about. "Never mind, my darling. Come, we will have something to eat and then we will play a game."

"I'm sleepy, mama," he said, yawning.

"Didn't you just have your nap?"

"Yes, but I am still sleepy. I am sleepy all the time."

April frowned, then gathered him tighter in her arms. It was so unlike him to complain of being tired. He'd always been so active, and hated having to be put to bed. They'd done something to him, she was sure. If only she knew what had gone on behind those golden doors.

"Get out of your clothes," Wu Lien yelled as he stomped into Mei Fei's apartment and began pulling off his tunic.

"Wu Lien," she said in surprise as she jumped to her feet. "You are returned from the Forbidden City?"

"I said get into bed," he bellowed.

She stood staring at him, not understanding his anger. It was Wu Lien to whom she'd lost her innocence by decree of the Empress—a gift to Wu Lien for his loyalty to her. She did not mind the

102

loss of her virginity at the time because she was promised to Wu Lien in marriage.

Then, when she was told she would not marry Wu Lien she was both pleased and ashamed. Freedom from an unwanted husband was welcomed; the loss of her virginity was a shame that could never be remedied.

Despite his anger, Mei Fei did not move. "You have no right any more to demand my favors. I am no concubine."

"You are the bastard daughter of a traitor to the Empress. You will do as I say."

"No," Mei Fei snapped. "I refuse to permit you to treat me like a common whore."

He grabbed her roughly and ripped open the front of her loose robe, baring her breasts. Mei Fei tried to cover herself. Wu Lien slapped her across the face and shoved her onto the bed. He stood over her, stripping himself naked, then fell on her like a ferocious beast.

He forced her thighs apart impatiently and wedged himself between them as he tore away the rest of her clothing. With one fierce lunge he entered her, not caring about anything but the need to hurt. He shut his ears to Mei Fei's whimpering cries of protest. Again and again he pushed himself into her, his eyes tightly closed as April's lovely face focused on the backs of his lids.

Mei Fei found that the more she struggled the more painful it was and so she forced herself to relax and endure his onslaught, blanking her mind to the humiliation, the torture of him. She lay with her face averted, her eyes closed, her mind stilled as Wu Lien drove into her with frenzied intensity. She heard him groan and felt his body stiffen.

With a long, low growl he pushed himself deep inside her as spasm after spasm wracked his body.

Then it was finished. He lay quiet for a moment, then heaved a sigh and fell away from her.

Slowly, quietly, Mei Fei gathered her tattered robe about her and moved off the bed. She went behind the latticed screen and dressed herself in a silk robe the color of saffron. When she emerged Wu Lien was seated on the side of the bed, still naked, his head in his hands. When he heard her move about he stirred and started to get dressed.

"You have no right to use me as you did," Mei Fei complained. "The Empress will be told."

He grunted and ignored her.

"I will never forget this insult, Wu Lien. Just remember that the lioness is far more deadly than the lion."

"Be quiet, and spare me your silly platitudes."

"See this hand," she snarled, raising the hand with the beautiful jade and pearl ring. "If ever again you force yourself on me as you just did, there will be a dagger in this hand that I will plunge into your back while you are laboring over me."

"I will take you whenever I wish," he said, but he cast a nervous eye on her upraised hand.

"I warn you, Wu Lien. You had better make me your enemy as I now make you mine."

"Be careful, Mei Fei. Remember, it is I who have the Empress's ear." He looked at her hand again as she lowered it slowly. A thought occurred to him. "Princess April leaves tomorrow. The Empress has expressed a desire that she be given a token, a reminder as to where her loyalties lay." He kept looking at the pearl and jade ring on Mei

Fei's beautiful hand. "I believe I have found a perfect reminder."

He walked out with an evil smile curved on his mouth. Outside the door Mei Fei heard him begin to laugh.

Chapter 9

Little Adam slept through the night. His sleep was so sound April found herself waking in the night, sensing that his breathing had stopped. Several times she shook him gently until he stirred, but he never woke up.

As she stood over him, moonlight streaming through the windows, she came to the conclusion that the child had obviously been given some type of drug. It was unnatural for him to sleep so soundly and the hour or two he had been awake he'd been so lethargic.

April slept little, part of her mind worrying about Adam, the other excited over the prospect of finally getting away.

When the sun was well over the horizon she threw back the covers and went quickly to Adam's bed. Her heart leapt when she saw him sitting up, his eyes bright, his face glowing.

"I'm hungry."

"Of course you are, my little man," she said, lifting him. "And you must eat a hearty breakfast, for today we leave for the the harbor and for the big ship that will take us across the ocean."

"Won't the soldiers stop us again?"

"Not this time, darling. Everything is arranged. And before the month is out we will be in your grandmother's big house in San Francisco." She carried him across the room. "Did you have a nice time when you stayed with the Empress?"

"I don't remember."

"You don't remember any of it? Surely you remember something . . . you remembered the toy soldier the physician gave you."

"He gave me sweet water that made me fall asleep."

So they had drugged him, April told herself angrily. But *why?* she wondered. "And do you feel sleepy now, Adam?"

"No. I never want to sleep again."

April laughed.

"And I will never drink sweet water again. It made me dizzy and sick and I threw up a lot."

Again April laughed, thinking, *Good, I hope he made it as difficult for them as possible.*

"Do you feel sick now?"

"No."

"Then we will have a bath and a big breakfast. After that we will dress in our heaviest clothing and the bearers will take us to Shanghai harbor."

"I want to go with the Marine soldiers."

"Not this time. The coolies will bear us in chairs. It will be much more comfortable than that hard, old wagon Uncle Eddie had us ride in."

She suddenly thought of Eddie Wells and supposed he was well on his way to Washington by now. April rang for the amah. "The child's bath water, prepare it."

"It is already prepared, Princess. I saw he was

awake and took the liberty." She reached for the boy.

"No, I will bathe him. Finish packing what I told you we would take and do not forget the travel documents I laid out. Then see that breakfast is prepared. We will also take food with us. See to it."

The amah bowed herself out of the room.

"Now, here we go into your nice, warm bath," she said as she carried Adam into the small adjoining room that was snug and cozy with a small, round porcelain tub set close to the brazier, the water steaming as it rose into the morning air.

April stood him beside the tub and pulled his loose-fitting nightdress over his head. As she lifted him into the tub she saw the ugly patch of skin on the inside of his thigh. Her breath caught in her throat as she leaned close to examine it.

At first glance she thought it to be a bruise, but on closer inspection she saw the intricate lines, the delicate traces of a tattoo pattern. It looked swollen and sore. She touched it gently. Adam seemed not to notice so obviously he felt no pain, she told herself.

Behind her the amah said, "It is the crest of the Manchu, the symbol of the family."

April looked up sharply, her expression angry.

"All male children wear the tattoo. It is the law," the amah said.

April leaned down again and studied the mark.

"The child felt nothing and feels nothing now," the amah said.

As April traced the design with her eyes she saw it formed the petals of two open poppies, one atop the other, encircled by a band of connecting dots.

"Seeds of the twin poppies," the amah explained. "The source of the Manchu wealth, the flowers that the world seeks to possess."

A shudder ran through April as she stared at the design. It wasn't exactly ugly; in fact, after the discoloration disappeared the design would be quite attractive but she wished with all her heart that it was not there. For the whole of Adam's life it would always be there to remind him that Oriental blood flowed in his veins.

Was this the Empress's way of reminding her of who she was? April sighed, resigning herself; the deed was done and there was no way it could be undone. She lifted Adam into the warm, soapy water and tried to close her mind to the tattoo and concentrate on the long, arduous journey that lay ahead—and of what lay in waiting once she reached the end of the journey.

Still, as she bathed the boy she found her eyes constantly moving to the poppy design on the inside of the little thigh. It was a strange place for a brand—and that is how she thought of it . . . as a brand.

When she lifted Adam out of the tub and wrapped him in heated, fluffy towels the amah came in to tell her the packing was finished and that the table was set for them.

"Do all Manchu men have the poppy brand in the same place?" April asked her amah.

The old woman nodded. "Close to the seed from which future generations grow. The seed of the man must pass the symbol of the family. As it passes it is reminded of its name and of its purpose so that as it rests in the womb of the woman it meditates on its destiny. When it matures and is

109

brought forth into the world, its purpose in life has already been instilled in its soul."

April found herself smiling in spite of herself. She thought of Kim Lee, her old tutor who lived over the bake shop in San Francisco's Chinatown and of all the lore with which he enraptured her. He'd never told her of the twin poppies and their seeds and as she looked again at Adam's thigh she suppressed a laugh, knowing why the old man had kept the story from a girl hardly into her teens.

The morning grew late and cold. There was no one in the courtyard except the bearers who were to carry the one sedan chair to be shared by April and Adam and to tote her two bundles of possessions. They were a scrawny lot of peasant men, thin and gaunt and looking as if a single pound would be a burden to them.

April had gone to Mei Fei's apartment to say good-bye but Mei Fei was with the Empress, she'd been told by Wu Lien. His tone had been hard and angry and he had laughed, which April did not understand.

"Please tell her I said good-bye and that I wish it were possible to delay my departure so I could tell her myself, but all is arranged."

Wu Lien gave her a stern nod.

"Tell her I only wish she were coming with us, and remind her that I will always remember her."

Wu Lien laughed again, louder than before. "I am certain you will," he said with a sneer. There was something cruel and ominous in the way he'd said it.

"Good-bye, Wu Lien."

"We will meet again."

"Yes, I am certain we will. I will return as I promised," she lied.

As she walked out of the palace and settled herself and Adam in the sedan chair, idle curiosity made her wonder if the twin poppies decorated Wu Lien's thigh. She supposed it did, as it also did that of Li Ahn, her brother. She was suddenly ashamed of herself for thinking such a thought.

Huddled in their rugs, Adam was overly excited and asked question after question about the things he saw as the bearers carried them along the road that skirted the rice fields and the bamboo thickets. He seemed never to tire of staring with delight at the endless forms of decoration of which the Chinese are so fond. Even the poorest village held charming evidences of intricately carved archways and doors, and lovely trellises—barren at this time of year—constructed in complicated and graceful patterns. Not a single bridge that they crossed had been overlooked by the hand of some local artisan—stones so laid as to make a simple straight span a work of art.

Nothing, April noticed, was built that did not compliment its surroundings. Villages were picturesque little tableaux set before carefully selected backgrounds of yews and birches, firs or mist-ringed mountains.

Yet, after several days on the seemingly endless road, their admiration for the beauty of the Chinese landscape began to lag and with each passing hour the boredom of the swaying chair became almost unbearable. With every river they crossed, every village they passed through, April asked the bearers the same question and received the same answer.

"How much farther?"

"Not far, Princess. Not far now."

The days stretched into a week. Hundreds of miles had been traveled and still there seemed no end to the long, boring days, the uncomfortable nights spent in inns that were no more than partially covered courtyards with rooms opened on two sides and lit by smoking oil lamps. The small cubicles were always windowless, with earthen floors and wooden pallets covered with matting.

During the days the coolies spoke hardly at all; at night they became a clanging orchestra of yells and talk and raucous laughter as they unashamedly stripped themselves naked and sluiced themselves with water from a well, washed their feet, and smoked their long pipes. After the dinner meal—always rice and tea, and some sweet-and-sour-tasting meats—a quiet gradually fell over the inn. Then came a stillness so heavy its weight carried sleep with it and nothing stirred until the inevitable crow of the cock or a blare of trumpets if the inn were in a sizable village.

Toward the end of the second week April sat forward in her chair and drew back the curtains as the unmistakable smell of salt air assailed her. She clutched Adam to her and pointed down the steep slope at the ocean far in the distance.

"At last," she said. "That is Shanghai," she told him, faintly making out the sprawl of buildings and the clutter of vessels that were blurred against the land's edge. Never had a sight been more welcome.

"Shanghai," she breathed, her pulse racing as happy little pangs throbbed in her breast.

After an hour they came to a row of dried mud huts, flimsy and dilapidated, that lined the road leading to the gateway of the city. A moment later they found themselves in the middle of crowds of people and carts and animals, all trudging back and forth, moving in all directions. The people looked tattered and poor, but every now and then a pair of gentlemen in long black figured-silk gowns and silk jackets could be seen looking imperious and untouchable. Ragged boys raced and hooted and jeered at passersby.

The street to the harbor was lined with shops of every shape and size, all manner of things being offered for sale in their dark recesses. Hundreds of people surged along the footwalks. April's coolies began shouting in sharp cries to clear the way.

The harbor itself was a confusion of workers and half-naked peasants operating blocks and tackles, loading and unloading, lugging, scurrying, arguing. April saw a large sailing steamer with masts for the emergency sails. It sat at the far end of the wharf and had the name *Columbia* painted in bright red letters on its bow. She directed the bearers toward it and was then set down.

Taking Adam by the hand she went up the gangplank and inquired of the ship's destination and whether or not passengers were being taken aboard.

"We're bound for the States," the seaman told her, "after a stop in the Philippines and another in Honolulu. From there we sail for San Francisco harbor." He nodded to the wheel house. "You'll have to speak to the captain about passage, Miss."

She found the captain to be a crusty old salt

113

steeped in the tradition that women aboard ships were bad luck. April's string of pearls and ruby pendant overpowered his superstitions, however.

The cabin assigned them was small, but luxurious in comparison to the hovels in which they'd been forced to sleep during the past weeks. After settling herself in and seeing that Adam was tucked in for his nap, she paid off the coolies and ordered them to return to Peking.

The captain tapped on her door and told her that they would be sailing on the morning tide. He eyed her critically. "If you have something a little less 'Chinesey' to wear, I'd suggest you put it on. There's the other passengers to think about." At dinner she found the other passengers were mostly Americans, but there were several Orientals, richly dressed and wearing authoritative airs. She was sorry she had chosen her plainest gown.

After a dinner of roast chicken and vegetables, followed by a chocolate pudding, all eaten in silence, April took Adam's hand and started back toward their cabin. As she turned the corner of the deck she stopped short. Wu Lien was leaning against the rail waiting for her.

"Wu Lien!"

He bowed.

"What are you doing here?"

"I came on orders of the Empress." He held out a purple velvet box with silver fittings. "She wanted you to have this."

April looked at the box and took it from him. She tried to raise the lid but found the box locked.

Wu Lien gave her a crooked smile and held up the tiny key.

April motioned toward her cabin and ushered

114

Wu Lien inside. She placed the box on the table and lifted Adam up onto the edge of his bunk.

"A gift?" she asked as she took the key Wu Lien handed to her.

"A reminder, Princess."

The key turned easily.

Wu Lien said, "Her Highness wanted to be certain you would not forget the vow you made to her."

April lifted the lid. Her eyes widened and a sickening scream tore from her throat. She stared at Mei Fei's beautiful severed hand, the blood soaking the purple velvet lining, the pearl and jade ring still on the third finger.

The room began to spin around as she clutched the edge of the table. She screamed again.

Wu Lien caught her as she collapsed in a dead faint.

Part Two

San Francisco—1894

Chapter 1

Lorna MacNair had always been a vindictive woman, one who never relented until she got what she wanted, no matter the price or how long it took. She was tall and thin, lovely in an austere way, though her stiffness was becoming a little less rigid as she grew older.

Lorna MacNair was a woman to be feared.

She'd be forty years old next month, on November 10th, but her face was as unlined and unblemished as a woman's fifteen years younger. She was slightly near-sighted but never wore spectacles except in the privacy of her own home, and even then usually when she was completely alone. At a glance anyone could see that Lorna MacNair was the epitome of snobbishness—haughty, cold, and accustomed to money.

The man seated opposite her in the fashionable, though over-crowded Victorian sitting room was precisely her opposite. Mr. Ramsey—everyone called him simply "Ramsey"—was short, paunchy, and balding. There was little about him that Lorna found attractive, with the possible exceptions that he was extremely interested in money and, like herself, had few ethics.

She had first met Ramsey when she'd hired the detective to spy on her husband, Peter, and Lydia Moonsong.

He'd done a good job, but he hadn't wanted the pay she offered him. He'd demanded—and she gave him—her body as the price for his services. As difficult as it had been for Lorna to settle that account with Ramsey, it had been worth it. She had disgraced Lydia Moonsong, exposed her secret marriage to a Mandarin, and told the world of her two Oriental children.

Unfortunately, Lydia Moonsong continued as a threat to Lorna's marriage and every time Lorna needed to subvert Lydia further, Ramsey was only too willing to help her—for the same price. Now, of course, she had no choice but to pay to prevent his exposing their relationship to Peter.

Lorna fidgeted with her cocktail, then nervously put it aside. "You didn't summon me here without a reason," she said to him. "What is it that you want, Ramsey?"

He put his cigar in the ashtray and tamped it out. "You," he answered simply.

"Really," Lorna said with an indignant shrug. "Since when have I become your chattel?" She knew his answer without hearing it and reached again for her cocktail. She sipped it, waiting apprehensively.

"I'm sure your handsome husband doesn't know the truth about us, Lorna."

"Nevertheless, I have no intention of being beholden to you for the rest of my life."

He chuckled. "Why not? Secretly you delight in

the way I force myself on you. You know, Lorna, deep in your heart you are nothing but a slut."

"How dare you!" She jumped to her feet and grabbed her hat and gloves.

"Sit down." It was an order.

She looked at him and saw the threatening expression, the cruel twist of his mouth. Slowly she lowered herself back into the overstuffed chair.

"Don't pull that haughty bit on me, Lorna. I know you too well. From what I hear he'd like a good excuse to divorce you, so behave. You're so damned determined to stay married to Peter you'd do anything, even take abuse from men like me." He grinned. "That husband of yours must be one pretty terrific man in bed to make you such a slave to him."

"You're despicable."

It was true though, she reminded herself. There wasn't anything she wouldn't do for Peter. It was seldom he came into her bed, but when he did he awakened feelings deep inside her she did not know existed. Beneath him she lost all control, blushing with shame afterward at how she'd writhed and clawed and groaned aloud like a common whore or one of those Chinese singsong girls he was so fond of visiting. She was enslaved by her husband's sexuality. And the worst of it was when she looked into his eyes and saw that he knew the power his body gave him over her.

Ramsey laughed. "I don't know why I want a woman like you, Lorna, but I do." He fanned out his hands. "I guess it's because you represent class."

"This situation cannot possibly continue forever," Lorna said.

He moved his head slowly from side to side. "You will always need someone like me to do your dirty work, Lorna. We are alike, you and I. I suppose that is why we really don't like each other much but can't do without each other."

He got to his feet and extended his hand to her. "I did not invite you here to chit-chat," he said. "Come on, let's go into the bedroom." When he saw her draw back he cocked his head, keeping his hand extended.

"Don't force me to give Peter an excuse to divorce you," he threatened.

He beckoned her. Lorna hesitated, then reluctantly placed her hand in his. He pulled her from the chair and led her into the adjoining bedroom.

Everything about Ramsey repulsed her, yet she could not help responding to the brutalness of his assault. He treated her as he would treat a streetwalker, a cheap prostitute from the Barbary Coast, forcing her to do the most humiliating and degrading of acts. Yet she submitted and even found his dominance reminiscent of the way Peter treated her. She closed her eyes and gave herself up to her fantasies, responding as she knew she shouldn't. But the animal force of him made her a helpless victim to her own carnal needs.

Though she would never admit it, even to herself, she knew when Ramsey summoned her to his flat this evening what he wanted of her. And she had come without hesitating, eager to play her part, knowing he'd give her the release Peter was depriving her of, the release she so desperately needed.

Afterward, Ramsey lay unashamedly naked on top of the tangle of sheets. Lorna found it impossible to look at him. She held fast to the vision she'd invoked of her husband's hard, muscled body—trim of waist, broad of shoulders; his torturously magnificent manhood.

She slipped quickly from Ramsey's side and began to dress herself. "Now tell me what you've found out about my husband."

"If you had gone to Lydia Moonsong's party you would have seen for yourself."

"They were together? He told me he wasn't going."

"They were together . . . like love birds cooing in a corner."

Lorna's anger made her hands shake as she buttoned her bodice. "That wretched woman," she growled. "I swore once that I'd kill her and I will, if I must."

"There are ways of dealing with Lydia Moonsong without getting yourself involved in a murder charge. She can be manipulated. The lady is in a bind."

"How do you mean?"

"She can't run after Peter without angering that Frenchman who's always hanging about. Without Monsieur Andrieux, Lydia would be in a pretty poor situation. Her company's success hinges on that Frenchie and she knows it."

"It's a disgusting business, her carrying on with her own son-in-law."

He had to hurt her. "It's your husband she carried on with." He saw her wince and smiled.

"You mentioned Peter wanting to divorce me. What do you know? Surely he can't marry Lydia. She has that Chinese husband."

"No longer. I'm surprised at you, Lorna. The dissolution of the marriage was all hush-hush, but it seeped into the inner circles of San Francisco's better drawing rooms. You'd better be careful not to alienate too many of your snobbish friends. That scene you caused at the Hearsts' was a mistake." He scratched himself indecently. "Lydia Moonsong is a free woman."

"Peter wouldn't dare divorce me. For one thing, I'd never permit it and the scandal would ruin his business."

"From what one of my informants overheard at the party, the word 'divorce' was indeed mentioned. And then your husband escorted the lovely Mrs. Moonsong to her home, where he spent several hours—and not in the drawing room."

Lorna began to seethe. She'd thought Peter's affair with Lydia was finished, especially since he'd been so attentive to her and the children after she gave him the money for his new enterprise. Suddenly it occurred to her that Ramsey could well be lying. Lorna knew Peter needed her financially, especially now when he was just starting up again. He wouldn't jeopardize everything by taking up with Lydia again. He thought too much of his own success for that.

"I find what you say difficult to believe, Ramsey. Peter is too wrapped up in making a success of his business to risk it all by resuming a sordid affair with that woman."

Ramsey scratched himself again, then put his hands behind his head. "If he doesn't want to be involved with Lydia, why then is his new line of cosmetics called 'Lady Lydia'?"

Lorna stared at him. "Lady Lydia?" she stammered.

"I saw the labels with my own eyes and they did not read 'Lady Lorna.' I double-checked just to be sure my eyes weren't deceiving me or that the printers hadn't made a mistake. The new line is called 'Lady Lydia' all right."

"He wouldn't dare!"

Ramsey looked smug as he watched her resentment of him turn against her husband. "Your husband is manipulating you again, whether you want to believe it or not. He and Lydia Moonsong had their heads together for quite a while the other night. Even the Frenchman was fuming at them. You can bet your last nickel they weren't just talking about their sexual attraction for each other."

Lorna stiffened and walked hurriedly out of the bedroom. She put on her hat, pulled on her gloves, and draped her cloak about herself.

Ramsey appeared in the archway, still unashamedly naked. "Don't upset yourself too much, Lorna. You will say things you'll regret. Take my advice and let things ride. You have your husband all tied up financially. He can't make a move without you unless *we* let him."

"You don't know my husband."

"Let me keep my finger on the pulse of things. I might be able to manipulate it so as to force Lydia into the Frenchman's arms."

"Monsieur Andrieux has a wife, remember."

"A wife who deserted him. Surely I needn't remind you of that."

"No," Lorna said sadly as she remembered the

death of her son. A shiver of disgust ran through her. "That entire Moonsong family is a disgrace. They shouldn't be allowed to associate with decent people."

"Lydia Moonsong has become a very powerful and very influential woman in this town. Her money has worked miracles. As I told you earlier, I wouldn't make your hatred of her so obvious, Lorna. It will only work against you—and against your husband."

She started for the door.

"Despite all the scandal, Lydia Moonsong is a very fine figure of a woman and well-liked in both society and the business world. And bear in mind that moneyed people always associate with other moneyed people."

"My family name goes back a very long way."

He scoffed. "These are modern times, Lorna. You can stick your family name up your nose for all it's worth. You aren't in Europe. This is the United States of America, where the All-American Dollar is what counts." He shook a warning finger at her. "Now you take my advice and be a good girl. Let me handle things. Be more like Lydia Moonsong—cool, reserved, and very likable."

Lorna opened the door and started outside.

Ramsey called after her. "And keep reminding that husband of yours that you are holding the pocketbook. That'll keep him in line for the time being."

As she climbed into the carriage and started toward home, Lorna kept hearing Ramsey's words: "Be more like Lydia Moonsong." When she thought of it, they weren't all that dissimilar, both victims of their own circumstances. They were both women whose hearts ached for the love of the same man, women who needed wealth, security, position. Lydia could no more divest herself of all she'd gained than she herself could, Lorna told herself.

She thought of the sordid scandals in which Lydia had been involved. But were they any more sordid than those in which she, Lorna MacNair, was involved? The only difference was that Lydia's affairs were public knowledge. Lorna smiled to herself, knowing that she'd been responsible for that. Her smile didn't stay long, however, when she thought of Ramsey, her spying, her conniving to try and destroy Lydia in everyone's eyes, even the driving urge to see Lydia dead.

Lorna sighed and leaned back, letting her body move with the gentle sway of the carriage. She supposed she'd always been an unscrupulous woman, always determined to have what she wanted by whatever means. And no one, especially not the likes of a woman like Lydia Moonsong, would ever keep her from having what she wanted.

Above all else, Lorna wanted her husband and her children. The only sure way she knew to ensure having them was with money. The children were too accustomed to wealth and comforts to manage without it and Peter needed it. It had been the way she'd gotten him to marry her originally, and as the carriage turned into the circular drive she vowed that it was the one way she would keep him, even if it meant sleeping with a hundred Ramseys.

Chapter 2

Susan MacNair looked at her father sitting at the head of the breakfast table, then at her mother seated opposite him. It was easy to tell that her mother was angry about something. Whatever it was, her father sensed it and was ignoring her, concentrating his attention between the morning newspaper and the poached egg in front of him.

"Eat your breakfast," Lorna scolded when she found Susan studying her.

"I'm not particularly hungry. Besides, I'm thinking of dieting. I've been putting on a little weight lately."

Peter said, "It's stylish for little girls to be a bit plump."

"I happen to be twenty-one years old, Father. Plumpness on a little girl may be considered cute, but on a woman it is definitely not acceptable."

He gave her an endearing smile and set aside his paper. "My, my, I had no idea you'd become a woman all of a sudden."

"A woman?" she said incredulously. "For heaven's sake, Father, I'm practically an old maid in some people's eyes. And I didn't grow to be this old all of a sudden."

Lorna set her mouth in a firm line. "If you'd spend more time with your family, Peter, perhaps you'd be more aware of how they are growing up."

"Speaking of family," Peter said, nonplused. "Where's Efrem?"

"Sleeping in again, I suspect," Susan answered. "He was out with some of the boys from his school last night."

Peter clucked his tongue and wagged his head at Lorna. "And you allowed him to go somewhere without YOU, Lorna? I am surprised. I didn't think you ever let Efrem out of your sight."

"You are being purposefully caustic, Peter," Lorna warned.

Peter just smiled. "You do coddle the boy far too much, Lorna."

"I suppose I should have given him a free hand, the way you insisted David have."

Susan saw the old argument starting up again and rolled her eyes. "Please don't get onto that again," she said as she pushed back her chair. "I'm going to my room."

As she walked out of the room Peter found himself looking at her with different eyes. She was all grown up, he saw. And a very beautiful woman, he had to admit, with soft brown hair and a stunning figure. She floated rather than walked, with her head straight on her shoulders, her back stiff. There was something royal in her carriage and he felt very proud that she was his daughter.

"She is indeed a very beautiful girl," he said to Lorna as he again picked up his newspaper.

"Maybe you're right. Perhaps I have had my eyes closed to everything but my business."

When she didn't answer he looked over the edge of his paper and said, "All right, what's bothering you now? You might just as well get it out while we're alone. Susan and Efrem, I'm sure, are tired of hearing our arguments, which you always start when you have an audience."

"There would be no need for arguments if you were any sort of a decent father."

"More 'decent husband' is what you're getting at, I assume."

He noticed the blush in her cheeks and began reading his newspaper again.

"If you were a proper father you would notice something peculiar about Susan."

"Peculiar?" He frowned at her.

"She's so . . . independent. She has dozens of very nice young men courting her but she says she isn't interested in marrying for a while. She's twenty-one, for heaven's sake. I believe you heard her admit that some people already look upon her as a spinster. All her school chums are already married, or at least engaged to be."

"Really, Lorna, the girl obviously enjoys being single."

She paused, debating with herself as to whether she should admit her prying into Susan's affairs. After a moment she said, "I want you to have a talk with her, Peter. I found several pamphlets in her room."

"What sort of pamphlets?"

"The kind sent out by that Susan Anthony and her friends. The National Woman Suffrage Association they call their movement."

"Oh," Peter said, his frown deepening. "Women's right to the vote and all that bunk."

"Yes. Susan's been attending meetings and rallies. Lord only knows where she'll wind up. In jail, more than likely."

"All right, I'll talk to her. There'll be none of those goings-on in this house," he said angrily. "If there is one thing I will not tolerate, it is a woman who refuses to accept her place." He turned back to his paper, then a thought struck him. He looked at Lorna again. "How do you know Susan's been attending lectures and going to meetings?"

The color rose in her cheeks.

"Oh, I see. So you're back to buying the services of Mr. Ramsey? Isn't that it?"

Lorna said nothing, but she couldn't stop the blush from deepening.

Peter studied her, noticing that she was suddenly nervous. Her hand trembled ever so slightly when she put her cup down on the saucer.

"But you didn't hire Ramsey specifically for Susan, did you, Lorna?" he asked accusingly.

She said nothing.

"Did you?" he almost shouted.

She clanged her fork on the edge of the plate. "No!" she said with defiance.

"You're checking up on me again." It was a statement. Their eyes locked.

Lorna let out her breath, her eyes suddenly flashing. "How could you?"

"How could I what?"

"I know all about that new cosmetic line you're coming out with. How dare you name it after that woman?"

"Oh, so that's what you really hired Ramsey

132

for? Susan was just something he stumbled on. Surely you have better things on which to spend your money."

"It's decent of you to acknowledge the fact that it is my money," she said vindictively. She watched as his eyes narrowed in anger. She narrowed her own. "And so long as it is my money you are spending so freely, the new line will be called 'Lady Lorna,'" she announced.

"Like hell it will. It stays as it is."

"I won't permit it."

"I don't give a damn whether you'll permit it or not. The line stays 'Lady Lydia.'"

Merely hearing him say her name infuriated Lorna all the more. "How dare you purposely humiliate me like this? Do you get pleasure from it, Peter?" A sob caught in her throat. "Right from the very beginning I knew it was my money you wanted, never me, and I gave you whatever you ever wanted."

He returned to his newspaper.

"Peter, in the name of decency . . . I have never asked much of you. Is it so much to ask that you change the name of the line to my name—or to anyone else's?"

He didn't answer.

Lorna clenched her hands, then slammed a fist down on the table, rattling the dishes. Still he did not look at her. "I know you've been going to her home. You spent several hours there after her anniversary party. I warned you once before of what I'd do if you ever took up with that woman again."

"What was that?" he asked, casually turning the page. "Divorce me?"

"Never," she spat.

"What then?"

"I'll pull out every cent from MacNair Products. I'll make you a pauper again."

He chuckled. "You are a very stupid woman, Lorna. For your information my company is doing extremely well, so well, in fact, that I will be able to repay every dollar of your God-blessed money, with interest. Then," he said evenly as he leveled his eyes on her, "I have every intention of divorcing you and marrying Lydia Moonsong."

"I'd ruin you!"

He shrugged. "You'll try, I am sure, but I believe I'll survive."

He suddenly remembered Lydia warning him about the same thing when he'd spoken to her of his plans to divorce Lorna. He also remembered Lydia's ordering him out of her life and smiled to himself. One look in her eyes told him she hadn't meant it, but as he had so often before, he played her game. He'd let her pout and fuss for a while. She'd come back to him when he felt the time was right. She always did.

Lorna said, "In the name of heaven, Peter, what do you see in that woman? She has a sordid past and is practically living with her own son-in-law," she lied, hoping to rile Peter. "She is a complete disgrace."

"She is not *practically living with her son-in-law,* as you say."

It pleased her to see she'd struck a nerve. "I happen to know that she is," Lorna said, continuing the lie.

"More of your friend Ramsey's snooping?"

"Yes, as a matter of fact, it is."

"Well, he is wrong. Lydia is in no way involved with Raymond Andrieux." He paused and then added, "Much as Raymond would want her to be."

"You're the one who is wrong."

"They are no more than business partners, Lorna, which requires they spend much of their time together. If you didn't have such a sordid mind you'd recognize that fact." He refused to think about the proprietary way Raymond had acted toward Lydia, and wondered if Lydia had lied to him about Raymond's proposal of marriage. She was capable of it, he reminded himself. He gave the newspaper an angry snap.

The maid came in with fresh coffee. Peter and Lorna went silent until they were again alone. Lorna said, "I'll see that harlot dead before I see her married to you."

"I'd be careful of remarks such as that, Lorna. You've made your hatred of Lydia much too public. If anything happens to her you will be the first person people will suspect and I will be the first one to point my finger at you."

"You really hate me, don't you, Peter?"

"No, I really don't. I'm not in love with you, but other than that I have no feelings toward you whatsoever." He folded his paper and laid it aside. "I honestly can't understand why you insist on remaining married to me, Lorna. You're still a very attractive woman. There are dozens of men who'd be only too happy to marry you. I'm not the husband for you. Divorce me, Lorna, for both our sakes."

"No. Besides, you know how society looks upon divorced women."

"To hell with society. I certainly don't give a damn about them." He sipped his coffee. "Rather than injure that stupid pride of yours, you'd knuckle under to propriety and gladly ruin your life."

"Both our lives," she reminded him.

"Not mine. If you refuse to divorce me, I am perfectly willing to live openly with Lydia."

"She'd never agree to such an arrangement. Common as she is, she knows she and her precious company would suffer. No one would have anything to do with her."

"I think I could convince her to give up Empress Cosmetics, consolidate it with MacNair Products, and keep discreetly in the background."

To his utter amazement Lorna laughed. "You don't know her, then, if you think you can accomplish that. You may have influence over her, but I doubt if you have that much of a hold on her. From all I know about Lydia Moonsong, she is not the type of woman who will take a back seat to any man—not even to you, Peter."

He tried to hide his uneasiness by looking smug. "We've already discussed my new line. She has agreed to help me launch it," he lied.

"How cozy," Lorna said with a sneer. There was something about the way he was watching her that told her something was not quite right. "Just bear in mind, Peter, that having Lydia as a business partner is one thing, having her as a wife is another. I'll never give you your freedom and I will see you in hell before I permit you to go to her." She raised her coffee cup to her lips. "Thanks to her example, our son is dead."

If her own hurt hadn't been so great she'd have smiled at his pained expression.

Efrem quietly entered the breakfast room and pretended he hadn't heard what his mother had said. He was a handsome boy, almost pretty, with dark, thick hair that curled and waved about his ears. Though he'd recently celebrated his nineteenth birthday, he was usually taken for no more than sixteen. People were always asking when he was due to graduate from high school.

He slipped into the chair beside his mother and mumbled a good morning.

Lorna forced a smile, after giving a warning glance to Peter that their discussion was far from decided. She said to her son, "You were out awfully late, dear. How was the Gordons' party?"

Peter looked up sharply. "Which Gordon?"

"Paul," Lorna said sweetly. "Tim's and Helen's boy."

"I don't know them," Peter said.

"No, you wouldn't," his wife answered, keeping her voice like syrup. "They're on the Symphony Board. Timothy is one of the trustees of the Art Museum."

Peter shuddered inwardly. "No wonder I never heard of them. They obviously don't work for a living."

"They don't have to. They are very old family."

"Figures," Peter sneered.

Lorna assumed the snooty air that annoyed Peter so much. "Paul is a school friend of Efrem's." To her son she asked, "Did you enjoy yourself, darling? And did you remember to extend my regards to Paul's parents?"

"They weren't there."

"You mean the party wasn't chaperoned?"

"Really, Mother. It wasn't any formal-type af-

137

fair. Just a few of us guys got together. We watched a lantern show of some pictures he'd brought back from his trip to Paris."

"Paris postcards," Peter joked. "And no chaperone." He clucked his tongue.

"Peter!" Lorna adminished.

Peter continued to grin as he dabbed the corners of his mouth and put down his napkin. He pulled his watch from his vest pocket. "I've got to leave."

"I have a great deal more to say to you," Lorna said coolly.

"It will have to wait. I have an appointment at the bank at ten." He started out of his chair. Lorna got up also and went with him out of the breakfast room. "I meant what I said, Peter," she whispered. "You might just as well make up your mind to forget all about that Moonsong woman."

"I told you what I plan," he answered.

"You will never have her. I'll never stop reminding you that she was responsible for the murder of my son."

She saw him square his jaw.

"Perhaps the next time you are alone with her, you can have a private little talk over how she set the example that poor David followed. It should give you a lot to be proud of."

He wanted to strike her. "You are an evil, malicious woman, Lorna. Lydia had nothing to do with David's death. If you persist on blaming anyone, blame me. God help me, I've blamed myself enough."

"David's body will always be between you and that woman. Can't you see that, Peter? She'll always be a reminder that if it hadn't been for her your son would be alive today. How could you want a woman such as she?" Lorna pleaded.

Peter scowled down at her. At the moment he almost did hate her. He turned and walked out of the mansion, closing his ears to Lorna's voice calling after him.

The San Francisco weather was brisk, but at least the fog had finally been swept away. He dismissed the coachman, deciding to walk down Nob Hill and try to get his wife's voice out of his head.

Perverse as it was, the fact that he and Lydia were connected, regardless of how remotely, with David's death made him closer to her. They both had a sorrow to share, a sorrow Lorna could never understand, even though David had been her son. China was what made the difference. Lydia understood, as he did, creating a solid bond that held them together more tightly than he and Lorna could ever be. Like a stitch in a tapestry there was that unbreakable silver thread that connected him and Lydia forever. China. That was what tied them inseparably.

As he crossed the street he glanced left toward the Moonsong mansion. He again remembered her slapping his face and ordering him out. They would always be at odds with one another because they both realized they were hopelessly in love and that their love represented a weakness neither wanted to reveal.

He would call her and ask her to lunch, he decided as he strolled along toward Powell Street. No, not yet. She'd not accept him yet. Better he stay away for a while and then stop in unannounced on the pretext of asking her advice.

Chapter 3

After her luncheon with Peter, and after several more lunches and dinners, Lydia didn't much care where he'd gotten the money to back his new venture. Their argument had been silly; she blamed it on her being upset by Raymond's domineering attitude that night. After all, she rationalized, Peter was right; it was only natural that he permit his wife to bail him out after all the money he'd poured into her charities over the years.

She still did not feel comfortable with the "Lady Lydia" name, but since he insisted that he was still intent upon making her his wife, she wasn't as strenuously opposed as she had been.

She would not allow herself to believe him completely, of course, much as she wanted to. As far as consolidating their companies was concerned, perhaps it wouldn't be such a bad idea. It was one way of getting out from under Raymond's increasingly difficult pressurings, she told herself. And if she lost Moonsong to either one of them, so she lost it. What difference? She had all the money she could ever spend and if need be, with or without Peter she could always make more.

One major objection Lydia had was that she considered "Empress Cosmetics" to carry far greater prestige than Peter's company and that it would be disasterous to discard her corporate name and image, as Peter wanted to do.

Lydia heard the bell and listened as Nellie went to answer it. A moment later Raymond walked into the study.

"You work too hard, Lydia. What are you poring over now?"

"Something I promised Peter MacNair."

"MacNair," he said, turning down the corners of his mouth. "I wish you'd stop involving yourself with that man. You know what a snake he is, always using people and then tossing them aside like spoiled meat."

Lydia had to smile to herself, wondering if Raymond knew he was describing himself as well. "Really, Raymond," she said with disdain, but knowing the truth in what he said. She supposed it was because she was getting older, but she'd made up her mind to have Peter for as long as she could, no matter what. She and Peter were both playing by the same set of rules. She knew they both enjoyed the contest between them because they were so evenly matched. Their competition would always go on until one of them finally tired and gave in. After that it would simply be a matter of settling down and living out the rest of their days happily together. At the moment, however, Lydia felt far from tired.

Lydia said, "I'm using Peter just as much as he is using me. I've never been foolish enough to trust any man," she added pointedly.

She heard him chuckle. "Including me?"

"Especially you."

He laughed as he looked down at the notes she was making. "You're right, you know. That new line of his would sell far better if he had women going door-to-door, though I admit I find the whole concept most distasteful. It has no sophistication, but then neither does Peter MacNair," he added with a grin.

"It will be a success. There are an awful lot of lazy women in this world, not to mention those who just don't have access to stores that sell cosmetics." She bent back over her work.

"You are seeing too much of Peter MacNair, Lydia. The talk is starting up again."

"The talk never actually stopped." She put aside her pen. "I really don't care, Raymond. People will always gossip, even when there isn't anything to gossip about."

"Then it isn't true?"

"What?"

"That you're sleeping with him."

She frowned up at him and purposely returned her attention to the papers in front of her. "I won't even dignify that question with an answer."

"You are, aren't you?" he accused. "You're sleeping with him!"

She didn't look up. She kept staring at the figures and thought of yesterday's luncheon and the afternoon that followed. The memory of the strength of his arms, the power and masculine smell of his body, was suddenly so strong her senses reeled. *Yes*, she wanted to scream. From no one else could she ever experience the thrill of sex that Peter made her experience.

"You needn't answer me," Raymond said. "I can see it in your face."

"My personal life is my own business, Raymond."

"You know it isn't. I love you, Lydia. I want you to be my wife."

Again she put aside her pen. "We have been over and over this. You are not free to marry me."

"Neither is Peter MacNair," he threw back at her.

That didn't seem important to her, Lydia found. Marriage was just a ritual, after all. What she and Peter had was so much more than a need for ritual. They could look at each other across a table, or walking on the street, or sitting at a business conference, and the present realities were obliterated. All that existed for them were the memories, strongest of which was their deep love for each other.

She said, "Actually, I don't think I want a husband. I happen to like things just as they are."

Raymond pretended to be shocked and Lydia wondered if he realized what a hypocrite he was. "Think of the children, Lydia," he said. "What kind of a life will they have growing up without a father, a man's influence or example?"

That made her smile as she returned to her work. One of the children upstairs was his own and he never so much as came to take her for a walk in the park.

Raymond persisted. "It's right that you and I marry. Caroline is my child, Marcus is yours, so being their parents would be natural."

Without looking up Lydia said, "Your logic is slightly warped, Raymond. Why not suggest that

Peter MacNair marry April. Marcus is his, Caroline is hers." Suddenly she realized her terrible slip.

Years before, when Lydia asked April to take her illegitimate baby it was agreed between them that no one would be told that Peter was the baby's father, not even April's husband, Raymond.

He said, "Don't look so stricken, Lydia. I've always suspected who Marcus's father is."

Lydia looked uncomfortable. "I don't love you, Raymond. Furthermore, I seriously do not think you love me."

"That isn't true. I do love you."

"You love the idea of being in love. Frankly, if you want to know what I really think, I believe you're still in love with April."

"I despise her!"

"No, you don't. She injured your male pride when she walked out on you for another man. The way you treated her, what did you expect, Raymond? I know that you beat her, abused her. I saw the marks on her myself. I told April at the time that a husband had certain rights. Now," she said reflectively, "I'm not so sure."

She leaned back in the chair. "April is a headstrong, resolute young lady who is determined to make herself happy at whatever cost." She gave him a faint smile. "You are much alike, you and April. That, Raymond, is why you will always love her, despite how much you deny it."

"She would never come back to me."

"In her heart she believes she has good reason not to. Nonetheless, that doesn't necessarily stop anyone from loving another." She was thinking of

145

her own relationship with Peter, a man she'd openly hated, secretly adored.

Lydia got up from the desk in a rustle of skirts. "You haven't started proceedings toward dissolving your marriage," she told him.

"That is true, I have not—not yet."

"Have you tried corresponding with April to learn how she feels? Perhaps the years have changed her."

"Correspond with her? Where?"

"Through the American legation in Peking. Though I have not received any reply to my letters to her, they must know where she can be reached."

"If I correspond, it will be through my attorneys," Raymond said bitterly. He made a disgruntled sound deep in his throat. "If April cared anything for me, she'd have returned by now."

There was the sound of the front door opening, then shutting, followed by footsteps crossing the marble foyer. The footsteps faltered, but proceeded toward the study.

Lydia turned toward the doorway, half expecting to see Leon. Raymond looked up when he heard Lydia's gasp. Both of them stared, wide-eyed in disbelief when they saw April standing there, holding a little boy by the hand.

"April!" Lydia cried as she rushed toward her and gathered her daughter in her arms, letting the happy tears roll unchecked down her cheeks. "Thank God. Oh, thank God," Lydia breathed as she embraced her. "It's like a miracle. We were just speaking of you and—and here you are."

"Hello, Mother," April said in a cool, matter-of-

146

fact voice. "I found I'd kept my house key so I just let myself in."

Lydia was too flabbergasted to say or do anything more than hug her tightly and mutter, "Thank God, thank God."

Raymond kept staring at his wife. She was more beautiful than he remembered, yet there was something very different about her. Then he knew what it was. Her clothes. She was dressed like any other chic American woman with her hair piled high on her head, a flowing blue cloak concealing a lighter-shaded blue gown.

"Hello, Raymond," April said evenly as she tactfully moved from Lydia's embrace. "Our ship got in just a short time ago. I came straight here."

"Oh, darling," Lydia gushed. "It is so good to have you home." She looked down at the little boy who was staring up at her.

"This is Adam," April said. She knelt beside the child. "And this is your grandmother, darling."

Lydia did not have to look too closely to tell that the child was obviously David MacNair's son. He looked the image of both his father and grandfather.

"And this is your Uncle Raymond," April added to the boy.

The introduction wrangled Raymond. Still, he couldn't take his eyes off April. She was the most exquisite woman he'd ever seen and looked nothing like the Oriental girl she'd once been.

April returned Raymond's stare, interpreting it as one of disapproval. "Adam is David's son, Raymond, though his papers say otherwise. It is all very confusing. I'll explain it later. Right now we are both ravenous and completely exhausted. The crossing was not very pleasant and very, very long."

Lydia hurriedly pulled the bell cord to summon Nellie, asking her to prepare a supper.

"It is fantastic seeing you again," Raymond said, his eyes staring wide with admiration.

"That surprises me. After what happened in Paris, you are the last person I thought would be pleased to see me."

He gave an indifferent shrug. "You were impetuous." He paused, continuing to look at her. "You're ravishing."

Lydia quickly hid the smile that threatened her lips.

April ignored him and turned to Lydia. "I've come for Caroline—and Marcus."

Lydia's happiness at seeing April began to slip. "Caroline and Marcus?" she asked, confused.

"I want them back, naturally."

Lydia gave her head a firm shake. "No. You abandoned them once. They are happy here in my house and here they will stay."

Lydia saw her daughter's lovely face turn hard as the eyes narrowed and the mouth drew itself into a thin line. "They are my children. I have every legal right to them. Raymond and I adopted Marcus, remember. Technically, he is ours."

If it was possible for one to be amused and annoyed at the same time, that was how Lydia felt when Raymond immediately sided with April. "She's right, Lydia," he said. "They are our children. We have every right to take them home."

Lydia bristled. "You are not taking those children out of this house, so make up your minds to

148

that. Besides," she said to April, "where on earth do you intend taking them at this hour of the night?"

Raymond said, "We're taking them home, of course." He looked sheepishly at April. "If that's what you want, dear," he said.

"we—" April told him coldly, "—are not taking them anywhere. *I* am taking them. I want to make it perfectly clear right now, Raymond, that I am going nowhere with you . . . ever again."

"You're my wife."

"I was your wife, but only because I was tricked into it. I never want anything more to do with you, Raymond. I consider myself David Mac-Nair's widow, and that I will always be."

"By American law you're married to me, and you are in America now, not in that heathen country where you were given to a man through some heathen ritual. So, as your husband, I demand you come home with me. now!" he punctuated.

"Go away, Raymond," April said as she moved away from his reach.

"Raymond is right," Lydia said. "You are still legally his wife."

"A piece of paper will never make me his wife." When their eyes met Lydia thought she saw a pleading in April's. April said, "Give me back my children, Mother."

Lydia stood firm. "In good conscience, I can't do that, April. Where would you go, if not with Raymond? How would you manage with two . . ." She glanced at little Adam, who was clinging wide-eyed to his mother's skirts. ". . . with three little ones?"

The pleading disappeared and was replaced by

a jutting chin. "I have money. We will manage. Besides," she said with malice, "knowing you, I doubt if you'll permit us to starve."

"I'm sorry, April. Naturally, I will see to your every comfort, but Caroline and Marcus remain here with me. Adam too, if you'll permit it."

Raymond tried to put his hand on April's shoulder. She shrugged it off. He said, "Let the children stay here, darling. They're happy with Lydia. Perhaps," he added looking down at Adam, "it might even be better if you left this little one here too, as Lydia suggested. We could go on a trip back to Paris again, just the two of us. We'll make a whole new start, April. I've never stopped loving you. Never."

His outpouring was sickening. Lydia had never realized what a weak man Raymond was.

April sneered. "I've traveled enough. Besides, I will never come back to you, Raymond, so forget me. Divorce me. I'm surprised you haven't done so by now."

"April," Raymond implored again, trying to touch her.

Nellie came in. "I've laid out supper in front of the fireplace in the sitting room."

Lydia looked down at little Adam. "The child is obviously exhausted and frightened by out bickering." To Raymond she said, "Let April and the boy stay here with me for a while until we can sort things out."

April said, "There's nothing to sort out. If you refuse to give me back my children, then Adam and I will live alone." As she started toward the sitting room she glowered at Raymond. "Make up your mind to the fact that I want nothing more to do with you, Raymond."

He angrily reached for her, but Lydia intervened "Go home, Raymond. April and the child need food and rest." He didn't move. "Please, Raymond. We'll talk tomorrow."

"I want her to come with me now," he insisted.

Lydia saw his lust. He didn't care a bit about April; all he wanted was her body.

April took Adam's hand and started out of the study. "We are staying here for the time being," she said over her shoulder, leaving Raymond scowling after her.

"Go home," Lydia repeated, patting Raymond's chest. "I'll talk to her when we are all a bit calmer."

Chapter 4

The following morning April refused to see Raymond when he called. She heard him storming and thundering in the hall downstairs, but she sat contentedly with the three children in her old bedroom.

After all she'd been through, she had to admit that it was good to be inside the comfort and security of the mansion, especially this room with all of its memories, even the bad ones.

When Lydia came in April asked, "Is he gone?"

"Yes. The children's nurse asked permission to go out on an errand. You don't mind sitting with the children if I have to go out too?"

"Of course not."

Adam sat huddled against his mother while Caroline and Marcus tried to tempt him off her lap with the variety of toys they'd brought from the playroom. The two older children had taken immediately to Adam. As for April, neither of them remembered her and like so many children were shy at first. But gradually, they grew braver with her, especially since she seemed so eager to play and had declared to their nurse that today was to be a holiday from their lessons.

Six-year-old Caroline considered herself in charge, though Marcus reminded her often enough that she was only a year older than he and that he was a boy, which made a great difference.

Seeing Marcus and Adam together gave Lydia a pang. They looked so much like brothers. They both had Peter's hair, the same square, stubborn jaw, the same deep brown eyes. Caroline looked like Raymond. She'd grow up to be an extremely beautiful woman. Already she had traces of that elegant flair so prominent in French women.

Lydia seated herself on the slipper chair beside the windows. "Raymond is a problem you can't ignore, April. He won't just disappear."

"Then I will, if I must." She failed to coax Adam to play with Marcus's wooden train, but succeeded when Marcus opened a box of lead soldiers.

"While you were away, Raymond had talked of having your marriage nullified. He thought it less scandalous than an out-and-out divorce."

"Since when have you been concerned about scandal?" April asked caustically.

Lydia ignored her. "He never did, of course, because down deep he is still in love with you."

"He is in love with his own comforts and you know it as well as I. He doesn't truly want me; he simply wants a built-in bed partner."

Lydia felt she should argue but could find nothing to say. No doubt what April said was true.

April watched Adam as he began to relax with Marcus and Caroline. The three of them chattered on, Caroline telling the other two what to do, Marcus countermanding her orders. Thinking of why she was here, April realized she had to keep Adam and herself separate from the others, despite her demands of last night. She'd been tired and hadn't been thinking clearly, she told herself. There would be time afterward to reunite her children.

Lydia nodded toward Adam. "The boy will present a problem, you realize, April. There is no mistaking he is David's son. You know the MacNairs will try and claim him the minute they find out about him."

"They'll never get him. I'm his mother."

"Nevertheless, Lorna MacNair is a very determined and formidable woman. I know what a bitter enemy she can be."

"And Peter MacNair?" April asked, giving her mother a knowing look.

Lydia felt the color rise in her cheeks "He will want his grandson, naturally, but Peter always liked you. He'll be more reasonable to deal with."

"There is no way they can prove Adam is their grandson." She went to the bureau and took the travel documents out of her reticule. "According to these official entry records, Adam is the son of Edward J. Wells, III. His father is an important politician in Washington. Eddie is with the State Department."

Lydia frowned as she read the papers, then handed them back to April. "I don't understand."

April tucked the documents safely away again. "Like you, Mother, I did whatever was necessary for my child's benefit. Isn't that what you claimed to have done for me? Eddie Wells was attached to

154

the American legation. I had no papers for either myself or for Adam. In exchange for certain favors, Eddie arranged for the necessary permits to enter the United States."

Lydia placed her hand on her breast to try and stop the sinking of her heart. There was nothing she could say by way of reprimand or admonishment. Hadn't she done something similar for the sake of April's safety?

"This Edward Wells," Lydia questioned, "will he present a problem later on?"

"Not Eddie. He most likely has forgotten all about me by now. He isn't exactly a paragon of propriety or one who remains constant for any length of time."

"Papers or no," Lydia said, "Adam is too much like David and Peter to be mistaken for anyone else's son. Peter himself told me you and David were married in China. Common reasoning will prove Adam is their grandson."

"Official entry papers will prove that he is not."

"It will mean a court fight, you realize."

She gave her mother a vindictive look. "You can afford it; unless, of course, you'd prefer to see Adam with Peter MacNair."

Lydia tolerated April's bitterness. "I can afford whatever you want, April." She thought for a moment. "But perhaps you really should consider returning to Raymond. It could help your current situation."

"Never. I'll never live with Raymond again."

Lydia let out a deep sigh. "Naturally, I'll respect your wishes." She smiled at the three children, now playing contentedly together. "They certainly are handsome children. Stay here with

155

me for as long as you like, if that is what you want, April. We'll fight Lorna MacNair."

April was quick to notice that she had not included Peter MacNair in her remark. Rather casually April said, "I get the impression you and Peter are on friendly terms again."

Lydia looked down at her lap. "Yes," she admitted. "He has had a very unfortunate setback and is starting up a new enterprise. I've been helping him with it."

"His wife must like that," April said sarcastically.

"It is strictly business," Lydia lied.

"Of course." She thought again of her need for revenge on this woman. "You always were in love with that man, Mother." She gave Lydia a mischievous grin and watched her expression. "You still are, I see."

Lydia deliberated with herself for a moment, feeling a terrible need to confide in someone. "He's asked me to marry him," she finally admitted.

"And just how does he intend to dispose of Lorna?"

Lydia stood up and went to where the children were playing. "I told Peter it was an impossibility." She helped Marcus and Adam straighten the contingent of soldiers and position the cavalry.

"But you'd marry him if he were free?"

"Yes," she answered quietly.

Good, April thought. Lydia and Peter would never be happy. She'd make them the two most miserably unhappy people on earth, she swore. Glancing at Adam she knew precisely how she would accomplish that.

Looking sweet, April said, "I'm surprised Raymond hasn't proposed as well, especially after finding you in his arms as I did before leaving Paris."

"That was an innocent embrace. He was very drunk and upset about you and David."

"And you have just been very good friends all these years?" she asked pointedly.

Lydia felt herself growing annoyed with her daughter's repeated barbs. "Raymond is a very integral part of Empress Cosmetics. Without him there would be no Moonsong, as you very well know. I need Raymond more than he needs me."

"Which is why you want me to go back to being his loving wife?" April turned toward the window. "You always did look out for your own interests, Mother."

"That isn't true, but please let us not go into that old argument."

April fell silent, looking at the barren trees in the yard and suddenly thinking of the palace garden and of the Dowager Empress. "How is Li Ahn?" she asked.

"Fine. Still at college. He comes home every chance he gets. Oh, he'll be so overjoyed to see you. You'll hardly recognize him. He's grown like a weed, and is quite the All-American college boy now and extremely popular."

"The Empress asked about him," April said rather nonchalantly.

"Oh?" Lydia creased her brows.

"Naturally, she isn't pleased about his failing to return to China with you in tow." She glanced toward the bureau drawer. "She has rather persu-

157

asive ways of reminding her subjects of their loyalty to her."

"From what I've read in the newspapers, the Dragon Empress has enough domestic troubles to occupy her time without worrying about an errant and disinterested heir to her throne."

April patted her elaborate coiffeur. "I was permitted to leave China only after giving my solemn promise that I would return with both you and my brother at my side."

"And just how do you propose to accomplish that?"

"I have no intention of accomplishing it because I have no intention of going back to China. I've seen the last of that place. And from all reports, my father will be forced to flee as well or he'll lose his head."

"Ke Loo is out of favor?"

"It is Ke Loo who is encouraging these rebels you've been reading about in your newspapers. I was told he will escape to Hawaii if it can be managed." She told her mother about Dr. Sun Yat-sen and of Prince Ke Loo's desire to put himself on the Chinese throne after the revolution.

"Your father was always too greedy," Lydia said, thinking of how he'd tried to poison April and herself so that he could be free to run off with a concubine.

"He won't succeed in dethroning the Empress. And if I were he, I would think twice before trusting Sun Yat-sen. The man despises the Manchus, I've learned. He is only proposing to use Father for his own purposes."

"Which are?"

"A Chinese republic, they say. And there are no

royal houses in republics. If Father has any sense he'll run to Hawaii and stay there."

All the terrible memories of her Mandarin husband made Lydia shudder. As far as she was concerned, if he met a cruel fate, he deserved it; he was a cruel man.

April went on with what she'd learned through court gossip about the Boxers and about how different China had become. She told her of Mei Fei, her half-sister, glancing sadly at the bureau drawer.

Lydia said, "The girl sounds like an enchanting little creature."

"She is. She's all I miss about China. I would have taken her with me had I been able to." Almost to herself she said, "She must despise the Empress now."

"What do you mean?"

April hadn't thought herself capable of so dastardly an act. Hardly aware that she'd stood and walked to the bureau, she opened the second drawer and took out the handsome velvet box with the silver fittings. She carried it like an offering over to where Lydia had reseated herself in the slipper chair. Without a word she handed the box to her mother.

"Exquisite," Lydia remarked, admiring the delicate workmanship of the fittings, the beautiful texture of the purple velvet.

"A gift from the Empress," April said. Her eyes grew hard and her heart began thumping with a perverse, almost sadistic pleasure. "Open it."

Lydia raised the lid. For a moment she simply stared at what she took to be an expertly executed ivory sculpture of a feminine hand, with the most beautiful pearl and jade ring she'd ever seen. It was a macabre subject for so artful a piece and without thinking she lifted it from the box.

The moment her hand touched the object she realized what it was. Lydia screamed as flesh connected with hardened flesh. She saw the dried blood stains in the velvet. Throwing the hand and box to the floor, Lydia dashed into the bathroom. Wave after wave of nausea convulsed her as she clutched her stomach and bent over the basin.

When she finally emerged, ashen and drawn, the hand and box were again hidden away inside the bureau drawer.

"It is Mei Fei's," April said as if she were speaking of some trivial gift she'd been given.

"Good God, April!" Lydia gasped. She lowered herself into a chair and dabbed the beads of perspiration from her forehead.

"It was the Empress's way of reminding me of my vow of loyalty."

"Horrible," Lydia shuddered, wrapping her arms about herself. "Horrible."

April kept watching her mother. "You should be familiar with the Manchu ways," she said, returning to the subject.

Lydia closed her eyes and tried to push the grisly sight out of her mind, but she only found it replaced by the sight of the pearl concubine's severed head impaled on a pole near the main gate of the city.

"Yes," Lydia managed as she fought to keep down the nausea.

With hatred dripping from her words April said, "Unfortunately, it was not David's *hand* that the Dragon Empress demanded."

"Please," her mother said, feeling faint. "Put it out of your mind, April. Destroy that . . . thing." She gestured toward the bureau.

"No. I want to keep it as a reminder of what China is really like under the rule of that maniac. And one day perhaps, I will be able to return Mei Fei's precious ring. She was extremely proud of it."

"April, I beg you. Stop. It's obscene to keep such a thing."

The children began arguing loudly about something Caroline was insisting upon. Lydia was only too happy for the distraction and saw an excuse to leave the room.

"Come along," she said to the little ones. Her voice was unsteady, as was she herself, she found, when she stood up. "Let's take Adam into the playroom and show him the hobby horses. He will have to have one of his own, of course." Lydia couldn't look at her daughter as she herded the children out of the room.

At the door Lydia forced herself to turn back. She felt she had to say something and not leave the room with the lingering memory of what lay inside that velvet box.

"Raymond said he would come back later this afternoon. What shall I tell him, April?"

"Tell him to start divorce proceedings, or whatever is necessary to invalidate our marriage. I will contest nothing he instigates."

"Are you certain?"

"I've never been more certain of anything in my life."

Chapter 5

Raymond arrived just before four o'clock. This time April did not hide from him. Somehow Mei Fei's forced sacrifice gave her a kind of renewed courage, fortifying her with a determination to accomplish everything she'd come here to accomplish, including destroying the husband she despised.

Raymond found her seated in the cosy library just off the drawing room, engrossed in a recent novel by Zola. April rather enjoyed the cruel, vulgar Nana and her disdain for men, her greed and her immorality. It was scandalous, she realized, for her to be reading such a book and she had rather enjoyed the look of disapproval on the bookseller's face when she asked for it on her lunchtime shopping trip.

She didn't look up from the page when Raymond spoke her name.

"Put that blasted book aside. I want to try and put a little sense into your head."

She continued to read.

"Damn it, April, you are exhausting my patience."

Slowly April placed the tooled leather bookmark across the page and laid the novel aside. "I would have thought you'd have lost your patience with me a long, long time ago. Why do you persist in trying to have something you've long since lost?"

"I love you, damn it. You're my wife and I want you to continue to be my wife."

"Raymond," she said softly, patiently. "I abandoned you and my children and ran off with a younger man." She was pleased when he flinched at the reminder that he was at least ten years older than David had been. "Surely you can't respect me still or continue to love me for having humiliated you as I did?"

"I don't care about the past," he argued, gazing with lust-filled longing at her beauty. Her black, silken hair was handsomely arranged in a luxuriant bouffant that framed her face. The silk gown was of the palest lavender, a perfect compliment to her. "I've never stopped loving you," he said as he came and knelt on one knee beside her chair.

"Get up, Raymond. Humility was never a part of your character. It makes you look more ridiculous than you are."

As he rose his face glowed with a rage he fought to hold back. Seeing her, inhaling the intoxicating perfume of her hair, of her body, made him blind to everything except his need to possess her, to ravage her body. He wanted to tear the dress from her, rip away her underthings, and force himself into her as brutally and cruelly as possible. He wanted to show her that he was a man, not some adolescent boy who hadn't a notion as to how to satisfy a woman. He almost laughed imagining how the boy must have fumbled and groped and hurried, only to leave April unfulfilled.

"April," he pleaded, trying to keep himself calm.

"There is nothing you and I have to say to one another." She turned her back and folded her arms across her bosom.

"I do not intend losing you again," he threatened.

"You never had me."

"You are my wife, damn it," he repeated. "You are going to stay my wife."

She glared at him, fire dancing in her eyes. "I would suggest we dissolve our marriage as quietly as possible. There has been enough scandal in this family without your creating more."

"I will not permit a divorce."

"Then I will make you the laughing stock of San Francisco."

He stared at her, not understanding.

"Either we dissolve our marriage without fanfare, Raymond, or I will publicize all of my disgrace. I will tell the world how I ran off with a teenaged boy, how I took my mother's illegitimate son into my house and then abandoned him as well as my own daughter. I will drag every ugly stitch of dirty laundry out into the open air and hang it high enough for everybody to inspect. I'll destroy you, Mother, your precious corporation, everything—unless you agree to end our marriage."

She reminded herself that she was going to do that anyway, but Raymond didn't have to know that just yet.

His mouth dropped. His face grew white. "You wouldn't," he stammered.

"I most certainly would, and if you don't believe me, then try me."

He continued to stare at her in disbelief. "You'd be destroying the children as well as yourself, your mother . . ."

"I don't give a bean about my reputation. As for the children and Mother, they'll survive."

"Survive what?" Lydia asked as she entered the library.

April reached for her novel.

Raymond stood, speechless.

"What's going on?" Lydia asked anxiously when she noticed Raymond's pallor, and April's brazen, defiant pose. "Raymond, answer me."

It took several starts before he managed to tell her of April's threats.

When he finished, the silence in the room pressed against Lydia's eardrums until she thought they would puncture. To April she said, "You're mad. Surely you're only speaking in anger."

"I meant every word of it. I want to be free. I want my children. I want to live my own life with them and I couldn't care less how all of that is accomplished."

Lydia couldn't speak. She watched her daughter casually return her attention to the book. "You can't do this, April."

"I can and I will," she said, pretending to read.

"Do you hate yourself so much?"

April raised her eyes and gave her mother a look that made Lydia take a step backward. "I don't hate myself at all," she answered, letting the rest of her meaning go unsaid.

"I have always . . ."

"Mother, please," April cried, slamming shut the book. "As you said this morning, let us not go over that old argument. We were never overly fond of each other to begin with."

"That isn't true."

"Passing me off as your maid is, I suppose, your way of showing how proud you were of me."

"That was years ago. Times were difficult. We were starving. I had to do what I did."

"You were ashamed of me, so why are you suddenly so surprised that I don't act the part of the loving, adoring daughter?"

"But this hateful thing you threaten would not only ruin me but yourself, Raymond, and especially the children. The MacNairs would take Adam and Marcus in a moment with every possible blessing a court of law can grant."

"I'll take the children where they can't be found."

"Such a place doesn't exist. And you can't run forever," Lydia reminded her.

Raymond found himself recovering. His face was flushed, his hands and teeth clenched tightly with rage. "I'll give you your freedom, April," he snarled. He turned to Lydia. "However, I do not intend remaining here to be the brunt of this scandal. I'm returning to Paris and so help me God, Lydia, I will do everything I can to have my revenge on this . . . this . . ." he motioned toward April. ". . . Bitch!"

April laughed in his face.

166

He took three long, angry steps toward her and slapped the laughter from her mouth.

She didn't lift a hand to ease the stinging of her cheek. "I hope that helps appease your male vanity. It was always one of your stronger points, Raymond—striking women."

He raised his hand to strike her again but Lydia shouted his name. Raymond stood there for a moment, his hand raised. Finally he let it fall, turned sharply, and stormed out of the room.

"Raymond!" Lydia called, but he was gone.

April had gotten to her feet and both women stood staring at each other. Lydia then made a helpless gesture and went toward the windows, pretending to see the carriages and people passing by the wrought-iron fence that bordered the big house with its handsome front lawn and carefully shaped topiaries. She stood with her back to April, feeling weak and slightly sick. In spite of what she'd endured for her daughter's sake, it had all been for nothing, she realized.

For the first time in a very long while, Lydia lost her composure and burst into tears.

"You needn't cry, Mother," April said, not unkindly. "My marriage to Raymond can be quietly and quickly ended. You have a lot of influence in San Francisco with judges and congressmen and the like. Surely it shouldn't be difficult."

Lydia pulled a handkerchief from her sleeve, dried her eyes, and softly blew her nose. "Hardly anything of that sort can be kept quiet, but I'll try." A complication occurred to her. "And what of Caroline?"

"I believe I can convince Raymond to renounce her as his."

Lydia turned so abruptly she almost knocked over a small cabaret with two porcelain figurines. "Will you stoop to any depravity to get what you want?"

"Any," April assured her. "And don't look so appalled, Mother. We aren't so different from that old Dowager sitting on the Chinese throne. The three of us have much in common."

Lydia turned away again, trying not to listen.

"I doubt if you will ever marry again, Mother, because like me and like the Empress, you enjoy power too much. Oh, we may both marry out of necessity, for the sole purpose of keeping our power, but I don't recognize that as being married, if you know what I mean. I admit it when I say I was pleased to see the fear in Raymond's face, how he crumbled under my threats. You like your independence, Mother, so why can't you understand my need for the same? We've both been steeped in the Chinese culture and will never shed our feeling that a woman who once gives up her proper role as a woman and seeks power—as we have done—becomes like that vicious Chinese tyrant, all power and no woman."

Lydia stood unmoving. "And what power do you have?"

"More than you think. I can get anything I want. My defiance of Raymond proved that. Don't underestimate me, Mother. I tricked the Empress into giving me what I wanted. If I can trick her successfully, I can trick anyone in the world."

Her voice was like the hiss of a snake.

"No, April, I will never underestimate you," Lydia said. She realized suddenly that April was more Chinese than American. Lydia could understand the analogy she'd drawn though she did not agree with it. It was true, the three of them were similar, like three individual branches attached to the same trunk, each testing the will and strength of the others. The aged and powerful Empress, though distant, would always remain a threat, like some sinister phantom that could destroy with the pointing of a finger. April was too strong-willed for her own good and obviously had a passionate thirst to avenge the murder of David.

Lydia sighed and kept staring out the window, seeing nothing. She'd never considered herself in the light in which April had placed her. She'd always thought of herself as a loving, protective mother who only wanted all that was good for her children.

She turned slowly. "Just what is it you want, April?"

Without hesitating she answered, "All the happiness I have been denied, starting with our leaving China and ending with the loss of my husband."

"David, you mean."

"I never consider myself as ever having had any other husband."

"I'll give you whatever happiness I can give you."

April shook her head. "I am the only one who can give myself that happiness."

"And just how do you propose to do that?"

"I want my children and a life of my own."

"I can't let you take Caroline and Marcus. They

are happy here. You are a stranger to them. Besides, as I told you earlier, three little ones would be a terrible burden on you."

"Really, Mother, I certainly don't intend living like a fishwife without comforts and servants," April said haughtily.

"You may take Adam," Lydia conceded. "The other two must remain here with me."

"All right," April was quick to agree.

"You are being a stupid little fool, April. The minute the MacNairs learn you are back, you will have a fight on your hands over the custody of Adam, especially if you try to brazen things out alone."

"Tomorrow I will begin looking for a suitable flat," April answered stubbornly. "I'd appreciate it if you'd look around for a possible amah for Adam. I'll do the same, of course. I thought perhaps my old tutor in Chinatown might have a relative."

"You want an Oriental?"

"Why not? Adam is very accustomed to the Chinese, which I'm sure you can understand." She bit down on her lower lip as she thought. "It's best I find a place as far from Nob Hill and the MacNair mansion as I can, without going into some seedy neighborhood."

"Try Portsmouth Square. It's quite fashionable," Lydia found herself saying. Reluctant as she was to agree, April did make sense in that regard. Her comings and goings would quickly be observed by Lorna. The longer the custody battle is delayed the better, Lydia thought. Besides, it would give Lydia time to plan her strategy and perhaps try to cool April's vindictiveness.

＊　＊　＊

The apartment was on the other side of China-town overlooking Portsmouth Square. It was spacious and new and sunny with airy rooms and vaulted ceilings. There was a formal sitting room with a small but adequate balcony and sufficient adjoining rooms for a nursery and two servants, though April decided she could manage with only a nurse and a woman to come in during the days to manage the cooking and cleaning. Her plans did not call for live-in servants, with the exception of the amah.

The apartment's main attraction for April was its proximity to Chinatown, where she could take Adam and have him learn all the stories and legends her old tutor, Kim Lee, used to tell her. She wondered if he still lived over the bake shop just off Grant Avenue. It would be one of the first things she'd investigate after they were settled in.

She had every reason to despise everything about China and its horrors, yet April could not ignore the force of the magnet inside her that drew her to Kim Lee and his tales of mystery and romance, recreating for her the China she loved, the China that was a part of her dreams. She wanted to have Adam learn of his homeland as she had been taught.

The old tutor was seated cross-legged, puffing languidly on his long-stemmed pipe. The sweet smell of incense was thick in the room as April and Adam came in. Kim Lee did not move; in fact, he did not seem to be aware that he was no longer alone in his room.

"Kim Lee," April said softly.

The old man continued to stare straight ahead

171

through the haze of smoke, lost in some new fantasy that was more real to him than living.

April came closer and knelt so that her face was on a level with his and only inches away. "It is April Moonsong," she said. She noticed a movement in his eyes as they focused on her face.

It took a moment for the name to register. When it did he stirred and a slow smile touched his mouth. "April, my child," he said finally, giving his pipe a disdainful look and putting it aside. "I spend too much time with my dreams. But then I am old and am entitled to my dreams, am I not? Soon I will be living in them." He looked more closely. "April Moonsong," he repeated, studying her face. "Yes. There was something I had to tell your mother. A warning." He frowned and tried to think. Then he gave an indifferent shrug. "I forget." He suddenly stiffened and looked afraid. "Danger," he said sharply, clutching April's arm. "The Empress. Great danger."

April placed her palm against his cheek. "The danger is past, Kim Lee. My mother is well and happy."

He grew calm again.

"I have come from The Forbidden City and have brought you my son." She positioned Adam in front of the old man. "This is Adam. I want you to teach him all you taught me."

The Chinaman moved his head slowly from side to side and took up his pipe. He stared at it for several seconds, then shook his head again. "My home, like all of my memories, are locked inside me and will never come out again. I have no pupils because I have nothing to teach them. I have become a selfish old man, April Moonsong. I keep my stories to myself, right next to my memories."

The bamboo curtain that separated the little room from the one beyond parted in a whisper of sound. Standing there was a short, stout woman, not old, not young, in a pale yellow jacket and black skirt. Her face was like a mask, powdered and rouged, with thin, black eyebrows curved high over her eyes, like lines drawn with a pen.

Surprisingly, when she spoke her voice sounded almost childlike. In Chinese she said to the old man, "You should sleep now." She walked toward him, moving with the hesitant air of a woman not too certain of herself. To April she appeared embarrassed.

"My uncle," the woman said to April, "enjoys his pipe too much." She shrugged. "It is his only pleasure these days so I do not deny him."

As she helped Kim Lee onto his pallet in the corner, April looked more closely at the old man. She suddenly remembered the men in the opium den in which she and her mother had been forced to hide. She gave a sad shake of her head, then stood and took Adam by the hand.

At the door leading to the street she hesitated and looked back, but her old tutor was already deep into his own private world. The Chinese woman bowed respectfully to April.

She said, "I could not help but overhear your asking my uncle to teach your son the myths and mysteries of our homeland. I am very skilled in Chinese lore. Perhaps you would permit me." She held out her hand, palm up.

"No, thank you," April said speaking Chinese.

She looked at Kim Lee. "I . . ." She didn't finish her sentence as a thought struck her. "Do you live here with Kim Lee, your uncle?"

"No." the woman answered. "I come by to see to his needs from time to time." She made an obvious motion toward the opium pipe.

"And you know all the old legends?"

"Oh, yes. My uncle taught me well, as did my father and my grandfather."

April hesitated but not for long. "I am in need of an amah for my son." She laid a loving hand on Adam's head. "Perhaps you might recommend someone."

"I could recommend myself," the Chinese woman said. She bowed again. "I am not without experience. I am called Mayli."

April's eyes moved carefully, critically as she looked at the woman. She searched into her drawstring purse and wrote something on a card. "This is my address," she said, handing Mayli the card. "Come to see me tomorrow and we will talk."

As she and Adam went out the door and down the wooden steps that led to the alleyway, April felt pleased. She wasn't particularly in favor of Mayli's supplying the old man with opium but in her interview tomorrow she'd make it very clear that her duty to her uncle could in no way become involved with her duties as Adam's amah.

Chapter 6

It was late on a Saturday morning when April left her flat and walked the few blocks to Grant Avenue. She loved browsing through the quaint Oriental shops, relishing the sounds and smells of the China she preferred to remember. She felt pleased that Mayli was working out so well and Adam was enchanted by her storytelling, especially when she told him of the golden dragons that breathed fire and of the great dynasty in which his mother was a princess and whose mark he bore on his thigh. Mayli called him *Little Prince*. April liked that.

The Chinese shops were busy with customers and with the usual idlers lounging about looking bored and restless. April stepped from the shop where she bought her rice paper and writing supplies and started toward home with her neat package tucked carefully under her arm. When the young man in the smart gray suit and felt hat stepped directly into her path, stopping her progress, she frowned, not recognizing him for a moment.

"Don't you know me, Sister?" he asked.

"Li Ahn! Li Ahn!" April cried.

They hugged unashamedly, reveling in the wonderful feeling of the love that they had for each other.

April held him at arm's length, looking him up and down, then hugged him again. "Li Ahn I've missed you so." When she again looked into his face, beaming with happiness, April put two fingers against her lips. "But I must not call you *Li Ahn*, must I? Mother told me you pronounce it and spell it in the American way."

"Leon," he answered, taking away the soft Oriental lilt and giving it a more guttural sound.

She hugged him again. "But what are you doing here?"

"I'm home for a holiday. When my marks are high and my progress too rapid, they send me home until the other students can catch up with me."

She saw he was joking by his wink. Leon picked up her parcel that had dropped when she threw her arms around him. She linked her arm in his.

"Actually," he said, "I am between terms. I was on my way to visit you and your son."

"Mother told you about Adam?"

"Of course, but I understand we are not to advertise him to the MacNairs."

"That is what Mother wants. Personally, I'm almost anxious for them to know I have their grandson." She spoke bitterly.

"Why?" he asked, astonished. "I would think you would want to avoid any court action. The MacNairs are important people in San Francisco and you . . ." He left his sentence dangle.

April finished it for him. "And I have not exactly been the best example of what a proper mother should be."

Leon said nothing. She took his silence as agreement. She squeezed his arm. "I don't want to even think of the MacNairs right now. I don't want anything to spoil our being together again."

They stopped at the curb and waited for a carriage to pass. "I was surprised when Mother told me you'd returned."

"If the Empress knew of my subterfuge, I would certainly not be here."

"Subterfuge?"

"I made a vow to the old Dragon that I would come only for the purpose of finding you and returning with you and Mother to Peking."

"As I was once instructed to do," Leon remarked, thinking back. "And are you determined to deliver us to our executioner?" he asked, laughing and letting his eyes slide sideways toward her.

"No. That is what I meant by subterfuge." Her thoughts suddenly grew dark. "I remember only too vividly the terrible sadness that woman caused me. I see her now for the cruel, heartless thing she is. She had David beheaded before my very eyes."

Leon lowered his eyes.

"It was not a pleasant ordeal," April continued.

"Don't speak of such things, April. Put them completely out of your mind. Though we are both from the royal house of the Manchus we must be proud only of our honorable history. We must always remember the good and what is happening in China today is far from good. The old legend that a woman will ultimately destroy the great Manchu dynasty is being realized. Tz'u Hsi will bring about the death of the China we both love."

177

She smiled in spite of herself as she listened to him, wondering if he too carried the twin poppy tattoo on his thigh. She was too embarrassed to ask. "Then you are not as Americanized as you appear to be."

"I will always have a great reverence for our homeland and I will never be rid of this feeling of being misplaced here in America. But I will always remain here. I will never go back."

"Not even if our royal cousin is dethroned and our father becomes emperor?"

"That will never happen." They walked a few steps in silence. "Would you go back in such an event, April?"

She sighed. "Unfortunately, no. Our father does not look upon me as a daughter."

"He's renounced you?"

"No, he thinks of me as a woman . . . a woman he openly admits he would be happy to have as a concubine rather than as a daughter."

"I see," Leon said. He remembered all those years he'd lived under his father's roof, the utter disregard the noblemen had for any woman who attracted them, even the closest of relatives. It was not commonly practiced, but it was practiced often enough to be considered acceptable.

April laughed. "Strangely enough, the Empress protected me from Father without realizing what she was doing. She held me hostage in the summer palace, ordering that I was never to see Father again. Little did she realize how willingly I accepted that dictate. Here we are," she announced as she led him up the broad stone steps with the grilled double doors at the top. "Adam is out in the park with Mayli, his amah. They should be back shortly. You'll adore him, Leon, he is a darling boy."

"Being yours, he is bound to be."

"Tea?" She removed her hat and put it on the console in the foyer. "The housekeeper doesn't come in on Saturdays. I rather enjoy fending for myself once or twice a week."

"I came to see Adam and then take you somewhere smart for lunch." He walked around inspecting the luxury of the overcrowded room, which was all the rage. He concluded that it was an extremely handsome room.

"Then come sit beside me and tell me all about yourself," April said, patting the cushion as she settled on the divan.

"There's little to tell. I study. I enjoy my schooling. I look forward to joining the business when I've graduated."

"Business?" April asked, looking blank.

"Empress Cosmetics, of course."

"Mother's company?" she asked in astonishment.

"Our family's company," he reminded her. He saw the flicker of annoyance that came over her expression. "Really, April, I never could understand why you disapprove so of Mother."

"You were not subjected to the humiliations and abuse I had to suffer when she brought me here."

"You make her sound like some horrible old witch who beat you daily and made you beg for your food."

April pouted. "You always did take her part against me."

"I tried not to take either part. I admire Mother for having accomplished all she has."

179

"Do you admire the methods she used to gain her end?"

Leon shrugged. "We all are guilty of having to do things we aren't particularly proud of. You must admit that for a woman who arrived in San Francisco without a penny, she has to be admired for her success."

"Which was built up by going through a long, long line of gentlemen's bedrooms."

"April," he said sharply. "You are being unfair." He adored his mother and was provoked at April for her lack of understanding. Defensively, almost without thinking he said, "You haven't acted very conventionally, to say the least. I'd think you would be the last one to throw stones."

"I didn't use men the way Mother did."

"You didn't have to. She gave you everything you ever wanted, when she had it to give."

"All I ever wanted was David and she refused me that."

"You were a married woman with children," Leon scolded. "I was never particularly fond of Raymond, but he was—is, after all, your legal husband."

April pulled away her hand that Leon had been holding. She got angrily to her feet, scowling down at him. "How can you condone Mother and condemn me?"

"You were always too independent for your own good." He looked around the room. "What are you doing living here? Your place is with Raymond."

"Oh, now I see," April accused. "Mother sent you here to try and get me reunited with Raymond."

"No!"

"I'll never go back to that sadistic brute."

"If you were in China you would have no choice, would you? You forget your upbringing." Their eyes locked. Leon saw her fury and looked away. He slapped his thighs and got up. "We are arguing. It was the last thing I wanted." He reached for her and she came easily into his arms.

April rested her head on his strong young shoulder. "Why can't you see things my way, Leon?" she asked, still trying to bend him to her will.

"Because I believe what you are doing is wrong. Your abandoning your family was wrong. It is not what you were taught."

"I had to learn new ways when Mother forced me to come here, where I was treated no better than the lowest of creatures."

"If Mother had not gotten you out of China you would not have been allowed to live. She told me how they tried to poison you both."

"They?"

"Father. The Empress. Ke Loo had taken a new wife. He wanted to be rid of his American wife and half-breed daughter. I was spared because I was, at the time, his only male heir. You can't imagine the torture to which I was subjected in order to blot out every reminder that there was Western blood in my veins." He cradled her gently. "Ke Loo is a cruel and dangerous man, as well you know."

She desperately wanted to change the subject. "The Empress is taking steps to deal with Prince Ke Loo, our father," April said.

"He will never stop trying to put himself on her throne, but as I said, he will never succeed. Whenever I am home from school I like to spend a lot of my time in Chinatown listening to the latest news from Peking."

"Father is in league with a commoner, a Dr. Sun Yat-sen."

Leon held her away from him. "I've heard him spoken of. There is talk that he is coming to America and going to visit other countries throughout the world in order to solicit the help of foreign governments in an effort to make China into a republic."

"The man came to visit me when I was at the American legation. He was then leaving for Hawaii to begin his campaign for outside help. I do not trust him, Leon. He said he and Father shared a common ambition."

"To overthrow the dynasty?"

April nodded. "But I got the impression he was merely playing a trick on Ke Loo. Palace gossip is making Father responsible for all these uprisings, which is why the Empress wants him killed. Mei Fei says the Empress will succeed, that secret forces have been sent to Kalgan to destroy Father and his soldiers."

"Mei Fei?"

April smiled. "Your half-sister, don't you remember her?" April's smile faded. "Mei Fei is also a prisoner of the Empress's." She thought of the severed hand. "She must hate having to be the hostage of that evil woman."

Leon could only vaguely remember the girl. He eased April away and walked across the sitting room, thinking of his father. "Ke Loo is too clever to be caught in any trap of the Empress's. He will slip through her nets. He has before; he will again.

Besides, he has his fortunes and his Western trade to protect." When he saw April didn't know what he was talking about he added, "The opium trade. Ke Loo controls a very large percentage of it. For this reason the Empress has always permitted him more liberties than any other. He is responsible for a good deal of the wealth that is earned by China through opium exports."

"Sun Yat-sen hinted that their headquarters would be established in Hawaii."

"Of course. If Ke Loo is forced from China, what better place to establish his opium trade, smuggling it from Hong Kong to Hawaii? It is an ideal location for distributing opium to the rest of the world, and making a fortune in the process."

April suddenly thought of Kim Lee and the opium den in Peking. "How horrible."

"Opium is used for many worthwhile products, like medicines. It is in great demand. Ke Loo will never let go of his control of its distribution, even if it means relinquishing his ambitions for the Chinese throne."

"That is where Dr. Sun plans to use him, I believe," April said. "Sun Yat-sen wants China a republic, but he is using Ke Loo's money and power with the promise that after the Empress is deposed Ke Loo will be emperor and the republic forgotten."

Leon couldn't help but laugh. He rubbed the back of his neck as he thought of the intrigues of it all. "It should be interesting to see who ends up the most powerful."

There was a sudden clamor in the hall. "Here's Adam now," April said happily and China and all their father's machinations were pushed aside.

183

Chapter 7

"She's back!" Lorna MacNair fumed, bursting into her husband's study. The room was so like him, very strong and dominating. Everytime she entered it she could not help but be intimated by its strength and at the same time reminded of the handsome power of her husband's body that she found so impossible to resist.

"Who's back?" Peter asked, annoyed at the interruption.

"The Moonsong girl."

Peter's head shot up. "April? David's wife?"

"Don't you dare refer to her as David's wife."

Peter shrugged. "He married her, didn't he? He told me so himself."

Lorna put her hands over her ears. "I do not want you ever to speak of that to me. I will never stop blaming you and those Moonsong women for that whole incident."

"I'm sick to death of listening to your blame, Lorna. Why must you always dwell on David's death?"

"Because I can never forget it and I never want you to forget it either," she snarled. Seeing April

184

had enraged her and now she let all her rage show itself. "On my deathbed I'll raise my hand and point my finger at you and those Moonsong women and remind you all that you killed my son."

Peter slammed his fist down on the desk with such force that the Tiffany lamp jangled and a glass ashtray bounced from the edge and crashed to the floor. "Stop it, Lorna!" he shouted. "I am sick and tired of listening to your blame," he said again. "One more word out of you and so help me I'll strike you."

She refused to let him intimidate her. She knew the guilt he carried inside him and she would never let him forget it. As much as he deprived her of his love, she would remind him of his blame. "Go ahead, strike me. Kill me as you killed my son."

Peter towered over her. He grabbed her shoulders and began shaking her. "Shut up, do you hear me," he yelled.

"I'm not afraid of you, Peter. If it weren't for you and your damned selfish ambition, David would be alive today. But you never cared for him or anyone else except yourself and that disgusting Moonsong woman. And frankly, Peter, knowing you as well as I do, I am not sure whether you want Lydia or her cosmetic empire."

He raised his hand to slap her.

"Stop it!" Susan yelled as she rushed into the study to see what the ruckus was about.

Peter glowered at her and he lowered his hand. "How dare you interfere in your mother's and my personal affairs. Children . . ."

"I am not a child," Susan said angrily, stomping

her foot. "And it is about time someone interfered with your constant wrangling. The servants have ears."

"What of it? They're servants," Peter stormed. "If I hear any one of them utter one word of gossip about our household they will never work again."

Susan looked from her father toward her mother, still standing defiant and straight in front of Peter. Lorna knew she'd gotten to him and she looked radiant in her victory. "Will you two ever stop going at each other's throats?"

"You keep out of this, Susan," Peter warned.

"I refuse to allow you to treat me as if I were a baby who can be shuffled off to her room. For as long as I can remember there has been nothing in this house but anger and arguing."

Peter waved a threatening finger at her. "I'll tell you once more, Susan, to mind your place."

"I am minding my place. I happen to be your daughter. This is my home. If you prefer, it doesn't have to be my home. I am old enough to go out on my own." Her voice suddenly softened a little. "Please Father . . . Mother . . . I know how awful it is that David is dead." She felt the tears and let them come. "I miss him as much as you, but for heaven's sake let him rest in peace. You both owe him that."

Peter scowled. "The modern woman. Is this what you learn from those suffragists' meetings you secretly attend. Numb your feelings, forget tradition, kill and let die."

He realized immediately his last remark and turned aside, ignoring Lorna as she drew in her breath so accusingly.

Susan stepped between them. Her wasp waist and trim, sleek skirt was a dramatic contrast to her mother's Victorian flounces and her father's austere formality. "I only ask that this constant fighting stop. David is dead. You must not keep harping on who was to blame or who was not to blame. Knowing David, I am certain it was no one's fault . . . just an unfortunate happenstance."

Lorna sniffed contemptibly. "Happenstance indeed. If your father hadn't forced him into coming into PM Cosmetics there would never have been an unfortunate happenstance."

"Oh, Mother," Susan pleaded. "Even I know that the difficulty with David and April Moonsong began long before David joined Father's company."

Lorna stared at her in surprise.

Susan brushed away her tears. "Must I constantly remind you both that I am a grown woman? I wasn't blind to David's love affair with April. He told me all about her and that he'd never marry anyone else . . . ever. I was almost tempted to tell April about that fake wedding announcement you had published. All I could think of was how unhappy April must have been when she read it, how desolate." She moved toward the bookcase. "I felt helpless and so confused. Even back then I felt that it was wrong for anyone to interfere with another person's happiness, including parents with their children."

Peter said, "I refuse to have you talk like this. You will, from this moment on, refrain from involving yourself in even the slightest way with those women who in my mind, God forbid, are no more than a bunch of Amazons shaking spears and wanting to be men."

"Peter!" Lorna gasped.

"We don't want to be men," Susan said. "All we ask is that we have the same rights as men."

"Impossible!"

"Why?"

Peter raised one eyebrow. "You've just finished reminding me that you are a mature woman. Need I have to tell you there is a biological difference between men and women."

"That is no reason."

"Susan," her mother said patiently. "This is not the time to discuss the matter. Surprised as you may be, I happen to agree with your father. These meetings and the mailings you have been receiving are to stop. There have been arrests and it is only a matter of time before someone gets hurt. I do not want it to be you."

"I'm sorry, Mother, I must do what I must. I am not from your generation. Things are changing. This isn't the Middle Ages."

Her mother remained adamant. "For as long as you live in this house you will do as you are told."

"Then I will live elsewhere."

She expected the fearful look on her mother's face; what surprised her was her father's laughter.

He said, "And just what do you intend to use for money? You haven't a cent of your own."

"Then I'll starve."

His grin infuriated her. "One night on a park bench will put you in jail. I'll deny you're a relation if I'm contacted."

"You would too, wouldn't you," Susan charged, feeling close to tears.

Peter went over to her and put his arms around her, pulling her against him. "I love you, Susan, as does your mother, but what you are doing is illegal and dangerous. I will not allow you to move out of this house, nor will I allow you to involve yourself with these radical females."

The front door slammed and Efrem started across the foyer, passing the open study door. His presence drew their attention.

"Efrem!" Peter called when he saw the boy glance away from them and start for the staircase leading to the upstairs. "I want to speak with you, young man," Peter said in a stern voice.

Efrem stood hesitating in the doorway as he looked from his mother to his sister and finally to his father. He saw Peter's dark scowl and felt his whole body begin to tremble slightly. He'd always been afraid of his father, who he never remembered as ever saying a kind word. He was always criticizing and giving orders and running everyone's lives. Efrem had never questioned his mother when she'd told him his father had been responsible for David's death. In Efrem's mind, his father was capable of every cruelty.

"Yes, sir," Efrem said as he felt the palms of his hands begin to perspire.

"Come in. Close the door." He glanced at Susan. "You're a grown woman, you claim, so you might just as well stay and learn the type of people your brother is mixed up with; people, I might add," he said looking at Lorna, "of whom his mother totally approves."

Lorna took a step toward him. "What is this all about, Peter?"

Peter indicated his son. "Your youngest and the

189

Gordons. Aren't they those highly respectable friends of yours whose son, Paul, you encouraged Efrem to befriend?"

Susan said, "What's wrong with the Gordons? Paul's sister, Angela, is a friend of mine as well."

"Filth! That's what they are," Peter charged.

Lorna drew herself up, hating the smug, complacent smirk on Peter's face. "Will you kindly explain what this is about?"

Peter took a stance in front of Efrem, placing his feet well apart, putting his clenched hands on his hips, pushing back the open front of his jacket. "You see a lot of Paul Gordon, I understand."

"Yes," Efrem said with a nervous bob of his head.

"Did you see him last evening?"

"No."

"The evening before?"

"No. Paul is in Sacramento with a friend."

"A friend," Peter repeated with biting edge. He rocked on his heels and toes and put his hands behind his back. "Do you know this *friend*?"

"No." His voice was shaking. "I think Paul said he would be with a friend of his father's, a state senator, I believe."

"Not a state senator but a man who works in a State Senator's office, a man named Melkes, Clarence Melkes," Peter clarified.

Efrem looked blank.

"Oh, Peter," Lorna said impatiently. "Stop being so melodramatic. The Gordons are very fine people."

"Are they?" He put up his hand. "You have your Ramsey, Lorna and I have friends who have access to police reports."

Lorna clutched her throat. Susan tried not to look intimidated. Efrem visibly trembled and his father saw it.

"Unnerved, Efrem?"

The young man tried desperately to steady himself. "The police?" he managed in a shaking voice.

"The police," Peter repeated.

"For God's sake," Lorna gasped. "Will you kindly explain, Peter."

Peter paused. "Paul Gordon is a pervert!" he said.

There was a moment of stunned silence.

Lorna recovered first. "Peter, I demand that you please explain."

"A matter of indelicacy between two males, one older, one younger. A man and a boy. A *Greek* relationship," he said offhandedly as if it were an ordinary acceptable topic that people discussed every day. "Paul Gordon and Clarence Melkes shared a hotel suite. Suspicions were aroused when a maid reported that only one of the beds was being used. They were discovered . . . I believe the expression is *in flagrante delicto*."

"It's a lie," Lorna spat.

"One of the senior men on Hearst's newspaper told me himself. There's a devil of a fuss being put up to suppress it, naturally, but the talk was all over the Club yesterday afternoon. They are considering blacklisting any charity that Gordon is connected with."

Peter's pretended casualness disappeared. When he turned to Efrem his eyes were like flint, his expression terrifying. "I understand," Peter said evenly, "that your friend Paul is being sent abroad with his mother and sister. When and if he ever returns to this city you will have absolutely nothing whatever to do with him or any of his other friends. If I ever so much as hear a hint of anything like this about you, I promise you, Efrem, I'll see you dead."

Efrem backed away, his eyes wide, his body clammy. He swallowed hard and tried to say something in his own defense, as well as in Paul's, but the words just wouldn't come out.

Peter said, "I will never have that kind of scandal in this family. Do you understand me?"

Efrem managed a quick nod as he kept backing away toward the door. "Yes, sir," he finally stammered.

Peter said, "Starting next week I want you to come to the office with me, Efrem. It's time you began learning the business and doing something worthwhile with your time other than wasting it on your mother's friends."

Lorna huffed. "You sanctimonious hypocrite," she snapped at him. "So quick to accuse others and blind to your own weaknesses and your disgraceful behavior with Lydia Moonsong."

"At least it's normal," Peter said, unruffled.

Lorna persisted. "And so far as Efrem's coming into business with you, I absolutely forbid it. You took one son away from me; you will not take my youngest."

Efrem shifted his weight uncomfortably and tried to tactfully leave the room, but couldn't. He wanted to be alone to think about Paul. He'd known about Paul and his friend. Paul had made advances once or twice toward Efrem, but Efrem had been too frightened to let anything happen. All his life he'd thought of men in his fantasies, never women. The fantasies were never overtly sexual; he never allowed that because he knew it was criminal.

Susan said, "Why not let me come into the business, Father? I don't think you'd regret it. I'm very interested in what you do. I'd love to learn the cosmetic trade from top to bottom. I find it fascinating when I listen to you talk of sales gimmicks, which products sell better than others and why. I'd so like to be part of MacNair Products," she said enthusiastically.

"You," Peter said with disdain. "Your place is at home and at parties where you should be looking for a husband. I don't want an old maid on my hands, or a female prototype of Paul Gordon either," he sneered.

He heard Susan gasp and start to object.

"Get married, Susan," Peter said, "and stay in the place God intended for you to occupy, the place of wife and mother." He looked at Efrem. "Monday morning you start to work in my office. Is that understood?"

"Peter!" Lorna warned.

He ignored her. "Is that understood?" he asked Efrem again.

"Yes, sir."

"Damn you," Lorna swore as she turned angrily and stormed out of the room in a rustle of taffeta.

Susan stood glaring at her father. "Lydia Moonsong doesn't believe a woman's place is at home and you don't seem to resent her being in a man's world."

"Lydia Moonsong is none of your business."

Efrem cleared his throat. "May I be excused, Father?"

Peter waved him away.

Susan stood firm. "If you won't let me come into our family cosmetic business, perhaps I can persuade Mrs. Moonsong to take me on. I want to learn the cosmetic trade, Father."

"You so much as approach Lydia Moonsong and I'll have you walloped." When he saw she was going to argue he added, "The subject is closed, Susan. You can go. I have work to do."

Chapter 8

The fog had burned off and the afternoon was bright and warm as Lorna turned from the window and went toward Efrem's room.

He pretended to be reading a book on ships when she came in.

"I thought you might like to come with me to do some shopping. You could use some new shirts and Brooks Brothers have some new bolts of woolens in, your father tells me. You might like a new suit or two."

He seldom argued with his mother about anything because he had found out long ago that it was a waste of time. She always insisted he do what she wanted and it was easier and more pleasant to do it by immediately agreeing rather than suffer her cold domination all the time they were together.

He put the book aside and got off the bed. "I'll be with you in a minute," he told her as he went toward the bathroom.

"I'll wait for you downstairs, dear."

Efrem splashed cold water on his face and slicked back his hair. He looked at his reflection in the mirror over the washstand. Suddenly he wanted to be as good-looking as Paul Gordon. The thought unnerved him. Hurriedly he turned away and went to join his mother.

As their carriage pulled out of the drive Lorna said, "I will try to talk some sense into your father's head, Efrem. Perhaps you should think about going on to college."

"I don't mind working with Father. I'd much prefer it to college. You know how poor I am at studies."

"Well, if that is what you want, of course I'll abide by your wishes." She patted his hand.

As they approached the intersection of Taylor and California streets the carriage slowed and finally stopped. The trap door opened and the coachman said, "Sorry, Ma'am, but there's been some kind of accident up ahead."

Efrem peered out the side window. A crowd was gathering at the intersection and there were at least three or four carriages in a cluster just ahead.

"It looks like one of the cable trolleys broke down, Ma'am," the coachman said.

"Oh, dear." Lorna sighed and leaned back. "Well, there's nothing to be done, I suppose, but sit and wait until the congestion clears." She took Efrem's hand. "It just means you and I will have a little more time together. We haven't had a good private chat in ages. You are always out somewhere lately," she said, thinking suddenly of the Gordons.

She said, "What your father told us about Paul, it isn't true, surely?"

Efrem felt himself blush as he looked out the

window trying to avoid her eyes. "I have no idea. I've never seen any evidence of that sort of thing in him," he lied.

"Your father is so quick to judge and is always so callous about other people's feelings. To speak of such a thing in Susan's presence was unforgivable."

"I'm sure Susan wasn't embarrassed. She's quite the woman of the world, you realize. I doubt if anything could shock her."

Lorna made a face. "If there is any truth in that sordid story, it wasn't fair of your father to condemn the entire Gordon family because of a transgression on Paul's . . ." She stopped dead in midsentence and stared at the girl who came around the corner and stood at the curb. Lorna watched April Moonsong glance behind as if waiting for someone.

"April Moonsong again," Lorna said with a sneer. "And as usual unescorted. It's sinful the way she flounces about alone."

"Where?"

Lorna nodded to the girl on the corner.

"David said she was beautiful. He certainly didn't lie. She's quite a looker."

"Efrem," Lorna scoffed. "You know I dislike it when you use slang. And if you have any love for me you will take a vow never to have anything whatsoever to do with any of that Moonsong family. Swear to me that they will always be your enemies."

"Mother, really," Efrem hedged.

"Swear it!"

"Very well, if it means so much to you."

"It does."

197

"Then I swear it."

"Thank you, darling." She couldn't keep from glancing at April. She was tempted to get out of the carriage and throttle the brazen little hussy for all the grief she'd caused.

Lorna's hatred suddenly turned to wonder when she saw the girl start back along the street and a moment later reappear with a young man she knew to be her brother. But it wasn't Leon who captured Lorna's attention; it was the small, dark, curly headed lad who was toddling along between them.

Lorna felt her heart give a thud as she found herself carried back over the years and remembering the way David looked, the way he always toddled along, refusing any help, just as this child was doing.

She clutched Efrem's hand.

"What is it?" he asked seeing her mouth agape, her eyes staring.

"The child."

Efrem turned and looked, but he wasn't looking at little Adam. Never before in all his life had he ever seen so handsome a young man. He swallowed hard and tried to look away but his eyes refused to obey him. His entire body seemed to have gone numb. He felt nothing at all but a wild stirring in his loins.

"That's David's child," Lorna breathed.

Efrem hadn't heard her. All he could hear was the pounding in his heart. He was completely captivated by the beauty of the man standing looking down at a small boy and laughing.

Just then Leon happened to glance up and

caught Efrem staring at him. Leon thought he recognized the youth and smiled.

Efrem's head began to swim. He closed his eyes and tried to stop the trembling inside him. When he opened them again the man was gone. Quickly Efrem scanned the street and caught a fleeting glimpse of the tall, handsome youth now with a child on his shoulders and a woman on his arm, working their way through the jam of bystanders who'd gathered to watch the accident.

Too often of late Lorna found herself coming to Ramsey's flat, which doubled as his office. She found him sitting in the little study waiting for her.

Ramsey put his feet up on the edge of his desk and puffed on his cigar. "Why do you think it's your son's little boy?" he asked after Lorna told him about seeing April and the boy. "April and the Frenchie had a son, the one she abandoned in Paris. It was more than likely that youngster she was taking for a stroll."

"It was David's child. I haven't a doubt about that. He looked like David, he walked like David, he had David's thick, curly hair."

Ramsey chuckled. "I hardly think you could compare the walk of a three-year-old with David's."

"I didn't come here to be argued with. I know that child is my grandson."

"All right, Lorna," he said, putting down his cigar. "I'll check out the Moonsong mansion and if a new tot has been added, I'll trace down his papers." He got up and came around the desk. He tried to take her in his arms. When she resisted, pushing him away, he grabbed her and pulled her hard against him.

"You know, Lorna," he said, ignoring her fighting to get away. "I'm always flattered that you can't stay away from me." He laughed.

"Let me go."

"Actually, I think deep down you rather enjoy coming here to me. Maybe it's my lack of polish that attracts you, or is it my immorality you can't resist?"

"Let me go, Ramsey," Lorna insisted.

He grabbed the back of her head and kissed her hard on the mouth, forcing his tongue deep into its wetness. When he finished he smiled at her look of contempt and let her go. If it was possible for him to be in love with any woman, he knew it was Lorna MacNair. Though it was impossible that she could love him, there was an animal magnetism that drew them together in spite of themselves. She'd never marry him willingly, of course, but then he already had a wife over in Sausalito whom he didn't advertise.

There were too many times lately when he'd caught himself wishing he were single again so he could concentrate more fully on getting Lorna free from her husband. As he'd told himself, she'd never marry him willingly, but there was always a way to get people—especially women—to do things they would normally never do.

Lorna reached for her gloves. She squared her shoulders. "I think our relationship is ended, Ramsey," she said indignantly. "Forget about April Moonsong's child. I'll have another agency do the necessary detective work."

Ramsey was unimpressed. "You'll never stop needing me, Lorna. Why fool yourself? There isn't another detective in the country who'll do the dirty work you want done. You know in your heart that if that boy isn't David's, I'll figure some way to prove that he is, if that's what you want. No, Mrs. MacNair," he said with a leer, "you are stuck with me. Partners, that's what we are and we will always be partners regardless of how much either of us wants it otherwise."

He saw her look of surprise. "Didn't it ever occur to you that I might want to be rid of you as much as you want to be rid of me?" Ramsey asked. "I'm a lazy kind of fellow, Lorna. Right now I can't help wanting only you because you're accessible and lovely and satisfy me completely. Until some other more interesting woman comes along to capture my fancy, you're the only one I want, so get used to doing as I say."

Lorna pulled on her gloves, hating herself for her dependence on this odious man. He was as corrupt and as ruthless as a person could be, yet there was something about him that she found impossible to resist. He was far from handsome; however, there was a strength about him that was so like Peter. She was flattered by the lustful way Ramsey looked at her, the way Peter never looked at her. And Ramsey did sexually arouse her more than she cared to admit. He was a powerful, exciting man in bed, who did things to her no self-respecting man would ever do, including Peter. She knew Ramsey adored her, despite his hard, uncaring veneer. It thrilled her to be ravaged by him. Besides, what other man could she turn to for sexual gratification? Peter certainly did not give her any.

Ramsey must have recognized the sudden desire that shone in her face for he said, "Get out of that dress, Lorna. I want you in bed."

"Don't be disgusting."

He started for her and without realizing it she found herself backing toward the bedroom door.

He took her the way he always took her, roughly at first, then tenderly, patiently, moving with her, bringing her to climax after climax. His body was so thick and powerful, his sex filling her until it almost hurt—but it was a delicious hurt.

Ramsey never hurried. Every motion was calculated to please her. She especially loved it when he devoured her body with his mouth, touching every part of her, even parts that made her face burn with shame and her loins blaze with passion. Then, when she was weak and exhausted, he'd enter her again, driving himself hard and cruelly deep into her seeping warmth, sending her over the brink and down into the blackness of the void.

She lay quietly beside him and again the same question rushed back at her. Why was it so impossible for her to stay away from this crude man? She never liked the answer, but knew it well. She was bored with her life, her friends, her own security. With Ramsey she could let out all those pent-up needs that normally shamed her, needs she wanted to deny. Besides, Ramsey represented a solution—if only a temporary one—to her boredom.

She turned and looked at his relaxed profile. "You will get my grandchild away from that woman?"

He didn't stir. "If that's what you want, I'll get him for you."

"I'll pay whatever it costs."

Ramsey smiled but didn't look at her. "Since when have I ever asked for money? Still refusing to admit that you're doing something more disrespectable." He sighed. "I remember the first time you hired me and I told you what I wanted from you, you settled your account without a second's hesitation. I liked that, Lorna. And ever since my price will always be the same."

"And I suppose I'll always pay it," Lorna said bitterly. She felt cheap and dirty after giving herself so indecently to him. Especially at times like this when the feeling of complete satisfaction was beginning to wear off.

Ramsey said, "Speaking of money, I have stumbled on a scheme that will make me a sizable fortune, but I'll need your help."

Lorna sat up, turning her back so she would not have to look at his nakedness. She started getting into her clothes. "My help?"

"Well, not yours personally. Actually I need the help of your husband's company."

"MacNair Products? I don't understand."

"I heard of a supply of opium coming out of China destined for Hawaii. It's sitting there waiting for distributors to bring it to market. I can have seventy percent of the business if I can manage to get it into the States. Now, I was thinking, if MacNair Products suddenly started buying, let's say coconut oil or betel nuts from my friends in Hawaii, it would be a perfect way to bring in the opium without arousing suspicions. It's a natural cover."

Lorna adjusted the collar of her dress. "I don't even want to discuss it, Ramsey. The idea is out of the question. I may not be the most honest woman in the world, but I will flatly have nothing to do with any opium smuggling."

Ramsey watched her move toward the door. "Why do I always have to remind you of how I can force you to cooperate, Lorna?"

She turned on him. "Threaten all you like, Ramsey. On this I stand firm. Go to Peter with whatever disgusting stories you want, but I will not allow any part of my family to become associated with trafficking in drugs."

"The opium would go to the pharmaceutical firms, the hospitals. I'm alleviating the suffering, the pain of the less fortunate," he said, still smiling.

"I mean it, Ramsey. I'll give you anything you want but I will not help you with this. I find it despicable that you'd even consider preying on the weaknesses of others, but then you always have, I suppose," she said, thinking of her own weakness. She straightened to her full height. "I swear I will let everyone know everything you and I have done—are doing—before I let you corrupt MacNair Products. I mean that with all my heart."

He saw that she did. He'd touched on a nerve and decided it was best he didn't apply pressure. He knew a lot of people like Lorna, people who wouldn't bat an eye about knifing someone or hacking up their grandmother, but tell a dirty story about a priest or a nun and they'd blow the whistle on you in a second.

"Okay, okay, don't get all riled up about it. It

was just an idea I had. I'll think of something else. Forget I ever mentioned it."

"It's forgotten," Lorna huffed, then swung out of the room.

Ramsey scratched himself. "Too bad," he said to the empty bedroom after waiting until the front door shut behind Lorna. "Oh well, I'll think of something."

Chapter 9

Ramsey lay under the sheet, idly toying with the wiry hairs on his chest. Hard as he tried, he kept coming back to the only solution to his problem. MacNair Products was the only way through which he could bring the opium in without any hassle. It was the perfect cover and somehow he had to get Lorna to change her mind about helping him.

For a moment he'd considered Lydia Moonsong's huge enterprise, but they were too well-established and had their regular supplier in Hawaii. New shipments to Empress Cosmetics from an unknown Hawaiian supply house might look suspicious. No, MacNair's new company was just starting up under a new name. What would be more natural than for MacNair Products to begin importing supplies from a new young Hawaiian company whose prices were lower than that of the big name suppliers?

"How do I get her to cooperate?" he asked the empty room. The longer he thought the farther he was from an answer. Now that he had told her of his scheme, Lorna would have an eye out for anything unusual, any new face at MacNair Products. No, he would have to go through Lorna. He couldn't think of any other way.

He let out a sigh.

No, money had always been his god. Money bought his honor and respect and his conquests, like Lorna MacNair. He admitted that he was a slave to the world of drudgery without money. Only money could keep him free from that slavery.

A smile crept across his mouth when he remembered a funny little sign he'd once seen above a bar: "Remember the Golden Rule. . . . He who has the gold makes the rule."

He started to chuckle. There had to be some way of getting that opium into the States. He lay back against the pillows and reached for a fresh cigar.

The quiet of the flat was broken by the jangling of the door bell. Ramsey cursed silently and reached for his dressing gown. He hoped it wasn't someone who wanted action. He was not in the mood for moving about. He was in the mood for thinking.

A young boy of about fourteen stood with his peaked cap clutched in front of him. In his other hand he held a piece of paper, which he extended to Ramsey.

"The lady said you'd pay for delivering this note."

"What lady?"

"I don't know her name. She lives down the road from our house. She sent me. I think she's sick or something."

"And where's your house?"

"Princess Street over in Sausalito."

Ramsey cursed under his breath and took the note. "Wait 'til I get a coin," he said as he went toward where his clothes were draped over a chair.

"She said you'd give me the fare for the ferry back and forth," the boy called.

Ramsey irritably fished out half a dollar—a handsome price to pay for something he didn't want—and handed it to the lad. The boy's eyes lit up and he gave a hoot as he bounded off down the steps and up the street.

"It's important you come at once," the note read. There wasn't any signature. One wasn't necessary. His wife's childish scrawl he easily recognized.

He crumpled the paper into a ball and tossed it into the wastebasket. Then he retrieved it, put a match to it, and threw it onto the fire grate.

Why hadn't he gotten himself free of the woman years ago? he asked himself as he started to get dressed. He had cared for her once, he reminded himself—or had it just been pity? She'd never been well, but was always weak and sickly, and it had become a habit, taking care of her.

He paused, half tempted not to go, but then she never bothered him unless it was something important. The thought occurred to him that one of his several enemies might have found out about his wife and was making threats.

He resigned himself to making the trip.

When he left his flat it was beginning to grow dark. By the time the ferry boat left the dock and started across the bay night was all around him. Ramsey watched the fog thicken as he stood at the rail, a mist of angel's hair laying across the choppy surface of the water. The foghorns added to his gloomy mood, depressing him with their mournful, echoing moans.

Though he'd been born here in Sausalito he'd never liked the place. The "wharf rats," as the poor people who lived on the flat near the water were called, were always fighting the "hill snobs," most of whom worked in San Francisco and commuted on The Sausalito Land and Ferry Company's side-wheeler, *The Princess*.

It was here on the wharf where he'd learned to hold his own and was taught all the easier ways of making money. It was also here on this wharf in a whorehouse that he'd rescued Sylvia from the three drunken sailors who were determined they were all going to have her at the same time.

No more than seventeen, he was strong as a bull and more reckless than smart. He never loved Sylvia, but they were both young and he mistook sex for love. When he learned the difference it was too late. He contented himself for the time spending his days making money by spying and blackmail, anything that kept him away from home.

The house he'd bought for her was just off the main street, a short distance up Princess Street. It was a modest little place, but well kept and comfortable. Sylvia, he made sure, wanted for nothing. Luckily she never wanted much, just her medicine, her doctor's care, and himself.

He hated these visits. They always reminded him of those sordid, poverty-ridden times he wanted to forget.

Sylvia Ramsey was sitting in a rocking chair, staring into the fire when Ramsey let himself in.

He'd almost forgotten how gaunt and thin she was. Her once bright yellow hair now hung in white, dull strings over her shoulders.

Her eyes were lifeless, almost dead as she looked up at him and started to get up. "You've come," she said trying to smile.

Ramsey eased her back into the rocker. "You told me to come, so here I am," he said gruffly.

"Don't be angry with me, Ramsey. I had to see you. It's been so long."

"What's so important? Has anyone been here who shouldn't?"

"No," she said sadly, again staring at the fire. She should have known he'd be angry, she reminded herself. He was always angry.

"Then what is it you want?"

She'd only wanted to see him, but telling him that would only make him despise her all the more. Hard as she tried, she could not figure out what she'd done to cause him to dislike her so.

"I hope you didn't bring me all the way over here for nothing."

She gave her shawl a tug and scowled at the flames. "No," she said, getting annoyed. "I need more money."

"Why couldn't you have said that in your note? I would have sent it back with the boy."

She ignored the question. "I'm your wife, Ramsey," she said sharply. "Is it a crime to want to see my husband once in a while?"

He rolled his eyes. "Don't start, Sylvia."

"I have every right to ask you to come here. I could have the law on you for desertion."

Purposely Ramsey forced himself to grow calmer. Patiently he said, "You haven't been taking your medicine, have you? You always get irritable when you don't take it regularly." He put his hand on her shoulder. He could feel the bones under her stretched skin. "Sylvia, you know I give you everything you could possibly want. You know my work keeps me occupied almost every minute of the day. Time is money in my line of work."

"Your line of work," she scoffed. "What keeps a detective busy every minute? It's chasing women that keeps you too busy to spend time with your wife," she charged.

"You know better than that."

"Then why must you live in that fancy apartment over in the city while you have a perfectly nice home right here with me?"

"It's not a fancy apartment," he lied. "It's just an office with a cot in it and a gas ring to make coffee on and a toilet down the hall."

She thought of the large sums of money he sent her every month. "I don't believe you." She pouted. "I have a good right to come over there and see for myself."

Ramsey towered over her, his face red, his eyes on fire. "Don't you ever come over to my office! Do you hear me, Syliva? Never!"

"There's something you're hiding that you don't want me to see," she said slyly. "I bet you don't live in no rat trap at all. I bet you have a woman you're living with. Well, don't be too surprised, Ramsey, if one of these days you answer your door bell and find me standing on the stoop."

"Don't you EVER come to my office!"

When he saw the skeptical way she was looking at him he turned away and reminded himself to calm down. "You just don't understand, Sylvia.

211

You know the type of people I have to deal with in my business. Besides, you know you aren't strong and I want to keep you here out of harm's way on purpose. I have a lot of enemies who'd like nothing better to do than to do you harm, because they know it would be harming me. There are a lot of powerful San Francisco toffs who'd gladly pay to have my throat cut for what I know about them. I have to be wary everytime I go outside my office. I could never bring myself to place you in jeopardy, Sylvia. Too many men would enjoy making your life miserable. You'd be threatened, seriously hurt. Unfortunately, men like me make enemies. I can't expose you to risk."

He saw she was buying his story. He had to drive his point home. "Coming over on the ferry tonight I found I was followed. I gave the guy the slip by ducking into Jake's place and out the back door. I don't stay away because I want to, Sylvia; I stay away because I must, if I want you kept safe."

Sylvia sat saying nothing. She felt utterly helpless and completely frustrated. The tears came before she could stop them. Burying her face in her hands she began to sob.

"When will it all end, Ramsey? When will we be together again? I miss you so much. I'm all alone and I'm so tired. If only I had someone." She looked up at him through her tears. "A baby perhaps," she said as if snatching at straws. "I'm not too old. Oh, Ramsey, couldn't we have a baby? It would be so wonderful to have a little one to take care of."

The thought horrified him but he kept the kind smile fixed firmly on his mouth. "You know what the doctors said about that. You're not a strong woman, Sylvia. You know a baby is out of the question."

"Then maybe we could adopt one. Surely there are hundreds of unwanted babies, and I would be a wonderful mother. We could give it a wonderful home."

Ramsey didn't know what to say. He patted her tenderly on the shoulder. "We'll see," he answered.

"You'll think about it? Please, Ramsey, at least think about it," she begged, clutching his hand.

The hard, dry skin repulsed him as he eased his hand out of hers. "I'll think about it," he said not finding himself able to look at her sallow, more-consumptive-than-usual face.

"Now," Ramsey said brightly as he reached inside his jacket for his billfold. "How much money do you need?"

"I don't need money," she said. Her voice was meek and apologetic. "I'm sorry, Ramsey, I just didn't think. I only wanted to see you, to talk to you. It's so lonely here."

He put the billfold back into his pocket and patted it into place. He wanted to be away. Suddenly he thought of what had been occupying his mind most of the day and decided he might pacify her with something to look forward to, something to occupy her thoughts and keep her away. Though she was a physically weak woman, he knew how hard she could be if he crossed her.

He said, "Perhaps we can move away from here."

Immediately her eyes brightened as she sat forward, stilling the rocker. "What do you mean?"

"Now I'm making no promises, mind you, but there is a business matter I've been offered that would necessitate living in Hawaii."

"Hawaii? With those half-naked natives who live in huts and wear grass skirts?"

Ramsey forced a laugh. "It is much more civilized than you think. It's a very beautiful place with lots of bright flowers and palm trees and colorful birds that sing all the time."

"We'd go together?"

"Yes," he answered with a solemn nod. "I've been thinking of giving up the detective business," he lied. "If this business deal comes through we would get far, far away from all of my enemies."

"When? When will you know? When would we leave?"

"Soon," he said as he put his hand on the doorknob. "Now don't worry about anything, Sylvia. I'll be in touch as soon as I can. In the meantime just think about Hawaii and the palm trees and the beautiful birds. A paradise, Sylvia," he said, his voice soothing, hypnotic.

When he saw her relax against the back of the chair and begin rocking, he slipped quietly out of the door and hurried off down Princess Street toward the ferry waiting in its berth.

Something had to be done about Sylvia, he decided. It would not be much longer before he'd be incapable of pacifying her. She was getting more and more restless and her threats weren't idle ones, he knew. One day he *would* open the door to his flat and find her standing there. The solitude he'd forced her into was eating her alive and it was

214

only a matter of time before she'd take no more of it.

He toyed with the idea of sending her on ahead to Hawaii. She'd never consent to go without him, he reminded himself as the side wheel started to churn up the water and the ferry began moving toward San Francisco. She was weak and sickly, but she was not a stupid woman and she had a temper that matched his own when she let it loose.

No, his only hope was to play for time, he knew. *She's sickly*, a little voice told him. *Perhaps she'll die*.

It was his only out, he decided as he leaned against the rail and puffed on his cigar.

Chapter 10

His wife was the farthest thing from his mind as
Ramsey sat in the closed carriage opposite the
Moonsong mansion. He found suddenly that he
had a new puzzle on his hands, a puzzle that was
beginning to intrigue him. The comings and
goings of the Moonsongs had not included April
or the boy Lorna had described. He saw the nurse
often enough with the girl, Caroline, and the boy,
Marcus, but Marcus was older and had straight
hair cut in the currently fashionable Dutch fashion. Lorna had said the boy was about three and
had thick curly hair.

Ramsey saw Lydia come and go. He saw the
son, Leon. And, Ramsey remembered with a smug
smile, he saw Peter MacNair make frequent visits.
He wondered if he should mention that in his report to Lorna. She'd become angry and spiteful
and very often was more passionate, which he
took to mean was her way of seeking revenge on
Peter.

What was most curious, and the thing that most
intrigued Ramsey, was the fact that almost four or
five times during the day and evening Efrem

216

MacNair would stroll by the Moonsong house and then linger on the corner for twenty or more minutes, all the while watching the front door as if expecting someone to come out and meet him.

Here he comes again, Ramsey said to himself as he drew back into the shadow of the cab and watched through the slit in the side curtain.

Efrem slowed his steps as he crossed the street several yards before nearing the mansion. The door was firmly shut, the downstairs windows were blank. As usual, there was no sign of the young man he'd seen with April Moonsong.

"Her Chinese brother," his mother had answered when he'd asked casually who the young man was who was carrying the lad on his shoulders. Ever since seeing him, Efrem couldn't put him out of his mind. All he could visualize was the handsome face, the high cheekbones, skin like ivory, a trim physique that made Efrem's pulse quicken. He wished with all his heart he knew his name. Efrem was certain his mother knew it, but he was afraid he'd arouse her suspicions if he asked.

Straightening his already perfectly centered tie, he smoothed down an imagined stray tuft of hair and watched the door out of the corners of his eyes as he strolled past the gate. Once past he quickened his step and took up his stand at the corner of the street, which he recrossed so he had an unmolested view of the front door.

Efrem leaned against the brick wall for about five minutes, never realizing that not ten feet away Ramsey was watching his every move.

It was as if a bomb went off inside his chest when Efrem saw the door open and Leon step out into the brightness of the day. He was even more handsome than Efrem remembered.

Ducking quickly around the wall, Efrem watched until he heard the wrought-iron gate clang shut before chancing to peek to see in which direction Leon was going.

When Leon started down the hill toward Stockton Street Efrem waited until he was a block ahead before falling in behind him.

Inside the cab Ramsey frowned as he watched Efrem start off after Leon. He asked himself what it was all about and was tempted to follow just out of curiosity, but he reminded himself that he was to pay attention to April Moonsong and the little boy with the dark curly hair, both of whom were either staying indoors these days or didn't live here in the mansion.

At the bottom of Clay Street Leon turned left on Powell and paused to look in Black and Stone's window at a rather smart pair of boots. He was tempted to go in and try them on, but remembered he was already late if he wanted tea with April. She had her fixed hour for the ritual and if you weren't there on time you went without.

It wasn't until he crossed to the other side of Powell Street that he noticed the slight, boyish fellow stop quickly and pretend to be studying the contents of a window display. Ordinarily Leon would not have thought it odd, but the window was filled with a display of women's hats. He shrugged, passing it off with the thought that the lad might be window-shopping for a gift. But when Leon stopped again and noticed that the lad ducked into a doorway, Leon began to grow uneasy. He suddenly thought of the threats of the

Dowager Empress and how far her long, sharp claws were capable of reaching.

Deciding to verify his suspicions, Leon started down Sacramento Street, into Chinatown where he knew all the crossways and shortcuts and alleys. If the person behind him was indeed tailing him he'd find out soon enough, Leon told himself as he turned the corner of a silk shop and walked slowly down the dingy alleyway with its trash cans and burlap sacks of refuse. Halfway down he came to an intersecting path that led back to the main street. Leon turned into the narrow path and stopped. He peeked around the edge of the clapboard building.

Efrem was just starting down the alley.

"So I am being followed," Leon said out loud. He thought for a moment, then quickly moved out toward the street, then easterly toward another alleyway, narrower and darker than the first. This one eventually opened out onto Portsmouth Square and was referred to by the locals as "Waylay Alley." It was so-called because it was where men were often set upon, knocked unconscious, and awakened to find themselves "shanghaid" aboard some ship needing deckhands bound for God only knew where—usually Shanghai.

Leon pressed himself flat up against the rough wall of a two-story dry goods warehouse, hugging as much of its shadow as he could. He stacked two burlap sacks of scrap goods one atop the other, which served as a blind.

Efrem saw the sacks but paid them no mind when he thought he saw Leon go out the end of the alley and disappear around a corner. Heedlessly he hurried on.

Leon's fist caught him on the side of the jaw, knocking him against the far wall. A second later Efrem felt the second blow land squarely on his chin. His knees buckled and he fell down into the dirt. In an instant Leon was on top of him, straddling his chest, his fists pounding into Efrem's face.

When the lad stopped moving and stopped trying to defend himself, Leon sat back, breathing heavily, wiping away the sweat on his face with the sleeve of his jacket. It took a while before Leon calmed himself enough to look down at his victim. There was blood streaming from the nose, one eye was already red and puffy, and dark bruises were beginning to show on his jaw and cheek.

He wasn't Oriental after all, Leon saw; there was no mistake about that. He was no more than a boy, certainly not one of the Empress's hired assassins. Still, knowing the crafty old woman he wouldn't rule out her inveigling someone like this young American to do her dirty work for the promise of a handsome reward.

Leon put his hand on Efrem's chin and began shaking him. "All right, who the devil are you?" He shook him harder and saw Efrem's eyes flutter open, then close again.

Still sitting on top of him, Leon renewed his efforts to bring the boy around, though now that he looked more closely he noticed that he wasn't a boy. He was perhaps Leon's own age, he decided, but his delicate, almost effeminate features made him appear much younger.

Tears streamed out of the corners of Efrem's eyes before he opened them. The pain from his cuts and bruises was bad enough; the pain of his humiliation and shame was far worse.

"Don't hit me again. I didn't mean you any harm."

"Why were you following me?"

Efrem tried to answer but could find nothing to say. "I . . ." He turned his head aside and started to cry.

It was bad enough to see a woman cry, Leon thought as he turned away, but for a man to cry was abominable. "Stop that!" he said, feeling unnerved.

"I'm sorry," Efrem said as he choked back his sobs. "I feel so rotten."

When their eyes met, Leon saw something through Efrem's tears that ripped at his heart. Never before had he seen pure shame radiating from a man's eyes. His anger was replaced by pity without knowing why he should feel pity for the young man. He started to get off him, but remembered a lesson he'd been taught years and years ago in China: Never trust an assailant even when you know you've beaten him.

Leon settled his weight on Efrem's flattened body. "Who are you?"

"Efrem. Efrem MacNair."

"MacNair?" The name hit him hard. "Peter MacNair's son?"

"Yes. You know my father?"

Leon nodded slowly as his mind started working on why a MacNair was tailing him. Was it possible they had found out already about Adam and had asked their son to learn what he could about where April and Adam were living?

Hardly, he decided. If the MacNairs had

learned about Adam, surely they'd hire a professional to do their investigating.

"I still don't understand why you were following me."

Efrem's face turned red as he closed his eyes again, suddenly growing conscious of Leon sitting on top of him. He squirmed and tried to quiet the stirring deep inside him.

Leon got up. "You're a mess, I'm afraid." He extended his hand and helped Efrem to his feet. Not wanting to appear apologetic Leon said, "But damn it, you shouldn't be sneaking after people. Lucky you didn't follow somebody who'd beat you up worse than I did."

"I know who you are."

"Oh? Who am I?"

"Mrs. Moonsong's son."

"So if you knew who I am, I still don't understand your cloak and dagger stuff."

"I just wanted to meet you," Efrem said, his eyes lowered. "I've seen you around."

"Then why not come to the house and ring the bell?"

Efrem touched the cut on his lip and felt the sticky stream of blood under his nose. "A MacNair going to the Moonsong house? My mother would have a fit."

"Oh, yes, I see. Here let me look at that cut." He tilted Efrem's head into better light and studied the cut.

The face was even more fascinating and exciting close up, but its closeness made Efrem start to shake. He pushed Leon's hands away. "I'll be all right. It's only a cut lip and a bloody nose. I've had fights before."

There was something tragic about the lad, Leon saw. He was certain he'd had fights before—bigger boys, the bullies who always enjoyed proving themselves over the weaker ones. He'd had his own share of fights at school with boys who were taught to hate and demean the Orientals. Leon had to sympathize with the lad; whereas Leon had been strong enough to fight back and win, looking at Efrem he saw at once that Efrem wasn't a fighter.

"Come on, Efrem," Leon said tugging his arm. "I know a place here in Chinatown where we can put a plaster on that cut and clean up that blood." They started out of the alley, back the way they'd come.

Leon's first idea was to take Efrem to April's, but he discounted that. He laughed when they came out into the bright daylight and he saw the puffed-up eye and the dark bruises. "Holy cow, what is your father going to say?"

Efrem grinned, ignoring the hurt of the cut. "He'll be pleased as punch. It's my mother who'll fuss and fume."

Leon unconsciously put his arm across Efrem's shoulders. There was something about the boy that he felt an affinity for. Efrem had a sense of loneliness about him that reminded Leon of himself.

"Tell you what," Leon said as they walked along. "We'll invent some wild story. Parents love it when their sons do something reckless that wasn't their fault."

"Like stopping a runaway carriage with an old woman and a child inside," Efrem said happily.

"Or having to fight off attackers who tried to snatch your girlfriend."

"Father would like that one," Efrem said laughing. He'd never felt so good in his whole life.

The old Chinese woman who owned the tea shop saw to Efrem's bruises, then insisted she get them something to eat. Efrem didn't particularly like the raw fish, but ate it anyway and devoured the almond cookies that had just come out of the oven.

As they talked and ate Leon found himself talking more freely about his feeling of misplacement in America than he'd ever talked to anyone about before, even his family. He spoke of his love for China and of the strangeness of his never wanted to go back there, as much as he loved it.

"I think I can understand that," Efrem said. "There's something inside me that I don't understand. I feel too that I know I don't belong here. Oh, it hasn't anything to do with being an American or anything like that, it's just something inside my head that keeps reminding me that I don't belong. And I never will."

At first Leon didn't understand, but gradually he saw something in Efrem's eyes, in the way he was looking at him, that gave Leon a hint and made him most uncomfortable.

"It's like wanting us to be friends," Efrem continued. He lowered his eyes. "It's something that just isn't possible."

Leon heard a warning voice telling him to agree and end the matter right here. Shake hands and apologize and wish Efrem luck, saying you agree that the MacNairs and the Moonsongs could never be friends.

He found he couldn't do it. Efrem was being eaten alive inside and he needed a friend, someone who'd be able to help him. Leon blamed it on his Oriental nonchalance about such affairs that sometimes happened between men. He could never understand how one man could be attracted to another. He had never been and would never be, he was certain.

In Efrem he saw a cry for help, for a strong hand to guide him out of boyhood into maturity. Leon felt he couldn't just walk away from Efrem without at least trying to be that strong hand. There were too many unscrupulous men in San Francisco who'd be only too willing to take advantage of a vulnerable, handsome boy like Efrem MacNair.

Leon said, "Why isn't it possible, Efrem? Just because our parents don't get along, I see no reason why you and I can't be friends."

Efrem stared. "You mean it?"

"Of course I mean it. Tell you what. I'm invited to a dance at the Carlsbads at their estate in Belvedere. There's this knockout girl who I know will go if you ask her. I'll fix it all up. We'll double-date. It'll be fun."

It wasn't what Efrem had hoped but they'd be together which was all that he cared about. He shook his head. "My father is pretty strict about who I go around with."

"She's Ellen Stanton. Holy cow, your father surely wouldn't object to your going to a ball with the Stantons' girl—and I know the Carlsbads are top society, so how could anybody object?" He poked Efrem's arm playfully. "Come on, Ef. What do you say? Tomorrow night. Meet me down at

225

the wharf ten o'clock tomorrow morning and I'll let you know if everything's set. If Ellen's already dated then you can come with me and her sister. You'll still be with a Stanton girl. Your folks don't have to know there is a Moonsong in the group."

He couldn't refuse but his thoughts weren't on the party; all he could think about was that he'd be seeing Leon at ten o'clock tomorrow morning. Just the two of them down at the wharf with a whole day to spend together.

Chapter 11

Over the following weeks Leon's and Efrem's friendship grew, affectionate but totally innocent. Leon was sure he was making a man out of what he considered his protégé. Efrem was lively and fun to be with and the girls all flocked around him because he proved to be an excellent dancer and a great flatterer.

Both young men went to great pains to make sure their families stayed ignorant of their friendship. Leon often used this as an excuse to rebuff Efrem's wanting to be with Leon so much of the time.

"Mustn't give them a chance to see us together, Ef. It would only mean not seeing each other at all."

Leon was quick to see Efrem's disappointment, but he knew that eventually Efrem's attraction to him would make its natural turn toward girls.

It was a cold January and the heavy fog that blew across the city only made it seem colder.

"Well," Lydia said as she kissed Leon good morning. She slipped a letter she'd finished reading into her pocket and sat down across from him.

She poured herself a cup of coffee as Nellie came in with her plate of eggs and ham. "If I didn't know you better, Leon, I'd say you've been up to some kind of skullduggery."

He gave her a blank look.

"For weeks now you've been going out almost every other night to some party or other and you never tell me who you've been dating."

"No one girl in particular." He smiled at her. "When there is one, you will be the first to know."

"In the past you always went on so about the people and places you'd been with. I can't help getting the notion that you're trying to hide something."

He merely smiled. "To be truthful, I am."

She was pleasantly infuriated when he didn't elaborate. "You're exasperating."

He swallowed a piece of toast. "Truthfully, I'm secretly at work on a shy friend."

"What gender friend?"

"Just a chap I got into a fight with and am trying to make amends by fixing him up with the girls and families I know."

"Fixing him up? Where on earth did you pick up that vulgar expression? I hope not from this shy friend."

"You should get out more, Mother. How can you keep up on the new slang and the new dances closeting yourself in this house and in your office the way you do?"

"There're more important things in life than slang and dances." She made a vague excuse about her age and that business had fallen off since Raymond left for Paris a month before. Besides, the truth was that Peter was all the company she wanted, but she certainly could not tell Leon that.

She'd been seeing a lot of Peter—discreetly, of course. Once or twice they went off to some quiet out-of-the-way place where no one knew them. Still, she didn't completely trust Peter. She frankly admitted to herself that she loved him and in her way of thinking one had nothing to do with the other, much as she'd read to the contrary. It was possibly perverse for her to think it, but not trusting Peter made their love affair more exciting.

"So where are you off to this evening?" Lydia asked, remembering that Tuesday was Lorna's bridge night and Peter often walked over.

"Nowhere. I thought you and I might do something."

"Of course," she smiled, but her heart wasn't behind the smile. "Perhaps we should ask April to join us."

"She'd like that, I think. She is becoming a recluse like you."

"I heard good news that might brighten her spirits," Lydia said, reaching in her pocket for the letter that had arrived in the early morning post.

"Oh?"

"It's from Raymond's solicitors. April will be a free woman by the end of the month."

"That was quick."

Lydia frowned at the letter. "Of course none of it is to April's advantage. Their marriage is being quietly dissolved on the grounds that she admittedly deserted her husband and children." Sadly she refolded the letter and put it back into her pocket. "It's what April wanted, so she should have no regrets." She tasted the eggs and suddenly had no appetite for food. "That foolish girl," Lydia sighed as she put her hand to her cheek.

"But as you said, it is what April wanted."

"Can't you see, Leon, she is giving up everything. She has relinquished her right to any part of Raymond's assets and estate, she's given up Caroline and Marcus."

"She has Adam," he reminded her. "It is all she seems to want."

"It isn't natural." In her heart she understood. Caroline only reminded April of her unhappy marriage to Raymond and Marcus was never her child to begin with. Her life had started with David MacNair. His son, Adam, was all April had left of that life and it was all she wanted for herself.

A thought occurred to Leon. "Do you think the MacNairs know about their grandson?"

"That's the improbable part of it. April is anxious for them to find out and try to claim Adam. It's as if she's taunting them with the child. I know Lorna suspects."

"Oh? How?"

"Her husband mentioned it at a business luncheon we both attended around the holidays." She looked helplessly at Leon. "Can't April understand that she could lose Adam as easily as she lost everything else?"

"She has proof Adam isn't David MacNair's son," he reminded her.

"Proof," she scoffed. "Since when did proof stop the likes of Lorna MacNair?"

Leon had come to know quite a lot about Lorna MacNair from Efrem's conversations. It was a subject Efrem was always talking about and the more Leon learned of this woman, the less he cared for her. Often as Leon had tried to steer their talk back to Efrem's progress with his father and his work at MacNair Products, Efrem somehow brought his mother back into the conversation.

It had been during one such conversation the previous Saturday evening that Leon was talking about the cosmetic business and suddenly found Efrem talking about his mother. They had brought the Stanton girls to the Lobster Claw for dinner and the girls were off in the powder room.

"I can never understand, Efrem, why you seem to have this need to talk so much about your mother."

"Because he's a mama's boy," a girl said behind Leon.

He saw Efrem stare up at the girl at Leon's back and Leon heard her laugh.

Ellen Stanton said, "We found her in the powder room, Efrem. She had no idea you were here."

"Hello, little brother," Susan said. "Harry Fielding is waiting for me at the corner table. I just thought I'd pop over and say hello." He moved around Leon's chair as he got to his feet.

Efrem nervously introduced them. "Susan, may I present my friend, Leon."

She held out her hand to him and smiled. "Leon? Just Leon? Doesn't he have a last name?" she teased. She knew perfectly well who the handsome young man with the slightly slanting eyes was.

"Leon Moonsong," Leon told her with a touch of pride and defiance.

"The Empress Cosmetics heir. Well, well, Efrem, I had no idea you were friendly with the family's competitors."

Meeting him, Susan couldn't quite make up her mind as to whether or not she liked him. He was certainly good-looking, with just the barest trace of the exotic Orient in his features, which only added to his good looks. His eyes, dark and mysterious, thrilled her more than she cared to admit. His pinched smile, however, annoyed her.

Leon said, "Would you and Harry care to join us, Miss MacNair? We know each other quite well, Harry and I."

"Yes," Susan said eyeing him dubiously. "You are quite popular in the social whirl of the city, I understand."

"I'm their 'token' Oriental," Leon said through his pinched smile.

"It surprises me that we haven't met before this."

"That is perhaps because our families would not approve," he said as he held the chair for Grace Stanton, as Efrem did for her sister, Ellen. He didn't wait for her to reply. "Join us, please," he said. "I promise I won't tell my mother if you won't tell yours."

"Thank you, yes, I'd like to join you. I'll fetch Harry." She went off leaving a wake of such loveliness Leon found himself unable to keep his eyes off her. He finally realized he was standing staring and waved for the waiter to bring two more chairs.

For Leon the evening had just begun, but he saw Efrem visibly withdraw into himself. Leon realized suddenly that as far as Efrem was concerned, his evening was finished.

"Were you angry that I asked your sister and Harry to join us, Ef?" Leon wanted to know after the group had broken up and they'd escorted the Stanton girls home.

"No, of course not. Susan and I are great pals."

"I wondered, because you got so sullen after they came to the table. Is it Harry you don't like?"

"He's all right," Ef answered as they sent the cabbie off and decided to stop somewhere for a nightcap. "It's just that I wanted tonight to be my party to you, a kind of early celebration before your birthday tomorrow. I know your mother is planning a party. We received invitations."

Leon looked surprised. "Mother sent invitations to your house?"

"She always invites my parents. She and Father were an 'item' once, as they say. He might be there tomorrow but Mother would not set foot inside your home if it killed her and she certainly wouldn't permit Susan or me to come."

"That's too bad. I'd like it if you came."

"Me or Susan?" Efrem asked petulantly.

"Both, of course." He clapped his hand on Efrem's shoulder and kept it there. "Now, where would you like to treat me to this birthday nightcap you promised?"

"Anywhere you like. I'll let it up to you."

Leon thought. "How about Orleans, the new French place on Market?" He nudged Efrem. "They have those can-can girls. That should brighten you up."

"If you like."

"I like," Leon insisted, ignoring Efrem's lack of enthusiasm.

The place was raucous, but lively and fun with

233

a brightly lighted dance floor where the girls kicked high and flashed their bottoms. Both Leon and Efrem drank more than their share of the champagne Efrem insisted upon and by one o'clock they were both staggering—Efrem sullen, Leon exhilarated. The dancing girls and flashes of bare flesh had awakened a sexual need in Leon and whenever these urges grabbed him Leon went to Madam Foo's and her beautifully seductive singsong girls.

"Come on, Ef, old friend. I think it's time I introduced you to one of my very secret haunts. Nobody in the whole world knows I go there so you've got to promise that it will be our secret—just yours and mine."

Efrem felt happier all of a sudden. This is what he wanted—something secret and personal that only he and Leon shared. He went along only too eagerly to the rather secluded little house on the far edge of Chinatown. He found it a rather quiet, subdued place with ornately decorated rooms and tinkling beaded curtains. The heavy aroma of incense hung over everything. Lovely doll-like creatures sat demurely about the room catering to the men who talked a little too loudly, but who never seemed to laugh.

There was something serious about the whole atmosphere. Efrem liked that. It made him feel all the more closer to Leon.

A pretty girl in an elaborate costume served them drinks in white porcelain cups, poured from miniature porcelain bottles. The liquid was warm and sweet and smooth. After emptying several of the little bottles Efrem felt the room begin to spin around. One minute he was telling Leon how much he liked him and the next minute he was asleep on Leon's shoulder.

In the corner, surrounded by three lovely Oriental girls, Ramsey leaned forward and watched the two young men with an intent stare.

Efrem didn't have any idea how he'd gotten there, or where he was. The bed felt soft as feathers and the cold towels on his forehead reminded him of spring streams and the first crocuses. When he opened his eyes he found one of the Chinese girls smiling sweetly into his face.

"You are feeling better?" the girl asked in a voice that was like a serenade.

"Yes, thank you." Efrem tried to sit up, but his head throbbed and he let the singsong girl urge him back against the pillows. "My friend?" Efrem asked, looking about the room.

A sly, yet almost embarrassed smile curled her lips. "He is in the next room, sleeping I think, by now."

"How long have I been passed out?"

"Not long. Maybe an hour, perhaps two."

"I've got to get home," Efrem said feeling a sudden panic.

She coaxed him to lie back. "In a moment. I will make you feel very much better. Close your eyes," she cooed as her fingers began moving over his naked chest like the trailing of satin ribbons. Her lips pressed lightly against one shoulder, then she gradually moved down and encircled the nipple of his breast as her hands moved downward over his stomach, reaching for him.

Efrem's eyes shot open as he realized he was stark naked under the light sheet. His body began to sweat under her manipulations. A sickening, sinking feeling started in his groin and worked its way upward into his brain.

She fondled him, coaxing him to become excited; he only felt more nauseous. When the girl slowly lowered the sheet, moving it before the path of her lips, the nausea grew worse.

Her hands cupped his testicles, massaged his flaccid member; gradually, artfully her lips replaced her hand as she drew him deep into her mouth.

Efrem threw himself up from the bed, sending the astonished girl sprawling onto the floor. He yelled Leon's name and charged out of the room, forgetting that he was stark naked.

"Leon!" he yelled as the perspiration poured out of him and the raging terror began to claw at his brain. "Leon!"

Doors began to open and strange faces, some angry, some amused, stared out at him.

"Leon!"

He knew it was Leon's naked body that was holding him without seeing it. The powerful, bare flesh had Leon's scent, Leon's feel.

There was a mumbling of words, an angry exchange between Leon and a woman. A moment later Efrem was lying naked and sobbing in Leon's arms.

"Leon," Efrem breathed as he leaned close to Leon's face.

"It's all right, Ef. Go to sleep."

"Please, Leon." There was a pathetic pleading in his voice as he moved his mouth closer to Leon's. Leon didn't move. He felt the brush of the lips against his own.

It was all wrong.

"Please, Leon," Efrem said again, sounding in pain.

Leon closed his eyes and lay back.

Across the hall Ramsey quietly shut the bedroom door and crawled back into bed with the young Chinese beauty he hadn't really wanted but who occupied the only room where he'd have the best advantage.

"I thought it would end like that," he said.

"What is it you say?"

"Nothing, pretty one. I spent a lot of time trying to figure out the answer to something that had been puzzling me." He sighed. "For a moment, earlier tonight, I thought I'd been totally wrong, that I'd been wasting my time." He pictured Leon taking Efrem into his arms and leading him into the bedroom after ordering the Chinese whore out.

He glanced at the door as a thought struck him. "Perhaps I'm still wrong," he said getting out of bed.

"Where are you going?"

"I'll be back in a moment," Ramsey said as he left the room. He went across the corridor and pressed his ear against Leon's door. A smile stretched across his mouth when he heard the voices, the sounds.

"You mustn't, Efrem."

"Please Leon. I can't help it. Please."

Then Ramsey heard the telltale sounds, the soft moans, the creaking of the bedsprings, the sounds of sex. He laughed and went back to his singsong girl.

"No, I was right," Ramsey said as he settled himself beside the whore. He chuckled softly. "I don't know why I doubted myself in the first place. I always did have a talent for making money easily."

Chapter 12

Evelyn Clary dropped the latest profit and loss statement on Lydia's desk. As many years as Evelyn had served as Lydia's right hand, she'd never seen a financial report on Empress Cosmetics as bad as this one.

"We'll be out of business in six months at the outside," she told Lydia as Lydia scanned the figures, then threw aside the report.

"I was prepared for this," Lydia admitted as she got up from her desk.

"So what are we to do? There are an awful lot of people who are depending on your company for their livelihoods."

"Including me," Lydia said.

"I wasn't thinking about myself, Lydia."

"I'm sorry, I know you weren't, Evelyn." She sighed and went toward the liquor cabinet she seldom used. She poured herself a sherry. "I know now how Peter MacNair felt when his first company went under."

"We could always consolidate. He's been wanting that," Evelyn reminded her.

Lydia tapped her finger against the rim of the

239

glass and tilted her head. "Not as insistently of late as he once did. Of course, it has absolutely nothing to do with our not having Moonsong or Raymond Andrieux, understand," she said caustically.

"What about Raymond? I know he's in Paris doing everything possible to put you out of business, but what I don't know is, why?"

Lydia knew but didn't say. "I've cabled Raymond, Evelyn. I did it on my own because I didn't want you to get your hopes up."

"So?" Evelyn asked eagerly.

"He arrived last week in New York aboard *The City of Paris.*" She took a sip of sherry. "His train gets into the Oakland Mole tomorrow. I am *not*, however, going to be at the station. I'd like you to do that if you will."

"I understand." She paused. "Am I to assume that he is returning to work for us here?"

Lydia shrugged. "His cable merely said he was coming to San Francisco directly from New York and would listen to any proposition I had to make and then reminded me that he had one or two conditions of his own."

Evelyn watched her pace. "I hate to say this, Lydia, but we need him pretty badly. The creditors are already fighting one another over who is going to get what."

Lydia slammed down her glass. "What went wrong, Evelyn? Moonsong was only one of our products. We have dozens of others equally as good."

"But no Raymond Andrieux and his talented nose. You know he had the final word on everything that went out of here. Not to hurt your feelings, Lydia, but Raymond was—is Empress Cosmetics."

"I was making a go of things before he came along."

"That was quite a long time ago. People are more selective now. They want better and better quality for their money. We have to stand behind our prices or we'll lose the respect for our products. MacNairs can sell cheaply because his products are cheap. If we lose our prestige we lose everything."

"I know, I know," Lydia said impatiently.

"I'll meet Raymond's train," Evelyn said. "And if his conditions are even remotely reasonable, I'd advise you to meet them or give up everything you've worked for."

"I can't lose all this," she said with a sweeping motion. "I'm too old to start over and I have Caroline and Marcus, April, Adam, Leon. . . . Oh, God, I have many, too many obligations. Losing Empress Cosmetics would be like losing my life." She felt tightness in her throat and swallowed hard. She put back her head and blinked back the tears. "I can't help thinking that somewhere far across the Pacific there is that evil, vicious woman sitting on a golden throne laughing at me." She lowered her head. "Maybe I deserve to lose everything," she added thinking suddenly of David's death.

Evelyn put her hands on Lydia's shoulders and gave her a bolstering shake. "None of that now. I'll pick up handsome Raymond and bring him to your place. The two of you will have a cozy, friendly chat and I am sure everything will work out just fine."

241

She hugged Lydia tightly to show her support, then started out of the office. At the door she turned back. "Incidentally, Peter MacNair called a moment ago. He said to meet him for lunch at the usual place."

Lydia made a face. "He didn't ask to speak with me?"

"No."

Her mouth turned down. "He's been taking a lot for granted lately," she said bitterly. She paused, thinking. "Call him back, Evelyn, and tell him I'm already engaged for lunch."

"Right away," Evelyn answered. Giving Lydia a knowing look she added, "I'll have something sent in. Sandwiches all right?"

"Anything." She was hurt and annoyed. "Damn him," she said when Evelyn closed the door. "Damn!" She picked up the profit and loss statement, studied it, then crumpled it into a ball and threw it into the wastebasket.

About half an hour later she was finishing the first half of the corned beef on rye when Peter barged in, as usual with Evelyn at his heels looking helpless. Peter closed the door in Evelyn's face and strode toward Lydia.

She put the sandwich aside and glared up at him.

"What's this 'already engaged' nonsense?" he demanded, looking at the half-eaten sandwich.

"Frankly, Peter, I thought you presumptuous, as though I were to drop everything whenever you snapped your fingers."

"For God's sake, Lydia, we've been lunching together almost three times a week at the Crystal Court."

242

"Not very long ago you complained of Raymond's proprietary manner with me; now, you're acting the same way and I don't appreciate it."

He cocked his head and watched her expression; it was steady and recalcitrant. "You're angry with me about something. What did I do?"

"I just told you. You're taking me a little too much for granted lately, ever since . . ." She was unaware that her eyes moved toward the wadded up financial report in the wire wastebasket.

Peter noticed. "Ever since your empire started to fall apart," he finished. "Is that it?"

She despised the smug way he was standing there, head tilted, feet apart, hands on hips, his pelvis thrust forward accentuating his manhood.

Lydia purposely picked up her sandwich, but didn't bite into it. She looked at it then put it aside. "I see you have your industrial espionage ring keeping you *au courant*, as they say."

"There are never any secrets in competitive businesses such as ours, Lydia. Yes, I'm fully aware of the trouble you're in. I'm not the only one who knows creditors love to complain, especially when they're out to lose a bundle." He moved forward, leaning his hands on the desk. "So why not come in with me?"

"It's been some time since you've mentioned that idea. Were you waiting to see the full extent of my disaster, Peter?"

"You're avoiding my question."

"I won't come in with you for the same reason you wouldn't come in with me when you were in trouble."

"You're a stubborn woman."

"You forced me to learn all too well how to survive. And I will survive, Peter. I did it once without any help from you."

"Don't bring up old skeletons, Lydia. We were meant to be together. My company is thriving. With the prestige of your name coupled with mine, we'll be the most powerful cosmetic enterprise in the world."

"And Lorna? How would your wife take the news? I assume you've spoken to her?"

"I have. She knows I want to divorce her and marry you."

"You've been saying that for months and we both know that it's impossible. She'll never let you go and truthfully, Peter, I get the impression lately that you don't want to be let go."

"Of course I do," he said. "It's just that Lorna has this notion about April's child being David's. If it's true it puts me in an awkward position."

She kept watching him. "I can't see how."

He ignored the remark. "Your only hope is to let me take you over, Lydia." It slipped out before he could catch it.

She jumped to her feet, her eyes on fire. "Take me over! So that's what you've been plotting in that selfish mind of yours." Dramatically she pointed to the door. "Get out! The day you take ME over will be when I'm cold dead in my coffin." She remembered Raymond's cable. "And as far as anyone taking over, we'll just see who takes over who."

"Lydia," he said, "I didn't mean . . ."

"You never mean a lot of things, Peter. Now again, I'm telling you to get out."

He slapped his thigh. "All right. We'll talk about this later when you're more rational."

244

"I don't think we will."

"Lydia," he said again.

Mentally she put her hands over her ears. "Please leave, Peter—and as they say in the theatrical trade, don't call me, I'll call you."

"Theatrical trade?" he said raising his eyebrows. "I wondered where you'd learned your sudden dramatics."

"Get out!" She threatened him with an inkwell.

Peter held up his hands and backed toward the door. "You are being foolish, you know that? But then you always were rather lacking in common sense."

He ducked out the door as the inkwell smashed against the panels, splattering black ink into an abstract pattern.

Lydia dropped into her chair and rested her cheek in her hand, thinking back over the past weeks when she and Peter had been alone. She should have surmised that he knew of her financial problems and that he was just biding his time.

She thought again of Raymond, who held the secret to Moonsong and wondered, of a sudden, why he'd never marketed it for himself. After all, the Patent Office had refused to grant her exclusive rights to Moonsong because under the Revised Patent Law of 1870 her product did not fulfill their requirement: That Moonsong had not been developed "in a flash of inventive genius," to use the exact words of the law. According to their decision, Moonsong was merely a haphazard mixture of oils and scents that required no real genius to produce. Besides, cosmetics were not inventions, they'd concluded.

The following afternoon when she and Raymond settled themselves in the drawing room and Nellie had set out the tea tray, Lydia asked Raymond the question that she'd wondered about.

"Why haven't you marketed Moonsong on your own, Raymond? You're the only one with the talent to produce it."

He merely shrugged and crossed his legs, knee to knee. "I may be a selfish man, Lydia, but I am not without principles. Moonsong is yours. I would never reproduce it as my own."

She knew him well, and he was lying. He hadn't a principled bone in his body. He wanted something and had been playing for time, waiting for her to come to him, as he knew she must if she wanted Empress Cosmetics to stay solvent.

"What exactly would it take to have you come back to Empress Cosmetics? I won't be foolish enough to pretend I don't need you.

"The company is practically defunct, as I am sure you know."

He nodded.

"So what is it you want?"

"You," he said simply.

Lydia froze. Why it should come as a surprise she didn't know. She supposed it was the way he'd said it, not as a proposal of marriage, or even a desire for her; it was more of a demand.

"Me?" she asked, stalling, trying to think, trying to recover herself.

"Of course," he said in his charming French accent. "I still want to marry you. I've told you that often enough."

"Yes, I know," she stammered, feeling most uncomfortable. "But, Raymond, certainly you're

246

aware that there has been enough scandal about this family. It's insane to think of adding to it."

He shrugged to show his unconcern.

"It wouldn't be right my marrying my own son-in-law."

"The condition I mentioned in my cable . . . that is it."

Lydia sat there thinking. "It's impossible." She got up, one hand nervously toying with the cameo at her throat, the other fussing with her hair. "Raymond, when you were married to April I took your proposals as harmless little caprices. I never believed you were serious."

"I told you years ago that I should have married you. When we were in Paris and April ran away, I should have freed myself of her then and married you immediately." He smiled. "You were very vulnerable then."

He had no way of knowing of the scene with Peter yesterday and of their argument; that right now she was more vulnerable than ever. How dare Peter make demands? He had no intention of ever divorcing Lorna. He'd always find some excuse not to. Now he was going to "take her over" as he'd put it. Take her over, indeed! She'd show him who would take over who.

She stopped halfway to the fireplace and turned around, one hand still on the cameo, the other on her hair. She stood frozen as if posed for a portrait. "You are serious about marrying me?"

"I said I was and I am. Would it please you if I went down on my knee?" He started to move. She stopped him.

"Ignoring what the newspapers will say, what will April say?"

247

"April despises me. I realize that."

"What of me?"

Raymond showed a tight smile. "Surely you know she doesn't exactly care any more for you than she does for me so what does it matter?"

She felt pained and turned her back to hide it. "True, there was never any real deep love for me on her part," Lydia said, feeling she had to make a pretense of not caring. "There are reasons why our relationship was never close, but I don't think she despises me."

Raymond went to her and pressed himself against her back, putting his arms around her waist. "Of course she doesn't despise you, Lydia. I only meant, I doubt if she will care one way or the other about our marrying. Neither of us were ever permitted into her private world. We will always be visitors in her life, nothing more."

He touched his lips to her hair. "You know, I don't believe April will ever be happy with anyone. Even if David had lived, she would have eventually found he didn't belong in her dream. And it is a dream in which she lives. I suppose it is cruel of me to say, but I sincerely believe April looks upon David's death as a scene in that drama she's living. It makes her life more tragic, more dramatic."

He turned her to face him. "April will always see herself as the lovely princess in the ivory tower, a prisoner to her own fantasies." He raised one eyebrow as a warning. "Beware of her, Lydia. She is capable of some very dark and dire emotions. I think she'd even kill if she thought it was necessary to her plot."

248

The way he spoke unnerved her and thinking of April's coldness made her shiver.

"Are you cold?" he asked holding her tighter.

"No." The hatred she'd so often refused to see in April's eyes continued to haunt her. "I'll have to have time to think about your proposal."

He chuckled. "Why is that always the woman's standard reply to a proposal of marriage?" He paused and looked deep into her eyes. "You've had enough time. I want an answer." His voice was suddenly harder and in it was an unspoken threat. It was either Raymond or ruin, she knew.

"Yes," she said meekly. "I'll marry you."

She expected him to kiss her and say he loved her. He did neither. "I knew you'd accept." When he saw her hurt he softened his remark. "And I'm glad. We will make an ideal couple."

"Raymond?"

"Yes?"

"One favor."

"If it isn't too great a favor."

"Give me a few days before we make the announcement public."

He frowned. "Peter MacNair?"

"No, no, nothing like that," she answered, unable to meet his eyes. "There are so many important friends and business people who would be insulted if they hadn't heard the news from me before reading a cold announcement in the newspapers."

"All right," he agreed. He didn't trust her, but he saw no reason to argue. "I'll give you a week."

"Thank you, darling."

It was then that he kissed her.

As their lips met and his tongue explored the warm wetness of her mouth she found herself fighting back the pain in her heart as she thought about Peter MacNair.

Chapter 13

It was two days later when Lorna MacNair hurried home after her luncheon with Phoebe Hearst. She couldn't wait to tell Peter the news and was furious when the butler told her Peter had called to say he would not be in for dinner.

Lorna fidgeted all evening and refused to go to bed until she'd talked to him. Finally, she heard his key in the latch. She was standing inside the front door when he entered.

"Aren't you up rather late, Lorna? It's almost twelve."

"I had something I wanted to tell you."

"All right," he said, still feeling a slight glow from all the drinks he'd had with the two clients from St. Louis. "I'm going to have a nightcap. Would you like one?"

"You're in a pleasant mood."

"I closed a good business deal tonight."

"Obviously not with Lydia Moonsong."

His high spirits dipped. "What is that supposed to mean, Lorna?"

She clasped her hands in front of her, fighting

251

off the temptation to applaud the fact that he hadn't heard. "You had better change your product from Lady Lydia to something more French. Perhaps *Duchesse Lydia* or *Madame Lydia*. Yes, I think *Madame* suits her more."

He splashed some cognac into a glass. "All right, what is it you want to tell me," he said with annoyance.

"Haven't you heard? I thought everyone of any importance in the business world of San Francisco had been told."

"Lorna," he said threateningly.

She put her palms together and placed them under her chin and gave him the sweetest, most innocent of smiles. "Lydia Moonsong and her daughter's husband," she said. "Oh, I suppose I should say 'her daughter's *ex*-husband.'"

He watched her warily, not wanting to hear what was coming next.

"They're to be married," she announced in a burst of laughter. "Your Lady Lydia is marrying Raymond Andrieux. Isn't that the most amusing news?"

He squeezed the glass so tightly it broke in his hand. "You're mad!" He threw the fragments into the fire and ignored the several cuts on his palm.

Lorna put back her head and laughed hysterically. "Mad with joy," she told him.

"What kind of filth are you spreading around now?"

"Oh, but the announcement didn't come from me, darling. Phoebe Hearst had tea with Lydia and some friends yesterday afternoon. Of course, Phoebe said her heart went out to the poor woman when she explained that it was a marriage

252

of necessity . . . for business purposes only. Naturally," Lorna continued with a ugly twist of her mouth, "Phoebe would commiserate with Lydia rather than lose her financial support on all those charities the Moonsong money flows into."

"I don't believe you."

Lorna gave a little toss of her head and ran a fingertip across the top of the lamp table as if inspecting it for dust. "Don't take my word for it, darling. You can read the formal announcement for yourself in this Saturday's *Examiner*."

Peter glared at her, then turned and stared into the dying fire in the grate. It wasn't true. Lorna was just goading him with vicious gossip, he kept telling himself.

Lorna started to speak in a lilting, happy voice that gradually turned nasty. "I really would give serious consideration to changing those Lady Lydia labels, darling, unless you want your products associated with an obvious common whore, available to the highest bidder."

He slapped her so hard her head almost snapped from her shoulders. Lorna put a hand against the sting on her cheek, but when she saw his pain she put back her head again and started to laugh.

Peter clenched his hands as he towered over her. To vent his rage he swept the unlighted oil lamp off the table, sending it smashing against the wall, and he stormed out of the house.

At the top of the stairs Susan stood in her robe and slippers. She called after her father but he didn't hear her. The door slammed shut and Peter rushed blindly out into the night.

There was no one but the night porter at the

club. Peter told him he only wanted to make a telephone call.

Max Zentner, the night editor at the *Examiner*, confirmed what Peter didn't want to hear. "Ain't it somethin', Pete? Lydia Moonsong sure is some woman. Imagine marrying her own son-in-law. You'd think she'd be tired of seeing her name in the gossip columns. But you have to hand it to her, she's the best businesswoman in the country and one of the richest so I guess gossip don't make dents in her armor."

"It's good for business," Peter snarled and hung the receiver on the hook. He went out again to find someplace where he could get good and drunk.

By Saturday evening Susan decided she had to do something about her father's disappearance. It was three days now since anyone had seen him. Her mother had been no help.

"Drunk and feeling sorry for himself," she'd said when Susan mentioned her concern. "He'll sober up and come home when he's ready."

Susan didn't believe that. Too many things could have happened to him. Every day men were being shanghaied and were never heard from again.

Efrem was less help than their mother. All he did of late was sit in his room and mope about like some sick cat. She'd tried to get him to tell her what was bothering him, but that only seemed to frighten him farther into his hole. He never left his room; he never went out; he never saw anyone.

Thinking back, Susan remembered that Efrem had been acting very strange ever since she'd found him out with the Stanton girls and Leon Moonsong. He'd come home near dawn then and when she'd made some casual remark about it he'd snapped at her so she never broached the subject again. Except she did assure him that his secret friendship with Leon Moonsong was safe with her—that she herself rather liked Leon.

"Moonsong," Susan said to her reflection over the dressing table. She knit her brows together, bit down on her lip, and made her decision. She'd heard her mother gloating about Lydia's engagement and that was obviously why her father had stormed out.

"Well," Susan said to her mirror, "if my family won't help, perhaps Mrs. Moonsong might have a clue as to where to find Father."

Leon was so surprised when Nellie ushered Susan into the sitting room that it took a few seconds before he stopped staring at her and reached for the hand she held out

"I know, Leon. I'm the last person you expected to be calling here. I'm as surprised as you."

He saw the creases on her broad, lovely brow. "Something is wrong."

"Yes."

"Here. Please, sit down, Susan."

He waited for her to settle and gave her a few moments to collect herself.

"It's Father," she said finally.

"What about him?"

She gave a quick, nervous glance around the room. "Mother would disown me if she knew I'd come here."

"Never mind that, tell me, what's wrong?"

Susan gathered up her courage. "Father has dis-

255

appeared. He and Mother had a row about your mother's engagement to Monsieur Andrieux," she said in a rush.

"Mother and I had a tiff about that ourselves when she told me, but she insists it is what she wants and I am not to interfere." He looked up. "I don't understand the connection between your father's disappearance and my mother's engagement."

Susan gazed at him in astonishment. "Surely you know Father and your mother were . . ." She felt her cheeks burn.

"I don't listen to gossip."

"Father wanted to marry your mother. He told Mother that months ago but she swore she'd never allow it. I heard them with my own ears." Without realizing it she put her hand over his. "Leon, you've got to help me find him. I thought your mother might have a clue as to where he might be."

"She's upstairs in the nursery. I'll fetch her."

Susan had seen Lydia often enough, but always from a distance. Close up it was easy to see why men were so attracted to her. Despite the fact that she had a grown son and daughter, she looked no more than a young lady herself. The signs of age were there, of course, but on Lydia they only made her more beautiful. Her red, gold hair fell in a luxuriant cascade about her face and shoulders; her dark green eyes were a perfect compliment to the jade pendant that hung from a gold chain about her neck.

"Miss MacNair," Lydia said with a bright, happy smile. "Welcome at last to our home." She looked down at herself. "Forgive my slightly rumpled look; the children and I were playing cowboys and Indians." Her smile faded. "Leon tells me you're concerned about your father. How may I help?"

Susan retold of her overhearing her parents' heated argument. "He slapped her, it sounded like," Susan said. "Then there was the breaking of glass and he stormed out. No one has seen nor heard from him since. He hasn't been to his office, his club . . ." The tears bubbled over the rims of her eyes and ran down her cheeks.

Hurriedly, Leon handed her the handkerchief from his breast pocket.

"I'm so worried," Susan sobbed. "Something dreadful has happened to him; I know it has."

Lydia patted her hand. "I've known your father since I was a girl of sixteen when we met in China. If any man is capable of taking care of himself it is he." She studied Susan. How like Peter she was—the same color hair, the same deep, limpid eyes. Lydia squeezed Susan's hand. "What does your mother say?"

"Oh, she doesn't care. She said he's on a binge . . . I mean that he's staying drunk somewhere, that he'll be home when he stops feeling sorry for himself and sobers up."

"I hate to disappoint you, Susan, but I think your mother knows what she is talking about." She looked at Leon. "You know the city very well, Leon. Where could a man stay drunk for days on end and not be disturbed?"

Leon looked down, pretending to see the pattern in the rug for the first time.

"Leon, stop being coy. You are not a saint by any stretch of anyone's imagination. You spend too many nights out Lord only knows where, usually creeping up the stairs in your stockings at the first light of dawn."

Susan found herself frowning at him, seeing Efrem in her mind's eye.

"Where would Peter . . . Mr. MacNair be likely to hole up?" Lydia insisted.

"There're a few places I've heard about."

Lydia huffed. "Heard about, indeed. I'm sure your face will be very familiar to them when we show up."

"We?" Leon said, startled.

"Of course. If we are going to find Susan's father, we are going to have to do it together. If one of us can't convince him to act sensibly, perhaps another of us can." She started from the room. "I'll only be a moment. Have the carriage brought 'round."

It was in the third place they stopped at that Leon came back to Lydia and Susan in the carriage and said, "I think he's upstairs. At least the proprietress described a man fitting his description. He's been causing a bit of trouble. She said she hopes he's who we're looking for because she'd be only too happy to be rid of him. I'm going up and have a look."

"You may need my help," Lydia said as she started to get out of the carriage. "You wait here, Susan."

Leon stared at his mother. "You can't go in there. It's . . ."

"I know perfectly well what it is. Believe me, Leon dear, your mother has had to enter worse places," she said, remembering the opium den in Peking.

The only thing she could find agreeable about the horrid place was that the man lying on the dirty mattress amid a litter of liquor bottles was Peter. Lydia knelt beside the bed and brushed back the straggling hair that felt so familiar, so exciting to her touch.

"Peter," she said softly. She saw his eyelids flutter and her courage failed her. She turned and looked up at Leon. "You'd better try to raise him up," she said as she moved away.

Leon shook Peter's shoulder. "Mr. MacNair!" he said sharply.

Peter grunted and rolled over on his side, curling himself into a ball.

"Mr. MacNair!"

"Leave me alone," he growled.

"Peter," Lydia said.

She watched his whole body stiffen as if a sudden frost had deadened it. Gradually Peter uncurled and rolled onto his back. His head slowly raised from the grimy pillow and he strained to peer through his heavy, swollen eyelids.

"Lydia." He spoke her name as in a dream.

She couldn't trust herself to answer. "Leon," she said almost in a whisper. "Help him up. We must get him out of here."

Leon slipped his arm under Peter's shoulders and gently eased him up into a sitting position. He lowered his legs over the side of the bed, supporting Peter so that he wouldn't fall backwards.

Peter sat numbly, his head hanging down, his chin on his chest. Slowly Peter's head raised and his eyes tried to focus. "Lydia?" he asked. It was no more than an ardent prayer.

"Yes."

He turned toward the sound of her voice and as his eyes met hers he said her name again, this time with such anguish Lydia had to turn away.

"Please, Leon," she said, gripping tightly to the bedstead to keep from throwing herself at his feet. "Get him up."

Leon tried to lift him, but Peter pushed himself free.

"Come on, Mr. MacNair. We're going to take you home."

"Who in hell are you?" Peter mumbled.

"It's all right, Peter," Lydia managed. "We'll take you home."

"Home?" It sounded like he'd never heard the word. Then, when he recognized it and remembered, he shoved Leon away so forcefully he almost fell backward to the floor.

Leon began to lose patience, but tried to hide it from his mother. "Come on, sir," he said, as again he lifted Peter and managed to get him to his feet.

"Here, let me help," Lydia said as she came toward them, intending to support some of the dead weight of Peter's body.

Peter's eyes focused on Leon, unaware that Lydia was beside him. "Get the hell away from me," Peter yelled as he swung at Leon with his fist.

Leon dodged. Peter's fist glanced against Lydia's chin, sending her sprawling to the dirty floor.

Leon grabbed Peter and threw him back across the bed. "Mother!" he cried as he knelt beside her.

"It's all right, Leon. It was only a glancing blow. He didn't mean it."

As Leon began to help her up, Lydia glanced at

Peter, who was propped up on his elbows staring in horror at what he'd done.

"Dear God," Peter groaned when she got to her feet and looked down at him. "Oh God," he cried again.

He sat forward and buried his shame in his hands.

Chapter 14

Peter offered no resistance when Leon helped him into the carriage, except that when Susan tried to take him in her arms he rudely shoved her away. All the way back from the brothel on Powell Street he kept as far away from Lydia as the inside of the carriage permitted. Susan's pity sickened him; her look of understanding nauseated him more. He ignored Lydia completely, as she ignored him.

It was odd, but the only face Peter found himself staring at was Leon's. There was something strange in the way it brought him back to his youth, those exotic and undisciplined days in China, the only time in his life he'd ever felt free. It was where he'd been happy, living the crude, brutal life he'd lived amidst those violent, half-civilized people.

He leaned back and shut his eyes, trying not to feel the pounding inside his head and heart. Perhaps that was where he belonged, in that savage, ruthless country that was so much like himself.

The coachman steered the horse up the steep slope of Clay Street. Peter opened his eyes. He was suddenly sober and angry with where he was and what he was. He looked out the window and saw his house up ahead.

"Don't drive me home," he snapped and rapped on the trap door. "Stop here."

Lydia recognized the look on his face and knew better than to argue. When Susan started to object Lydia stopped her with a quick shake of her head.

Peter said, "Your mother may be up, Susan. It would only make things worse if I came home in Lydia's carriage."

He got out. For a moment he stood steady on the cobblestones, his hand on the open door, his eyes on Lydia. There was nothing to say, he found. He shut the door hard and started on up the hill.

"I should go with him," Susan said.

Lydia held her back. "Leave him alone, Susan. I think that's what he wants. We took a lot of his pride away from him tonight. It would be better if this incident were completely forgotten," she said looking at Leon.

He nodded.

Lydia touched Susan's hand. "Come home with us for a while, Susan. We'll have some tea—a drink if you'd prefer."

In spite of herself and what they'd been through, Susan found herself smiling. "How positively racy, Mrs. Moonsong."

"Lydia," she corrected.

"Mother would faint dead away at such an invitation."

Lydia laughed. "Then you'll accept, of course."

Susan found Lydia delightful, a woman much like herself, free and determined and motivated to be something other than a docile, weak female with no other purpose in life but to be what a man wanted her to be.

Leon excused himself and left the two women alone in the comfortable downstairs sitting room. "I think I'll walk for a while," he said. "I feel all tight inside."

"It's late," Lydia reminded him.

"I'll be all right."

"Very well, dear. And thank you for everything, Leon."

"Yes," Susan said, putting out her hand. She found herself reluctant to see him leave. "Thank you, Leon." When he took her hand and said good night she felt herself grow warm inside as if the air in the room had suddenly gotten thick.

"I hope," Leon said, "that your next visit will be under more pleasant circumstances."

"I promise it will."

When alone, Lydia asked Susan to tell her all about herself and Susan found herself talking more openly than she'd ever done with anyone else. With Lydia it was like speaking to her own inner self.

"I think," Lydia said, "women will always be treated as chattels, and I can assure you, Susan, that independent females such as we will never be accepted. I know from experience what I had to lose in order to gain what I did. No matter how noble your purpose, conventions are required to be met and abided by or else you are an outcast of society."

"I wouldn't exactly call you a social outcast, Mrs. . . . Lydia."

"Ask your mother and see what she has to say about that."

"But you're accepted in every salon in San Francisco."

"My money is accepted, not me."

Susan sipped her wine as an idea struck her. "I wonder, Lydia, if it would be possible for you to find work for me with your company. I want so to learn the cosmetic business. I asked Father, but he was outraged that I'd ever consider taking a position."

"Oh, my dear, Susan," Lydia said, feeling very frustrated. "I'd like nothing better, but it isn't possible. What would your family say? Your mother in particular?"

"I don't care. I'm of age to live apart from my parents. If I were employed I'd manage on my own."

"I wish I could say yes, Susan, but I can't. There is so much bad blood between your mother and me, I could never bring myself to hurt her by being responsible for taking you away. I have a daughter of my own," she said wistfully. "I know how much it hurts to have lost her."

She saw Susan's frown, but did not pursue the subject further. Lydia artfully changed the subject and later, after Susan had gone, Lydia lay in bed admitting her reason for not hiring Susan. It hadn't been Lorna she'd been thinking of when she refused the girl. Liberated woman or no, Lydia could never have brought herself to go against Peter's wishes. It was only for Peter that she'd refused Susan. In her mind, it made up in a way for some of the pride she'd stolen from him tonight.

* * *

265

Leon strolled on down the hill, wanting to forget the horror of having seen Peter MacNair knock his mother to the floor. Of course it had been accidental, but the entire episode had been so sordid, so squalid. It reminded him only too vividly of another brothel, an earlier night, another MacNair.

He hadn't seen Efrem since his birthday and knew he was being a coward for not facing his friend and setting the account straight. What he'd permitted had been a terrible mistake and it left Leon feeling unclean and totally responsible for corrupting Efrem.

Leon stopped midway down hill. He WAS being a coward, he told himself. He turned around and started back toward the MacNair mansion. It wasn't fair to either himself or to Efrem to treat the matter as if it hadn't happened.

As Leon passed his own house he saw Susan and Lydia still chatting. Quickly he rounded the corner and took the short cut across the side lawn to the next street and to the back of the MacNair mansion. He knew which room was Efrem's and noticed that a lamp was burning on the other side of the closed curtains. Leon took up a handful of pebbles and tossed them up against the pane. A moment later Efrem's anxious face appeared. Leon saw him light up as brightly as the lamp he held and motion to him

Seconds later Efrem came out through the servants' entrance and ran toward Leon.

"Come on," Leon said, glancing at the lighted windows on the main floor. The two of them started off on a run across the lawn and down the

266

street. When they reached a safer distance they stopped.

"I thought you didn't want to see me again," Efrem panted.

"I didn't, Ef. But we have to talk."

He tried to ignore the injured look on Efrem's face.

They walked along in silence for a block or two, not headed anywhere in particular. A trolley clanged by and instinctively Leon ran for it and hopped on, pulling Efrem up behind him The trolley wasn't crowded and neither seemed to care where it was going. They settled themselves in a far, empty corner and sat listening to the clamor of the wheels, letting themselves move with the sway of the car.

"It wasn't right, Efrem. I'm sorry."

Efrem said nothing. He sat staring at the boards on the floor, his heart pounding.

"I should never have permitted it to happen."

"It wasn't your fault, Leon," Efrem said finding his voice. "I've never done that to anyone before in my whole life." He fought back the tears.

"I'm sorry," Leon said softly.

Efrem couldn't look at him. "It's all right, Leon. It was all my doing. It's just that . . ." He choked on a sob.

The car rattled on down Mason Street and Leon could smell the salt air as they neared the wharf, the end of the line.

They walked for a long time and stood looking out at the water, neither of them speaking.

"We'd better head back," Leon said finally. "The last cable car should be leaving for the Hill soon."

267

Efrem merely followed doggedly along behind. Halfway between their houses Efrem stopped. He glanced up the street toward his home and saw the lights still on, his parents still arguing. He wished with all his heart Leon would reach out, take his hand, and take him home to his house.

"We're still friends?" Efrem chanced.

"Yes, sure, Ef. We'll always be friends." Leon hesitated, then put his hand on Efrem's shoulder. "We mustn't let that happen again, though."

Efrem dropped his chin. "I know."

Leon tilted his face up to his own. "I'm not angry with you, Efrem, or disgusted by what happened. We were just doing kids' stuff. We're too old for that."

"I know," he said again.

Leon gave him a gentle shake. "Go get some sleep. We'll go out someplace tomorrow night if you like."

Efrem beamed. "You mean it?"

"Sure I mean it." He put out his hand. "Friends?"

Efrem clasped Leon's hand tightly. "Friends," he repeated. Unable to control himself, he threw himself against Leon, kissed him quickly on the mouth, and raced on down the street.

Leon touched his fingers to his lips, feeling the moistness of Efrem's kiss. He knew he should be angry, repulsed.

He wasn't.

Efrem hummed as he finished putting the last of the vouchers in the wire basket and carried it into the bookkeeper's office.

"Your father wants to see you before you leave," Mr. Carson, the head accountant, told him.

At first Efrem had hated being called into his father's office. It always meant a dressing down about something. However, as the weeks passed he found the dressing-downs fewer and fewer. Of late, Efrem found he was actually enjoying his work.

He hesitated when Miss Adams pointed to her boss's private office and told Efrem his father was waiting for him.

"What did I do this time?" Efrem asked her with a tight smile.

"The only one who can tell you that is your father."

Efrem was glad to find his father looking pleasant.

"Sit down, Efrem. To put your mind at rest, I did not call you in here to complain, so relax. On the contrary, I am not displeased. You are doing extremely well, though Carson admits you don't have much of a head for figures." Peter didn't look concerned; in fact, he smiled. "I never did either, but in time I learned. As for keeping books, you can always hire professionals for that; all you need to know is how to read the books so you know you aren't being cheated. All that will come in time, Efrem. At present, I'd like you to change jobs. I want you to get to know more about the production end of the business. Starting tomorrow, report to Jeff Fredericks in Shipping and Receiving. Learn all our suppliers, where and how everything is shipped, get familiar with the faster and least expensive ways of shipping, and at the same time start using that head of yours to try and come up with suggestions as to how things can be improved."

In a week Efrem considered himself one of the happiest men in the world. The work was sometimes backbreaking, but he was beginning to gain muscle and put on some needed weight. He noticed he was losing the "little boy" look, which his mother complained to Peter about.

"You're working him like a field hand," she whined.

Leon thought he never looked better and they seemed to be closer than ever. The night in the brothel was never mentioned, though every once in a while when they'd both had a little too much to drink they'd hug and peck each other on the mouth when they said goodnight.

Leon kept telling himself they were harmless gestures of friendship, but when he saw the way Efrem looked at him, the dangerous depths of Efrem's feelings were all too obvious.

He'd have to put a stop to their friendship, Leon kept telling himself. But the thought of never seeing Efrem again meant automatically that he'd never see Susan again. It was the latter that Leon found he couldn't live without, even though he was certain Susan didn't know he was alive.

Friday was payday, and Efrem and Leon were taking the Stanton girls to the new minstrel show at the California Theatre. Efrem was whistling happily to himself and didn't pay any attention to the stocky man in the dark suit standing on the corner of the loading dock, chomping on the butt of a cigar.

"Master MacNair," the man said as he stepped in front of Efrem.

Efrem frowned. "Do I know you?"

"The name's Ramsey. I thought after so long a time you and I should have a little chat." He nodded toward a waiting hansom cab.

"Sorry," Efrem said, growing wary and not liking anything about the man, especially the shiftiness of the beady eyes. "I'm in a hurry."

"Then permit me to drive you."

"That isn't necessary." He tried to step around the man.

Ramsey blocked his way. "I thought we might talk about Leon Moonsong. I've been following your—friendship for several weeks now, ever since that night you spent together in the same room at Madam Foo's."

Efrem went cold all over. His face turned bone white.

Ramsey smiled and nodded toward the hansom. "Oh, have no fears, my boy, I'm not interested particularly in your somewhat bizarre relationship. My lips are sealed in that regard. I only wanted to have a talk with you about your present position with MacNair Products. The Shipping and Receiving Departments, isn't that where you're working? I'd be most interested in hearing about that. You see, I have a proposition to offer to you."

"What kind of proposition," Efrem asked, trying to stop himself from trembling.

"Let's just say we discuss trading one favor for another." He motioned to the hansom again. "May I drive you somewhere?" When Efrem resisted Ramsey forcibly took the lad's arm. "I would sug-

271

gest, for your sake as well as for Leon Moonsong's, you listen to what I have to say."

Efrem pulled himself free. "Leave me alone."

Ramsey again grabbed his arm and put his lips close to Efrem's ear. "Acts of perversion, especially with a Chink, can put you in prison for life," he hissed.

Wild-eyed, Efrem stared at him as Ramsey relaxed his grip. "Now, shall we have our little talk, my boy," he said sweetly.

Numb with fear, Efrem let himself be led toward the waiting carriage.

Part Three

Chapter 1

None of the Hawaiian Islands were to Prince Ke Loo's liking, and their government and politics he liked less. Chinese were looked upon as no better than slaves and even the extremely rich and royal Chinese like himself were disliked by the American sugar planters and distrusted by the native Hawaiians. The only ones treated worse were the Japanese, who were hated and abused by everyone.

Ke Loo kept reminding himself that this was only a stop gap, a way-station where he and Sun Yat-sen would begin rallying their forces before returning to China, where Prince Ke Loo would sit on the throne.

Honolulu was too rife with internal problems to settle in. The American sugar millionaires had recently succeeded in usurping Queen Liliuokalani's throne. Some Hawaiians wanted British rule; the United States refused to annex the Islands and wanted Queen Liliuokalani restored to power. The biggest problem was the exporting of Hawaiian sugar to America, which the sugar growing states in America disliked.

Ke Loo wanted no part of the Islands' troubles and so established himself on the less inhabited island of Maui, where the Chinese population was more pronounced and the natives more conscious of their ancient ties to the Orient through their Polynesian forebears.

Money was Ke Loo's first concern, particularly in view of the fact that the Dowager Empress had seized all his lands and properties, and he'd been forced to flee in the disguise of a peasant when her armies overpowered his forces. He was not disheartened; he'd left behind too many of his followers who'd vowed to continue their strife against the Empress. It was only a matter of time before the Boxers would regroup and succeed in ridding China of the female tyrant.

Meanwhile, the Boxers had to be financed lest they lose interest in their cause, and Ke Loo was quick to set in motion his trafficking in the opium trade. The island of Maui was a distance removed from the seat of the Hawaiian government in Honolulu and was more or less outside police jurisdiction, which made his smuggling operation less conspicuous and also less complicated.

"It is so hot," Mei Fei complained as she came into the large house of straw and thatch. "Does it never grow cold?"

"No," her father said, disgruntled. "From all I've learned of these accursed islands it is always warm. A sea breeze will soon come and refresh you." As he motioned for a servant to come and refill his wine cup he said, "It would be far hotter for you in China, Mei Fei, if you had not secretly escaped the Empress and come to me in Kalgan.

Not only your hand would be missing if you'd been caught."

Mei Fei looked down at the beautifully carved hand of exquisite ivory. Ke Loo's artisans had not failed in their difficult task. At first glance the ivory hand was hardly distinguishable from her real one, the one the Empress had so cruelly cut off without ever explaining why.

When the initial shock and pain had worn off, Mei Fei found her earlier devotion to the Empress replaced with loathing and the bitter taste for vengeance. She had gladly joined her father in his plot to assassinate the old woman and yearned as ardently as he for that day to come.

Despite all of Ke Loo's complaints about the balmy, brightly colored islands, Mei Fei was amused to see he was quick to take a new wife for himself within the first weeks of their arrival. Her name was Malama, a lovely Hawaiian girl of fifteen with long, black hair, perfect skin, and a figure so provocative Ke Loo found it impossible to keep from caressing her.

Sun Yat-sen had objected indignantly to the girl, but Ke Loo was quick to remind him of his being from peasant stock. "Besides," Ke Loo had told him, "my union with a native girl will only fortify our cause. Her people will be more prone to assist us."

Sun Yat-sen nodded and forced himself to bow low before his prince, silently swearing that one day he would be rid of this Manchu fool forever. For the time being he cautioned himself to be content. Ke Loo's connections with the opium traders were indispensable at present. And he would not be staying long in Prince Ke Loo's company, Sun Yat-sen told himself. He would begin his tour, his campaign to rally the world against the cruel Manchu dynasty and toward his own cause to make China a republic.

"Hong Kong," Ke Loo said. "The opium is best smuggled from China through that busy harbor where the British are kept too busy to watch every ship's movement. Our shipments will come directly here. I have already been told of a cove deep enough to set anchor and unload the bales by long boats. Here we will store the opium in a warehouse until the buyers are contacted and we are instructed on their arrangements for shipment. A market has already been established in Mexico, another in Canada. I have made contact with a source in San Francisco, an organization that proposes a safe channel across the continent of America. My agents in Hong Kong will handle the traffic into the Middle East and Europe. So you see, Sun Yat-sen, I have not been idle. You are free to continue now on your respectable geste. I will take over command of things here."

The following day Sun Yat-sen set out for Honolulu. Two days later he was aboard a ship bound for San Francisco.

"I don't trust him, Father," Mei Fei said when Sun Yat-sen was gone.

"Do you think for a moment that I do?" Ke Loo's eyes grew dark. "No, there is not a man on the earth whom I trust—nor a woman." He fondled Malama's lovely young breasts. "I don't trust even myself at times." He felt the age-old weakness for the child's body and his loins stirred with desire. Blatantly he lifted the girl's flowered skirt and began fingering her until he had her giggling and moaning, seeping under his manipulations.

Mei Fei was forgotten for the moment. She liked Malama as she liked most everyone, and was glad her father had taken her for his wife. Too often during the first weeks after she arrived safely in Kalgan, she began to grow uneasy at the way Ke Loo kept watching her. His eyes told her what he wanted. Luckily, circumstances had kept him away from her bed chamber and now that Malama shared his bed Mei Fei relaxed.

Though she disliked the monotonous climate and greatly missed her homeland, there were too many things in China she was glad to be rid of. First, the Empress; close behind her was Wu Lien, who had become the Empress's closest confidante.

Mei Fei hurried out of the house, crossed the wide veranda, and ran off through the grove of mango trees. Behind her she heared Malama squeal and Ke Loo roar with laughter. Malama's lovemaking was always so boisterous and completely uninhibited, which Mei Fei found so unlike the ways of Chinese women. Malama was shy about nothing and was proud when others watched the way she aroused her husband.

The native men, Mei Fei found, had the same lack of shyness. Usually they wore nothing but a skirt of colored cloth from waist to ankles which they called a "lavalava." Often when at the shore with their fishing nets or unloading the long boats they wore nothing but a loincloth. Mei Fei had even seen some of them completely naked.

They were a happy, carefree race of people, she thought, always laughing and dancing and as gay as the flowers and birds that teemed throughout the chain of islands. As she walked along the sand, letting the surf lap at her bare feet, she began wondering of her own destiny. She would go where her father commanded, but being here among these carefree people gave her the unfamiliar desire to be free, to go and live as she wanted.

She stopped short when she rounded a curve of the beach and came upon a trio of naked Hawaiian youths splashing and swimming about in the water. When they saw her one of the young men beckoned for her to join them. When she hesitated and started to back away he ran toward her, making no effort to cover his nudity. He took her hand and instantly held it up, inspecting it closely. He said something Mei Fei didn't understand, but he made it clear he was in awe of the ivory hand. He bowed over it and pressed it to his lips, as though it were something sacred.

The young man spoke softly, encouragingly, all the while pointing to his other two friends. At first Mei Fei didn't understand but when she came nearer she saw that one of the other two was a girl almost her own age. Now she knew what the youth was saying; he was trying to make it clear that she had nothing to fear and that they only wanted her to join them in their game.

He urged her toward the water, but Mei Fei hung back. The others, laughing, ran toward her. The first youth showed them her beautiful ivory hand. They, too, bowed over it and touched their lips to its cold, smooth beauty.

Then, of a sudden, the two young men lifted her and before she knew what was happening they laughingly carried her into the water and dumped her into the surf. Mei Fei came up sputtering and coughing and when she heard their laughter she found herself joining in. The boy said something in his own language to the others. From the way they kept looking at her hand she knew what they were talking about.

Her clothes were soaked, but although they coaxed her to remove them, she would not. She did, however, join their games. She'd always loved swimming in the large emerald lake at the summer palace.

She was too busy enjoying herself to notice that she and the handsome Hawaiian who'd taken her hand were suddenly alone.

"Where did the others go?"

He didn't understand, but when he saw her looking about he pointed to a grove of palms and ferns. Thinking it just part of the game, Mei Fei ran toward the grove and stopped dead when she stumbled across the young pair copulating on a bed of fronds.

She turned abruptly and bumped into the young man who'd come up behind her. He smiled a gentle, encouraging smile and reached out to her. It was the way he was looking at her that told Mei Fei not to fear him.

She heard the two young people writhing and moaning in sexual pleasure and felt the burning desire for this handsome youth standing before her.

When he touched the wetness of her hair and let his hands fall on her shoulders, she stood trembling with the need to feel his naked body against her own. Taking her hand in his, he led her a short distance away and laid himself on a mound of blue-green grass. He reached up to her. Mei Fei knelt beside him and put her hand on his bare chest. A moment later they were locked in a passionate embrace.

His name was Tehani and after learning some of his language she found that his friends were convinced that she was a goddess. Tehani never stopped admiring the lovely ivory hand, kissing it whenever they met, as one would kiss some divine relic.

For the first time Mei Fei was happy. Her father, unfortunately, resented the new ways she was adopting and, in his mind, the lack of respect she showed him.

"You are forgetting," he told her one evening, "that you are from a royal house. You mix too freely with these native people."

Mei Fei looked at Malama, but said nothing when she saw the extent of her father's displeasure.

"It is time for you to leave here," Ke Loo announced.

Mei Fei's head snapped up. "Leave here?" She watched his shifty look. "I thought it was not time yet for us to leave."

"I did not say 'us,' I said 'you.' "

"But where am I to go?"

"America."

"Alone?"

"Why not? You traveled from Peking to Kalgan alone."

"But I was in my own country. I speak English only falteringly. I only remember a little of what April taught me."

"You will manage."

She didn't want to leave. Not now. Tehani had

suddenly become her life, her love. She could never leave him. "What am I to do in America?" she asked, her voice frantic.

"There is business there you must do for me. You will be my emissary."

"Emissary?"

"You will find my son, your brother, Li Ahn. You will bring him here to me. Li Ahn must join me here and help with our revolution. It is his place, his duty as my only male heir." He paused and glowered at his daughter. "Never again will a woman sit on the throne of China." He made an impatient gesture. "Prepare yourself. You will leave as soon as it can be arranged."

"But . . ." All she could think about was Tehani.

"There will be no arguments."

"I should have an escort. Tehani?"

"No!" Ke Loo stormed. "Tehani will help me here. You go alone."

Mei Fei wracked her brain to think of some reason to stay with Tehani. She suddenly pounced upon what she thought to be a way out. "I am Chinese. The Americans are excluding us."

Ke Loo frowned and bit down on his lip. "No matter. I will arrange something. Papers can be falsified. I am not a man without influence here. The details I will attend to. Be ready to leave by the end of the month."

Chapter 2

Lydia's and Raymond's wedding was held in the garden of the Moonsong mansion. The setting was copied from a garden Raymond had seen on Capri. The back of the house was completely covered by thick blooming wisteria, with ornate iron balustrades and a lovely gazebo of delicate lattice where a small orchestra played. Huge tubs containing dwarf lemon and lime trees were scattered everywhere and lanterns glowed softly from the branches of all the trees.

Lydia wore pale yellow and carried a little bouquet of yellow roses. Raymond kissed her tenderly under the heart-shaped bower of bougainvillaea.

"I hope you'll be happy, Mother," Leon said as he kissed her cheek.

Lydia smiled and looked at the girl beside him. She was one of the Stantons, but she never could remember her first name. Later, when she found Leon alone she asked, "Where's Susan? I thought you told me you were bringing her. She'd accepted the invitation. She sent me a note."

He shrugged. "Her mother went into one of her rages this morning. To keep peace in the family,

Susan decided it would be best if she did not provoke her."

"What a shame. I so like the girl. I was rather hoping that you liked her as well."

He smiled back. "I do."

Of late Leon had been seeing a lot of Susan and, oddly enough, not very much of her brother, he noticed. It was as if Efrem were purposely avoiding him, always with a ready excuse not to be seen together.

"It's my late hours," Efrem had told him. "I'm just too tired to go out by the time I get home from work."

There was something amiss, Leon thought. Efrem never looked at him whenever they did happen to see one another. He would drop his eyes and hurry past with only a muttered "Hello."

Lydia linked her arm in Leon's and strolled among the guests, nodding and thanking them for their well-wishes. Raymond was holding court near the bar that had been set up along the hedge.

"I know you don't approve of my marrying Raymond," she told Leon. "Please try to like him a little, for my sake. April is being particularly unpleasant; don't make yourself difficult as well."

"I promise," he said. "I know why you married him, Mother. If that is what you want, then you have my blessings. As for April, she doesn't seem to mind at all. She may be short with you, but then she always has been. Actually she seems pleased that you're married. She said as much just last evening."

"Oh?"

"Better Raymond than Peter MacNair. They were her exact words."

Lydia's heart gave a little tug.

On the other side of the garden April watched her mother and brother and nodded pleasantly when Raymond caught her eye. It was all working out splendidly. Her mother was caged in with Raymond and April found herself free to move ahead with her plans for revenge. She would simply seduce Peter MacNair. He was vulnerable now. And when her mother discovered the affair—and April would be certain she discovered it—she would be heartbroken at the thought that she'd lost the only man she'd ever loved to her own daughter.

And Adam would be April's revenge on Peter. Somehow she had to think of a way to get Leon away from their mother. She'd think of something to accomplish that, she told herself as her mind clicked along. After seducing Peter MacNair, April would then lure Raymond back. That would be the easy part because regardless of how much he claimed to be glad to be rid of her, his eyes told her otherwise.

Then she'd take Caroline and Marcus eventually, and Lydia would be alone, Peter MacNair would be more miserable than he was now, and David could rest peacefully in his coffin.

In April's mind it was all crystal clear. Through her seduction of Peter she would destroy them both.

The wedding reception dragged on for another hour or more. April was completely bored. When Lydia mounted the terrace steps and threw her wedding bouquet in April's direction, she ignored it and let it fall at her feet.

And then they were gone. April moved herself into the mansion to look after things until they returned from their honeymoon cruise. It had been April's suggestion that she "house sit." In truth, April felt her chances of meeting up with Peter MacNair were more likely if she were in closer proximity to his home.

For several days she noted his daily routine. Saturday afternoons, she decided, were the best time to try and make contact. He went out alone on Saturday afternoon and usually walked rather than take his carriage.

Her timing the following Saturday was perfect. She was walking up Taylor Street just as Peter started down.

"Mr. MacNair," April said brightly. "How long it's been since we've met."

He doffed his hat. "April. How wonderful to see you. I knew, of course, that you'd returned from China. It's unforgivable of me not to have called on you."

She kept her smile fixed solidly on his face. "Under the circumstances, I completely understand. After David's death I grew homesick," she lied. She liked the way he flinched at the casual mention of his son's death.

"You have another son," he ventured. "Congratulations." Remembering Lorna's suspicions he decided this was as good a time as any to dig a little.

She didn't stop smiling. "Yes. Adam. You really must visit me one of these afternoons." Slowly, purposely she let the smile fade. "I think you'll find Adam an adorable little boy. So like his father," she said pointedly.

287

"Oh?"

"Edward Wells. Perhaps you know his father. He's very big in politics."

"The name is familiar."

"So," April said, smiling again. "When will you come to visit?"

Peter found himself without an excuse.

"I won't take *no* for an answer. I know your wife never approved of me, but I was always under the impression that you more or less liked me a little."

"Of course, I've always liked you. I told David how pleased I was that you two married. I . . ."

"Yes, David said you wanted us to return with you to America. It's unfortunate that it didn't work out." She looked hard into his face. "You are so much like David—the same eyes, the same handsome face, the same hair."

Self-consciously Peter ran his fingers through his hair. "Mine is a little grayer, I'm afraid."

"It only adds to your good looks."

She was flirting with him, he realized, and Peter found it not unpleasant, though he knew he should.

"I'm staying at Mother's," April said, nodding toward the mansion on the corner. "Just temporarily, of course, until she comes back from her honeymoon." She saw his hurt and pressed on. "You didn't come to the wedding. How unfortunate. It was a lovely affair."

"Yes, I read about it in the newspaper." He shifted awkwardly. "My wife, as you know, is not exactly a fan of your mother's."

"I do hope that won't interfere with our being friends." She fished in her bag and drew out her card. "I have a flat overlooking Portsmouth Square. I'll be back in residence next Thursday. Do try and find time to drop in. I serve tea precisely at four o'clock and I would so like for you to meet my son, Adam." She extended her hand. "Of course, you are perfectly welcome to call on me here," she said, again nodding toward the Moonsong mansion. "But if your wife happened to notice she might not approve."

He took her hand and her card. "I'll try to make a point of dropping by. I look forward to it, April."

It was a week after Lydia and Raymond returned before Peter called at April's flat. She'd never doubted for a moment that he would accept her invitation. He was dying to get a look at Adam, she knew.

"Mr. MacNair," she said sweetly when she opened the door and found him looking rather forlorn.

He grinned sheepishly and took out his watch. "It's five minutes before four. You did say tea at four o'clock."

"Come in, come in," she urged. "Adam is having his nap but the tea is just being set out." She took his hat and stick and ushered him into the tasteful living room. "I only keep a nurse for the baby, but she's also an excellent cook. I let the housekeeper go. Help is such a problem these days. Tea?" she asked, nodding to the tray. "Or perhaps you'd prefer a drink. I know David used to despise tea."

"Whatever," Peter said.

"You are an easy man to please, Mr. MacNair. I'd been told to the contrary." She smiled up at him. "Would I be too forward if I called you *Peter*? You're far too young to be addressed as *Mister*."

"Please. I'd like that."

She was lovely, he noticed as he settled himself across from her and watched as she went through the ritual of pouring the tea. Before handing him his cup she went to the sideboard, brought back a whiskey decanter, and poured several jiggers into the tea. "It's the only way David could tolerate tea."

"That was a terribly unfortunate thing," Peter said, his eyes sad.

"I will not permit you to even think about that, Peter. What is past is past. Everything must stay where it belongs. Our lives go on in spite of everything."

"Still, I can't help feeling responsible in more ways than one. I . . ."

"Please," she said softly, reaching out and laying her hand on his knee. "You mustn't blame yourself, Peter."

As she continued to speak, Peter was conscious of nothing but the pressure of her hand on his knee. She let it rest there for several minutes before withdrawing it. When she did remove it he looked at the spot where it had lain, expecting to see a burn mark on his trouser leg.

They talked pleasantly for half an hour and then April excused herself and went to fetch Adam.

She returned without him. "The nurse had him in the park later than usual. She says I must not wake him." She showed a charming smile. "But that only gives you another excuse to call again.

Perhaps this Saturday afternoon. I entertain hardly ever and get restless on Saturdays for some peculiar reason. It's my least favorite day of the week. Make it pleasant for me by promising you'll come by."

"I'd be happy to."

She teased him into several visits without his ever seeing Adam. There was always an excuse. "Lydia took him to a puppet show with the other children." Or, "Leon insisted on going to the new aquarium and wouldn't think of Adam staying behind."

But Peter was finding that he wanted to see April and was almost glad they had their tea alone together and that Adam wasn't there. Not seeing Adam always gave him the excuse to come back. After a while it had become his excuse to return, not hers.

When April was absolutely certain she had him more interested in her than in Adam, she finally produced the boy one afternoon when Peter arrived promptly at four o'clock.

Peter stood staring down at the child. It was as if he'd gone back in time and was looking at his own son. Lorna was right. There was no doubt that this was David's child, regardless of what his immigration papers said.

April watched Peter closely. She took added delight in seeing his dilemma. When their eyes met she gave him a challenging look. "A lovely little boy, isn't he, Peter?" she asked, daring him to question the child's parentage.

She could almost see his thoughts. They'd start to investigate, naturally, if they hadn't already. *Let them*, she told herself. *Let them check all they wanted.* In the end it would come down to one thing. If they proved Adam was their grandchild, there was no way they could take that child away from his natural mother. Lorna MacNair would burn in hell before she'd publicly admit to a Chinese daughter-in-law, April figured.

The next time Peter arrived at the flat Adam was not there. "He so enjoys romping around Mother's place with Raymond's children." She emphasized that latter point, making it clear they were no part of her. "I do admit I get very lonesome for Adam when he's away. He's all I have."

"You're a very beautiful woman, April." He'd almost said "beautiful girl," but when he looked at her he realized there was nothing girlish about this tantalizing creature.

April gave him her most seductive look. "I don't suppose you could possibly stay for dinner? I feel so lonely." Peter checked his watch. It was almost five-thirty.

"Stay? I'm afraid I can't." The way she was looking at him made him want to be with her. "If you'll premit me a few hours leave, I think I could manage to return . . . say, eight o'clock."

"Splendid. Eight o'clock."

He was fifteen minutes early and had the smell of liquor on his breath, both of which April took as encouraging signs.

His seduction was easier than she'd thought it would be. All her life she'd looked upon Peter as some kind of hero whom her mother had idolized. He was just a man with better than average endowments—something David had inherited from his father.

Peter MacNair had fantastic technique, something else David had inherited. April kept reminding herself to pretend that this seduction was all part of a plot, just part of her overall design. Still, Peter aroused her more than she cared to admit. She blamed it on not having had sex for so long. Yet there was something in the way he undulated his hips, the way his shaft plowed upward, making it impossible for her not to respond. This was David in her arms, she kept telling herself, and as for Peter, Lydia was in his arms. They both knew the truth in what they fantasized and were content with that.

Over the days that followed, April found herself living for those times Peter would come and take her in his arms. She didn't love him, of course. It was his body, his sex she found impossible to resist.

She could tell that Peter felt guilty about their affair, but he kept coming back and she knew he'd continue to come to her because in his mind she was Lydia. He'd even called her Lydia during those delicious moments of passion.

April never corrected him. All she wanted was the affair. It was her only way to get even with them both.

Chapter 3

Mei Fei arrived in San Francisco one hot afternoon toward the end of August. From the docks she started immediately for the address her father had written on the sealed envelope.

It was a strange city and she found it difficult to understand why so many people wished to live in the tall square buildings built on the steep streets. The noise of the place was so foreign, not like the softer, singsong noises of China or the lilting, muted tones of the Hawaiians. Here everything jarred and clanged and moved at a hurried pace.

As her father had directed, she spoke the faltering English April had taught her and managed to make herself understood by one of the many coachmen lined up waiting for hire.

The address was on Market Street, up one hill, down another, past the strange cars with their harsh bells and grating steel wheels, miraculously moving under their own power.

Whether the driver overcharged her for the fare she had no way of knowing. When the hansom stopped she simply held out her hand with various coins and paper money. He took what he wanted and left her standing with the handle of her reticule draped over the ivory hand and the sealed envelope clutched in the other.

Carefully, she compared the number on the envelope with the number over the arched doorway. When they matched she slowly mounted the short stairs and banged the brass knocker.

Ramsey frowned when he saw the shy Chinese girl standing on the stoop looking so lost.

"I came from Prince Ke Loo," she said.

Taken slightly aback he stared at her, then scanned the street to make certain no one was watching. He'd been told a courier would come; he hadn't expected an Oriental girl in her teens.

"Come in, child," he said, carefully watching the street for signs of a tail.

"You've come from Hawaii or from Hong Kong?"

She extended the sealed envelope. "My father, Prince Ke Loo, is on the island called Maui. He said I should give you this. It will explain."

Ramsey motioned her into a chair as he went to his desk and slit open the thick envelope.

Mei Fei sat as straight and stiff as a rod, her ivory hand resting in her lap, her reticule on the floor beside her.

After carefully reading the several pages, Ramsey eyed her skeptically. "You know what Prince Ke Loo has written?"

"No."

Ramsey turned back to the pages that contained a complete detailed map of the exact longitude and latitude of the cove near Ke Loo's warehouse, also the times of the tides, the depth of the waters lying outside the cove, the directions for anchoring, the days and hours of police patrols, and the quantities on hand, together with prices and the conditions Ramsey's organization must meet if they wanted the opium traffic.

It was all as had been previously arranged. Ramsey smiled pleasantly at Mei Fei, glad that at last the operation could begin. The ships had been chosen, the required palms crossed, and Efrem MacNair was only too anxious to close his eyes to the additional bales, the forged manifests that would mysteriously disappear once the MacNair shipment was cleared by the customs officials.

"Now," Ramsey said as he rubbed his greedy, fat hands together. "Is there anyway I can help you, girl?" She was an extremely lovely little thing, he saw. "Do you return immediately to your father? Have you a place to stay?"

"My father says you are a very important man and know many important people here in San Francisco. I seek my half-brother. He is called Li Ahn."

Ramsey shook his head. "I'll need more than that to go on. He is most likely in Chinatown somewhere. Has he no other name?"

"He has a sister, my half-sister. Here she is called April Moonsong."

His eyes widened at the coincidence. Just this morning he'd had a report from one of his agents in Washington who'd finally tracked down Eddie Wells in connection with the Moonsong lady.

"I know where you can find April Moonsong, girl." He hastily scribbled an address on a piece of paper. "If the Li Ahn you seek is her brother, he lives with his mother when he is not in school. Your half-sister will be able to take you to him."

As he ushered her to the door he said, "I assume your father stressed the importance of forgetting that you came here. You are not to tell anyone of this visit."

"Prince Ke Loo was most explicit about that. As far as anyone is concerned, including myself, I have never seen you."

"Good. Good."

When April opened the door and found Mei Fei smiling at her, she gasped, then gave a hoot and threw her arms about the girl. "Mei Fei, Mei Fei," she said, trying to hold back the happy tears.

She eased the girl away and looked her up and down. "As beautiful as ever," April said, taking both her hands. When she felt the cool, hard ivory fingers she stared as the horror suddenly came back to her. April looked down and studied the perfect piece of sculpture so expertly attached by a large golden band that passed easily as a bracelet. "It's exquisite," April said, unable to believe that it was anything but real. She looked into Mei Fei's sad, smiling face; April's tears came in a rush and she again pulled the girl into her arms. "How terribly cruel. Your beautiful hand."

It was as if Mei Fei's soft warm body suddenly turned hard and cold in her arms. The young girl's mouth was drawn into a thin angry line, her eyes blazed with hatred.

"I will one day repay that evil woman," Mei Fei said. Except for the voice inside her own head, April had never before heard the sound of pure hatred, nor had she ever seen it so fiercely engraved on anyone's face.

"She has done us both a great harm, Mei Fei. She will one day pay for her crimes."

"That is why I have come."

April realized they were still standing outside the doorway. She picked up Mei Fei's bag, led her inside, and settled her on the divan.

"Before we speak, I have something of yours that I want to return," April said.

Mei Fei frowned as April hurried out of the room. Suddenly, she caught a shadow of movement from behind the divan and when she looked down she found Adam gazing up at her.

"Little Adam," Mei Fei cried. "Oh, surely you remember your Aunt Mei Fei and the beautiful palace we once shared in China."

The little boy struggled to understand the Chinese he'd not heard for so long. The amah had recently begun to refresh the little he'd known.

Mei Fei reached out to him and after studying her face he broke into a broad smile as he let her pull him up onto her lap.

She said, "We played so many times in the garden. Don't you remember when you fell from the plum tree and landed in the goldfish pond? I got all wet fishing you out." It all sounded familiar to the little boy, but he'd thought it had happened in one of his dreams.

Mei Fei cradled him to her and caressed his warm bare legs exposed by his short pants. Her eyes caught the Manchu symbol tattooed on his little thigh. She remembered again how that evil woman had taken the child and cruelly branded him even though she disclaimed him as an impure brat of a half-breed girl.

April came in and saw Mei Fei staring at Adam's tattoo. "Another reason that keeps my need for revenge kindled."

"He's grown so, and he's oh-so-very handsome," Mei Fei said as Adam squirmed out of her lap and trotted off onto another of his happy adventures that he was so expert at inventing. "Bang! Bang!" the women heard from the hallway as the child yelled something and raced away to his room full of toys.

April laughed. "Today he is off on a shoot. Tigers, I think he told me." She looked down at the ring in her hand. After a slight hesitation she held it out to Mei Fei. "This is yours. I hope I don't offend you by returning it. I do not do so to invoke painful memories."

Unmoving, Mei Fei stared at the ring. Slowly, questioningly she raised her eyes to April's. "But how?"

"Wu Lien brought it on her orders."

Mei Fei's next question went unasked. The look on April's face told her the answer.

April held out the ring. "Yes," she said simply. She sighed. "It was sent as a reminder that I must remain obedient to my vows."

The ring was as beautiful as Mei Fei remembered, but it held a different meaning now. Once it served as a reminder of her love; now it served as a reminder of her hatred. She fitted the jade and pearl ring to the artificial finger and held it out, admiring it.

"I know a countryman who will affix it permanently, if you like."

Mei Fei continued to stare at the handsome ring. "Yes," she answered, her voice tight with hate. "It will always remind me of what we must do."

April sat down beside her and took her hands. "Now you must tell me how you managed to come to me."

Her story—minus Ramsey—took them into the late afternoon. "So with your help," Mei Fei concluded, "I need to find Li Ahn."

"Leon," April corrected.

"Leon?" Mei Fei repeated, carefully copying the way April had pronounced it. "Prince Ke Loo commands *Leon* to join him in Hawaii and help with the revolution."

"He will not go," April said. "Leon does not share our need for revenge. Besides, he hates his father."

"He must take his rightful place beside Prince Ke Loo. He cannot refuse. Li Ahn is his only heir."

The ringing of the telephone startled Mei Fei. When April went to the wall and spoke into the brown box, Mei Fei kept frowning at her. She had never seen a telephone or even knew what one was until April explained it to her.

"Mother asked me to bring you to dinner this evening. In fact," April said, thinking suddenly of Peter MacNair, "she wanted me to ask if you would like to stay with her and Leon. They have a very large house on top of the hill. As you can see, my quarters are somewhat limited. But, of course, you are welcome here."

"If you think Li . . . Leon will resist his father's command, then I should stay near him where I will be in a better position to try and influence him."

"Good, then it's settled. Come. Rest for an hour. You must be tired. Then I will dress you as the Western women dress here. I am sure we are about the same size."

April chose a flowing chiffon of the palest pink and did Mei Fei's long black hair up into an elaborate bird's nest. She touched the cheeks with rouge and hung pearls about her neck and pearl pendants from her ear lobes.

Lydia embraced Mei Fei warmly and Raymond could only stare in admiration. She reminded him of that afternoon in this very drawing room when he'd first seen April.

"*Enchanté*," he said in his thick French accent.

Unseen, Lydia rolled her eyes, more amused than annoyed at Raymond's affected continental charm. He'd never change, she told herself. He would chase beautiful women until the day he died. She didn't care. He was attentive enough to her physical needs and Empress Cosmetics was as sound as the dollar.

"Mei Fei," Leon said, bowing respectfully.

When she looked at him her look was skeptical. "My brother?"

"Yes. You were but a small child when last we saw each other, but I am Li Ahn."

"But you are an American."

Leon laughed. "I only look very much like one."

"Prince Ke Loo, your father, will not be pleased," Mei Fei said bluntly.

Leon shrugged. "That is of no consequence to me."

301

Mei Fei looked anxiously toward April, who put her arm about the girl's waist and gave her an encouraging hug. "It will be all right, Mei Fei." To the others April explained. "Mei Fei has come from Prince Ke Loo. It seems he wants his children to come to him." She watched her mother closely.

"Ridiculous," Lydia said. "You are going nowhere, none of you," she said, looking directly at Mei Fei. "You are staying right here with me."

"But . . ." Mei Fei protested.

Lydia said, "It is very different here in America, Mei Fei. Come. Dinner is ready. There will be lots of time to speak of Prince Ke Loo and whatever deviltry he's up to these days."

As they gathered about the dinner table Mei Fei could not contain herself. "I have come on our father's command," she said to Leon. Hardly touching her food she told him of her escape from the Forbidden City, carefully keeping her ivory hand resting in her lap. She ended with her arriving in San Francisco, again omitting Ramsey. April sat quietly through the retelling. "My father has friends here who told me where I could find April."

"What is Ke Loo doing in Hawaii?" Lydia asked.

Mei Fei shrugged. "Trade of some kind. He has hired many natives." She thought longingly of Tehani and desperately wanted her mission accomplished so she could return to him.

Leon said, "This Sun Yat-sen spoke at a Chinese gathering just the other night. If my father is tied in with that man, there is something seriously wrong. Sun Yat-sen does not advocate the dynasty. He wants the Manchus annihilated. He is all for revolution, this is true enough, but I heard him with my own ears say he is soliciting help to overthrow the Manchus—all the Manchus. He wants China to be a republic. He will never consent to Father sitting on the throne. Ke Loo is being used and is obviously unaware of it."

"Then you must be at your father's side where you can protect him," Mei Fei insisted. "Dr. Sun will eliminate Prince Ke Loo after he has served his purpose. I feel it," she said, touching her breast with the ivory hand.

"I don't know," Leon hedged. "I . . ."

"I think you should go," April said, putting aside her wine glass. "You are, after all, his only male heir. It is only through you the Manchu dynasty can continue."

"Don't be ridiculous," Leon scoffed. "There are plenty of Manchu relations still in China."

"It is the Empress's side of the family that must be destroyed along with her," Mei Fei said firmly, unconsciously punctuating her anger by banging the ivory hand on the table.

At once every eye was upon it.

Embarrassed, Mei Fei lowered the hand out of sight. "I am sorry. I have selfish reasons for seeing the Empress overthrown."

Lydia and Leon understood immediately, but when Raymond asked her to explain, Lydia laid her hand on his and gently shook her head. "I'll explain later, Raymond."

"The new regime must begin with Father and you," Mei Fei said.

He couldn't look at her for fear she would see his refusal to want to go. There were too many terrible memories and too often the bad dreams crept into his sleep. "I'll have to have time to think on it," Leon said.

Again April voiced her opinion that he go.

"You must come also," Mei Fei said to April.

"No, I have no place in my father's house. If you recall when we were both prisoners in the summer palace you saw Prince Ke Loo's interest in me. It was not a father's love for his daughter," she said meaningfully.

To her surprise Mei Fei giggled. "But that was years ago. You are no longer a young girl. Our father has a new wife. Malama. She is a very pretty Hawaiian girl. Sun Yat-sen disapproved highly, but Father would not be dissuaded. He said it ties Hawaii to China more firmly."

"The lecherous old devil," Lydia said under her breath and saw Leon, sitting across from her, turn and smile.

April had no intention of leaving Peter until she'd had her revenge here, but she decided she had to encourage Leon to leave. Through him and Mei Fei the Empress would be destroyed, she told herself. She had to do whatever was necessary to persuade Leon to commit himself to his father and to the destruction of the Dragon Empress.

Chapter 4

Eddie Wells looked up from his desk as the heavy-set man in the tight-fitting suit removed his bowler hat and put out his hand.

"Mr. Wells," the man said. "I hope I'm not disturbing you?" He looked around the small but tastefully appointed office. "I understand you diplomats here at the State Department are kept pretty busy what with President Cleveland moving Mr. Olney from Attorney General to Secretary of State."

"Yes," Eddie said curtly.

"Your new boss is a tough acorn, I understand."

"Just what is it you want, Mr. Taylor? I told you on the telephone my time is limited."

"Of course, of course." The stocky man took a card out of his pocket and handed it to Eddie. "Mind if I sit down, Mr. Wells."

"Private Investigator!" Eddie said, reading the card.

Jack Taylor sank heavily into one of the two chairs in front of Eddie's desk. "Yes. Very discreet, naturally. Domestic matters mostly." He chuckled. "None of the dangerous stuff for me. I have a wife and kiddies to think about before sticking my nose into some dark alley."

Eddie frowned, quickly thinking back over the women he'd been with recently. One or two had been married. "Is this about a divorce action?" he asked warily.

"Not exactly, Mr. Wells. I've come to talk about a certain April Wells."

"April Wells? I know no one of that name. Does she claim to be a relation?"

"Actually," Jack Taylor said, putting his feet out and leaning back, "she's supposed to be your wife."

"My wife?" he asked incredulously.

Jack Taylor shrugged and pulled some papers from inside his coat. "These are copies of her imigration papers. They show her name as April Moonsong Wells and her son's as Adam Wells— father, Edward Wells."

Eddie rested his forearms on the desk and kept his hands steady as he recognized copies of the false papers he'd arranged for April.

"Oh, yes," Eddie said, trying to sound casual. "The Oriental girl from Peking. I remember now." He handed back the papers. "I was at the legation. It was one of those unfortunate things. She was alone. I was terribly homesick. You can understand how these affairs happen. Lovely creature. Didn't look a bit Chinese."

"And the child?"

"I wanted to support it when April told me she was expecting our son, but she was the daughter of a prince or some high muck-a-muck who wanted the child raised in the royal household."

Taylor knew he was lying, but let him ramble on.

"I begged April to come back to America with me when my term of service was up, especially with the boy looking so American. I knew the Manchu would never take him in as one of their own. She wouldn't hear of it. However, I arranged for immigration papers for her and little Adam in case she changed her mind."

"And she is your legal wife?"

Eddie looked uncomfortable. "It was a Chinese ceremony." Hastily he added, "But I intended to legalize it here once April arrived."

"Of course." Jack Taylor leaned forward and put his elbows on his knees. He propped his chin on his fingertips and thought for a while, watching Eddie begin to fidget with the ruby ring on his pinky finger.

When Taylor continued to say nothing Eddie stood up. "Now, if there is nothing more, Mr. Taylor, I really am a busy man. If April has entered the United States, naturally I will assume responsibility for her and the child." He searched Taylor's face for some clue to the reason behind the visit but found none.

"One thing that puzzles me, Mr. Wells."

Eddie hesitated, then slowly sat back down when he saw the narrowed eyes and the hard, accusing look.

"Yes?" His voice was unsteady.

"According to official State Department records, your two-year term of service at the American legation in Peking began in June of 1892. You returned to America in September 1894."

"September, yes. I wanted to remain and try and convince April to come home with me. My new assignment here would wait for me, I was told."

"It isn't your two-and-a-half month delay in returning I'm interested in, Mr. Wells." He scratched the side of his square head of plastered-down hair, which was parted in the middle. "What baffles me is your arrival in June of 1892 and your son, Adam, isn't it . . . ?"

"Yes."

"According to the birth records at the American legation, the boy was born in July of 1891, almost a year before you arrived in Peking. Don't you find that rather peculiar?" Taylor chuckled. "Or was it done by proxy?"

Eddie refused to be ruffled. "A mistake, obviously. The birth certificate is in error."

"Come, come, Mr. Wells. I've seen the boy for myself. Any good doctor could easily determine the present age of the boy. And the birth date on the immigration papers agrees with the birth certificate. You should have caught that."

Eddie ignored his sarcasm. "They are here in Washington?" he asked in alarm.

"No, no, Mr. Wells. The mother and child are in California. They have no desire to communicate with you, it appears. I am only here to make inquiries about the child's real father. I am convinced, most assuredly, that it is *not* you."

Eddie began to object, but Jack Taylor held up his hand. "I mean to cause you no trouble, Mr. Wells. All I want is the truth and you'll hear no more about it. You needn't sign any statements or make any affidavits. My client is well aware of

308

your father's influence, but you do have to admit that it would be very embarrassing for everyone in your family if the matter of your forging official immigration papers for a Chinese woman got into the newspapers."

"God!" Eddie breathed. "Surely that isn't possible."

"It could be if you aren't cooperative. You see, Mr. Wells, the boy's real father is dead and the grandparents want the boy very badly. They are extremely rich people and very determined. A scandal is the last thing any of us wants, don't you agree?"

Eddie sat for a moment. April meant nothing to him, nor did he mean anything to her. They'd agreed to that long ago. He owed her no loyalty and if offered he knew she'd refuse it. Suddenly he went cold. "But if there is a court case over legal custody, won't the immigration papers be brought into evidence?"

Jack Taylor grinned. "If they are false papers, those on file could easily be lost. I'm sure your father and you could arrange for that."

"And April's papers? The ones she's carrying?"

"Forgeries, of course. All you need do is deny any knowledge."

Things were looking too bright for him here in the State Department to jeopardize his position. Women, prestige, money, the promise of an exciting, interesting new assignment in England. He couldn't throw it all away for some hard-nosed Chinese girl who didn't care anything about him and who could easily destroy the new image he'd created of himself, Eddie thought.

He let out a deep sigh. "The boy was born after

I arrived. The father was an American. He was beheaded for stealing, she told me. MacNalley, McGuffy, something like that. I don't rightly recall."

"MacNair."

Eddie shrugged. "It could be. She referred to him as David. I do remember that."

Jack Taylor slapped his knees. "Thank you very much, Mr. Wells." He got up and put out his hand. "You'll not be troubled again, I assure you." He winked and leaned across the desk. "I'd remove any trace of those papers from Immigration if I were you . . . just to be on the safe side."

When the door closed, Eddie leaned back and tapped a pencil against his teeth. He should feel guilty, but he didn't. It had been no more than a business deal between him and April, he reminded himself. If it didn't work out to the girl's satisfaction there wasn't much he could do about that. Besides, he was being assigned to the Embassy in London as the Charge d'Affaires. He might be ambassador one day. How could he risk all that on some girl who cared for no one but herself?

He scribbled the words "Immigration Department" on his pad and promptly put April and Adam out of his mind.

"There isn't any doubt," Ramsey told Lorna. He picked up his cigar and reached for a match.

"I'd appreciate your not smoking here in the house," she said. "My husband always notices. I'd prefer he not know you and I are . . ."

"Intimate?" Ramsey asked with a laugh as he put the cigar back into its case.

"Doing business together," she corrected caustically. She walked toward the library table and opened a note book. "Edward Wells," she said, writing the name. "You're positive we will have no problems with him? The mother, naturally, will not give David's boy up without a court action. That will mean dragging Mr. Wells into the matter."

"Edward Wells's father is a very influential man. My agent assures me a statement of declamation will easily be obtained."

Lorna slowly shook her head. "I don't care how influential the Wells family is, I know April Moonsong well enough to know she'll make it all as uncomfortable as she can for everyone. After all, she has everything to lose. She will scratch and claw when threatened. No, we must avoid a legal fight if humanly possible. Besides, I want the child out of her custody NOW, not whenever some judge gets around to deciding the matter. The girl has skipped before. She may well do so again when she learns this . . . Edward Wells intends to disclaim any knowledge of her or Adam." She looked up at Ramsey. "We will change the child's name, of course, after we have custody."

He unconsciously reached for a cigar again, saw her disapproving frown, and put it back. "True, a court fight could get messy. The girl could bolt and by the time legal custody is given you, if it is, the boy might be too attached to his mother and that Chinese nurse. They're teaching him to speak Mandarin, you know."

Lorna looked horrified. "They're not!"

He nodded. "Oh yes. Making him into a regular little Manchurian prince from all I gathered."

"Oh, Ramsey," Lorna said, going to him. "You

311

must do something to get the boy away from that horrid woman."

He put his arms about her waist. "I guess I could snatch the lad."

Lorna stiffened as she stared at him. When she saw he was serious she turned and pushed herself away. "I want that child," she ordered, "but kidnapping is definitely out of the question."

"We wouldn't be kidnapping the boy. There would be no secret made of where he is. You have important friends who'd be only too happy to agree that you did the only proper thing for the child. After all, the boy is here under false papers, and the mother has proven herself irresponsible by abandoning her other two children, as well as a previous husband. She's Oriental, partly, and a bigamist. No one will accuse you of any wrongdoing. For the boy's own good you merely took him from an unhealthy environment."

Lorna stood quite still, letting the idea fix itself into her head. "I don't want the boy frightened in any way."

"He won't be frightened. He's a friendly little thing. Adapts easily to strangers." Ramsey gave her one of his coy smiles. "But the boy won't exactly be a stranger to this household."

"What do you mean?"

"He knows your husband, so I'm certain the boy will believe himself in safe hands."

"Peter?" she gasped. "How . . . ?"

Ramsey cocked his eye. "Now how do you think, Lorna?"

She stared. "You mean Peter has met the child? Knows him? Where? How?" His smugness infuriated her. "Don't play cute with me, Ramsey. I demand you tell me what you know."

"Peter and April Moonsong, of course."

Lorna clutched her throat. "The Chinese daughter?"

"His daughter-in-law." He took out the cigar and lit it. Lorna stood speechless.

Ramsey walked across the room blowing smoke up into the air. "I suppose he figured if Lydia could marry her son-in-law, he could . . . well, let's say, get acquainted with his daughter-in-law. All very family-like, don't you agree, Lorna?"

Her eyes were hard as stone. "He's been seeing the girl?"

"Several times a week, like clockwork."

"Surely not in the disgusting way you insinuate?" She flounced over to him. "Put out that disgusting cigar!"

"All I know," Ramsey said as he continued to smoke, "is what I see with my own eyes. Now, I saw your husband going in and coming out of his daughter-in-law's flat on many an occasion, and at usually the same hours of the day and night. Some visits were no more than an hour or more—the afternoon ones. Others . . ." He stopped and leaned against the mantlepiece.

"Yes, go on."

"The nightly visits usually lasted well toward one or two in the morning. I just put it down as their having a lot to talk about."

"The despicable beast!" Lorna snarled.

"Now I'm not saying . . ."

"Get out!" she shouted as she stormed toward the door and yanked it open.

313

Slowly Ramsey eased himself away from the mantlepiece, the cigar clamped tight between his teeth. As he passed her at the doorway he stopped. "Do we snatch the kid, Lorna?"

"Yes," she snarled.

Chapter 5

Peter hadn't intended to go to bed with April after dinner. It was all wrong and for days he'd been trying to find some way of breaking off their affair. But hard as he tried to stay away, in the end his resolve would weaken. He'd remember Lydia and the hurt she'd inflicted on him, and he would return to seek a perverse revenge in April's arms.

He lay staring up at the ceiling, his hands behind his head, a light sheet covering his naked body.

April slipped between the sheets and lay her head on his shoulder. "You seem to be far, far away," she said as she began playing with the thick hairs on his chest. "In fact, all evening your mind has been somewhere else." She let her hand move down over his flat, hard stomach.

When she encircled his flaccid sex he gave a little groan of protest and lifted one knee in an effort to discourage her.

"Tired?"

"Yes, very."

She put her mouth over his nipple and began

tickling it with her tongue. Despite all his determination, he felt himself start to respond, but he'd be damned if he'd do·anything to encourage her, he kept telling himself.

April forced his knee down and moved one leg in between his. She tensed her thigh, relaxed it, tensed it again, teasing him with the constant pressure of her leg.

Peter was conscious of the hardening of his shaft and knew there wasn't anything he could do to prevent its lengthening and growing into a demand. Her body felt warm and soft, igniting his brain, blanking out his resolutions.

She began to nibble at his ear lobes. Her tongue licked the side of his neck, moved over his broad, muscled shoulders and back to the pouting nipples on his chest.

Peter's whole body was drawn taut as April's lips continued downward. She eased away the sheet and when she reached his navel she paused long enough to get out of her filmy night dress.

He couldn't help himself, he found. A deep, almost tearful sigh escaped his lips as her creamy, smooth breasts brushed his groin. His rigidity jutted up between them as he pinched shut his eyes and surrendered himself to his own lust.

Moving as if under the control of some other's will, he put his long, virile fingers into her hair and began to writhe and moan under the hot sensations her mouth was producing. He tried desperately to unleash the torrid lava that bubbled deep down inside him and have it done and over with. Her mouth was tormenting his flesh and he never wanted the delicious torment to end, he found himself contradicting: Part of him wanted to be away; the other part wanted to stay forever.

Finally the torture became too agonizing. With a desperate push he raised himself into a sitting position and began running his hands over the tantalizing smoothness of her exquisite body. He played with the nipples of her breasts, pulling, caressing, his mouth suddenly craving the feel of them, the taste of them.

April raised her head out of his lap, her lips glistening like dew-drenched rose petals. She shifted her body, lowering herself into a sitting position on Peter's lap, sucking him hungrily deep inside her hot wetness. Their arms went around each other, her breasts smashed tightly against his chest as their mouths crushed together in a searing kiss.

Ever so slowly April began to rotate her hips, drawing Peter deeper and deeper into her hot, passionate body. She moved faster, swaying wildly as his shaft pulsed and throbbed. Tiny little groans of pleasure escaped her mouth, only to be sucked from between her lips as their mouths remained glued together.

She sensed his stiffening and moved more violently, bouncing, churning her body over Peter's exploding desires.

He gasped, tightening his embrace, lunging his hips, almost unseating her. April jammed herself down on her impalement and groaned out the last throes of her own ecstasy. She sucked his tongue into her mouth, groaning, moaning, almost screaming out the delight she sensed in her power over him.

Slowly, she allowed her grip on him to loosen. She fell against him, then slid easily to his side. The quietness of the bedroom enveloped them as they lay trying to bring their breathing back to normal.

April stirred finally, propping herself up on one elbow. She looked hard into Peter's face. His eyes were closed, his lips half parted. She knew he was thinking about Lydia.

She frowned. "Something is the matter."

He didn't open his eyes. "Oh?" He sounded bored and disinterested.

"It's not like you to let the woman take the initiative. You've been so passive of late. What's wrong?"

He put his arm across his eyes and sighed. He lay for a moment feeling drained and utterly disgusted with himself. "Everything is wrong," he said angrily.

"What do you mean?"

Peter found the courage that he thought he'd lost. He took away his arm and turned and looked at her. "*We* are wrong." He saw her eyes grow hard. "This should never have started, April. It isn't right and it isn't fair to you."

April scowled. "Isn't it rather unusual for you to become self-righteous all of a sudden? Or is it that you don't find the daughter as stimulating as her mother?"

"Please, April," he said as he got up and started to dress. "There is no reason to get unpleasant. What we are doing is completely wrong." He found that his resolve was getting stronger by the minute. "I honestly believe we should not see each other again."

To his surprise April laughed. "You truly believe it is as simple as that? What are you going to do when the need builds up in you again, Peter? Go to a brothel? You won't find my mother there," she spat. "I needn't remind you that she has a man in bed beside her every night. A husband. My husband," she shouted. "She doesn't want you."

"You're wrong. I don't care about Lydia being with another man because way down deep I know she loves only me, as I love only her. We will always be hopelessly as well as helplessly in love with each other and I mean to tell her that. She married Raymond because of Empress Cosmetics. She doesn't love him. I have every intention of going to her and confessing this sordid affair in which you and I got ourselves involved. If I have to get down on my knees and beg her forgiveness, I'll do it. I've been fooling myself all these weeks. I know now I only succumbed to you because I was hurt and angry and you were Lydia's daughter."

April rose up in all her fury. "How dare you! It wasn't my mother's body that you couldn't resist, nor was it Lydia's body that just satisfied you. Oh, you may have breathed her name once or twice, but you also breathed mine often enough at your moment of climax. It is I who you need, Peter," she snarled.

"You're mistaken."

When she saw the shoe he was searching for she picked it up and flung it at him. "Go to her if you are stupid enough to think she still wants you. She'll spit on your pleas for forgiveness, your protestations of love. And do you know why, Peter?

319

Because Lydia Moonsong cares about no one but herself. Mark me well, Peter. By going to Lydia you'll only be making a bigger fool of yourself than you are right now."

"I'll take that chance. If she orders me out of her life, it won't be the first time. I've lived with it before; I will again. No matter how she storms and rages, I know she loves me and that I love her."

He finished dressing. There was a sudden brightness, a buoyancy inside him that made him happy for the first time in a long time. "She may kick me out, April, but I will leave with a clear conscience," he said. "I never felt good about us. I was kidding myself. I know that now."

April started to blaze up at him. Gradually, she let herself relax and lay back against the pillows, enjoying the way he could not look away from her blatant nakedness. She put her hands over her head and smiled. "What a complete fool you are, Peter." She watched his tongue unconsciously touch the corners of his mouth as she pushed out her breasts.

He tore his gaze away and started for the door.

"And what of Adam?" she cooed.

Peter stopped. "What about Adam? What has he to do with any of this?"

"Really, Peter, surely you know Adam is David's child."

He throat grew tight. "Oh?"

"By never seeing me, you will never see Adam again either."

For an instant he was tempted to warn April of the legal action Lorna was planning to institute. Reason told him to remain quiet, to tell April nothing. She might run back to China and Adam would be lost to them forever.

He clenched his hands and looked at her with a show of disinterest. "As far as I am concerned, the boy's father is a Mr. Wells. Good-bye, April," he said. He turned and walked out of the room.

April pulled a pillow from behind her head and flung it at the closed door. She sat pouting, her mind seething with all sorts of horrible thoughts. One of her thoughts made her glance at the time of night. The clock on the night stand told her it was still early, not yet ten o'clock. April knew her mother's habits only too well. She'd still be up, working in her study, and chances were, being that it was Saturday night, she'd be alone in the house with only the servants and the children. Raymond always went to his club on Saturdays. Mei Fei had told her earlier that morning she and Leon were going to some revue at the Lyric.

Hurriedly, April put on the first street dress she pulled from the wardrobe. She didn't care how she looked; it was what she would say that she paid close attention to.

The amah was dozing in the chair next to Adam's little bed. April shook her shoulder and saw the glazed look. "Mayli, you've been smoking that damned pipe again!" April charged.

Mayli cowered back from her mistress's raised fist. "No, Mistress, no. I was at my uncle's house earlier, as you know. We talked. He smoked. Many times the smoke makes me drowsy after I leave."

April noted the hour. She had no time to argue. "I must go out. Find me a carriage. Hurry!" she said, trying to keep her voice down for fear of awakening Adam. "Go!" She gave Mayli a shove toward the door.

As the cab clattered over the cobblestone streets toward Nob Hill April forgot about her anger with Mayli and concentrated on what she would say to her mother. The moment for her revenge was close, only a few more streets away. It was going to be glorious to see the hurt in Lydia's face when she told her she'd taken Peter away from her, how much in love they were, and how he wanted to marry her and divorce Lorna. It would be a triumph, April thought, hugging herself with joy.

The Moonsong mansion was as she'd known it would be. The children were asleep upstairs, the servants were in their quarters. Lydia was working on a report. Raymond was out. Leon and Mei Fei wouldn't be home until quite late, Lydia told her.

April played her scene to perfection, starting with, "I know you and I have never been close, Mother, but I thought you'd prefer hearing the news from me."

"News? What news?"

"Peter MacNair and I are to be married."

She wanted to wrap her arms about herself and dance across the room. The color drained from Lydia's face, her eyes widened with shock, and then a terrible pain began to inch its way across her face.

"I don't believe it," Lydia gasped, tightening her hands on the arms of her chair as if to keep herself from flying at the girl and ripping her to shreds.

"We've been seeing each other for some time—

secretly, of course," April said, putting as much lurid inference as possible into her words. "I know now why you loved him. He's quite a marvelous man. But then I'm sure you will not argue with me on that point."

"I don't believe you," Lydia said again, feeling it was her only defense.

April flung back her light cape and helped herself to a glass of wine. "Peter insists on coming here to tell you himself. I told him I didn't think that proper, that it might pain you to hear it from someone outside of the family."

"I don't believe any of this." Lydia somehow let loose her grip on the chair and got unsteadily to her feet.

"Isn't it odd the way things worked out," April said, sipping her wine. "You end up with my lover and I end up with yours."

"Stop it!"

At that moment the door bell sounded. "That will be Peter," April said. "Shall I let him in?"

Lydia straightened to her full height and folded her hands in front of her as she faced the doorway. "Nellie will do it."

A moment later Peter MacNair was shown into the room. At first he saw only Lydia and started toward her. When he noticed April sipping her wine and grinning maliciously, he stopped short.

"How dare you?" Lydia demanded, eyeing him contemptuously.

"Please, Lydia, I only want to explain."

"I find nothing to explain. You've been engaged in an affair with my daughter. How can that be *explained*?"

"That's why I'm here, Lydia. I . . ."

"You came to deny it?" she asked coolly.

Peter looked helplessly from April to Lydia. "No, but . . ."

"Then there is nothing to explain. I think you are the most hateful, unprincipled man ever created and I demand that you leave this house forever. But you will never marry my daughter."

"Marry?" His chin dropped as he gaped at April.

She sashayed across to him and smoothed the silver hair at his temples. "I thought Mother should hear the news from me, darling. More family-like, you know."

Peter looked at Lydia. "What has April been telling you?"

"I know of your affair, of your proposal of marriage . . . a proposal you no more intend keeping than the one you offered me." To April she fought to soften her voice. "You were a fool to be taken in by this filthy cad. He'll never divorce Lorna for you or anyone else. I above everyone else know what a scoundrel he is."

"Now just one damned minute," Peter swore. "I never . . ."

"You never what?" Lydia demanded, cutting him off. "You never had an affair with my daughter?"

"No, but . ."

"You intend divorcing Lorna and marrying April?"

"No," Peter blurted out, "but . . ."

"Peter," April cried, pretending to be cut to the quick. "How could you?"

"April! Damn it, you know perfectly well . . ."

Again Lydia cut him off as he turned toward

April. "I won't listen to another word you have to say, Mr. MacNair. Now kindly leave this house. And if I ever see you so much as tip your hat to me or any member of my family I will have you in a court of law for breach of promise."

None of them heard Raymond let himself into the house and enter the study. "What in the devil is going on?" he demanded, glowering at Peter.

"Mr. MacNair," Lydia sneered, "is up to his usual skullduggery. Escort him out, please, Raymond."

Peter lost all patience. "Listen to me, damn it, Lydia," he said knocking aside Raymond's hand and banging his fist on Lydia's desk. "All I want is a chance to explain."

Lydia remained unmoved. She had never hated him more, even more than that night he'd traded her off to the Mandarin just to save his own skin.

She said, "Please leave this house, Mr. MacNair. You, sir, are a liar and a cheat."

Peter shook off Raymond's hand and knocked him backward. "You are the stupidest, most foolish woman I've ever known. God only knows why I ever fell in love with you."

"You never did." Her voice was like the sharp edge of a knife.

April stood to one side smirking to herself, her heart bursting with happiness at the looks of hatred passing between Lydia and Peter.

"Believe what you like. I don't care," Peter charged. "I can only see now what a self-centered, hard, dispassionate woman you are. One of these days, Lydia, you will regret not having believed in me. I came here to ask your forgiveness, but to hell with your forgiveness. I don't want it now."

"Come on, mister," Raymond said, grabbing Peter's shoulder and spinning him around.

Peter's temper flew out of control. He hit Raymond square on the jaw and sent him tumbling backward over a table.

"Raymond," Lydia cried, rushing toward him more out of concern than love.

Peter stood over them, giving free rein to his rage. "I'll ruin that bastard husband of yours. I'll ruin you and your precious company." His anger was so blind he hardly knew what he was saying. "My house-to-house business is making millions. One of these days very soon I'll be the most powerful, most popular cosmetic firm in the world. I have a new scent, Lydia, a far superior one to your damned Moonsong," he lied.

She glared up at him. "You've never been anything but second-rate, Peter, and you never will be." She patted Raymond's cheek as he started to come around. "Nothing will ever be superior to Moonsong and you know it."

Peter let an ugly smile cross his lips as he pointed to Raymond. "There's your blessed Moonsong," he gloated, kicking at the shoes of the semiconscious Raymond. "Without that Frenchman you are nothing."

"Get out!"

April casually drained her glass and refilled it. She stood with her arms crossed, the rim of the glass touching her lips. She'd never been so pleased.

"I'll leave when I've had my complete say." He looked down at Raymond, who sat up and rubbed his jaw. "You're the worst excuse for a man alive and you both deserve one another." He turned to

Lydia and said, "I wouldn't bank too heavily on that louse if I were you. You don't know, of course, but he's been bragging around the club about how he intends taking over your precious company, Lydia, closing down your American operation, and hightailing himself and the profits back to Paris. So let me warn you, Lydia Moonsong, you are going to have a war on your hands between Empress Cosmetics, MacNair Products, and a possible third front headed by that bastard in Paris. He'll bleed you dry and spit you out like a seed."

Raymond pushed himself up and lunged at Peter, forcing him backward over the desk. He pounded his fist into Peter's face. Peter raised his knee and kicked Raymond in the groin, doubling him in half.

Raymond staggered back. As Peter straightened himself from over the desk and smoothed his jacket, he glanced to find the muzzle of a pearl-handled revolver inches away from his forehead.

"Get out," Lydia rasped. "Get out before I kill you."

Peter gave a smug, polite little bow. He tugged at the cuffs of his sleeves and strode from the house.

April couldn't hold back any longer. She put back her head and began to laugh hysterically.

Chapter 6

Ramsey saw Peter leave. Ten minutes later April climbed into a hansom and dashed off. "That leaves the amah and the boy," he said to himself as he got down from his two-wheeled buggy and started toward the flat.

He'd waited several nights for the amah to be alone with the boy and touched his jacket pocket to be certain the packet of opium was safely tucked inside. Things were all working out wonderfully well. The MacNair kid was turning into an alcoholic, but he was doing as he was told, though Ramsey reminded himself he'd better keep a closer eye on Efrem.

"The mistress is not at home," the amah said when she answered Ramsey's ring.

She started to close the door, but Ramsey put the flat of his hand against it. "I would like to wait for her," he said in his most authorative voice. "I am from the government."

He saw her eyes stare up in fear. It was the one sure word to induce fear in any Oriental. He smiled kindly. "Don't be frightened, Mayli. It does not concern you or your . . . errr . . . little business." Ramsey saw her fingers grip the edge of the door. "Oh, I know about the favors you do for your uncle and others. It's all right. In fact, here," he said, reaching into his pocket. "I brought a present for you. We have something in common, you and I," he said, dangling the opium in front of her eyes.

The door opened and he stepped inside after she snatched the packet from him. "In there," Mayli said. "You wait there. I don't know when the mistress will return."

"I have plenty of time."

Ten restless minutes later Ramsey crept down the hallway until he came to the open door of the nursery. As expected, Mayli was deep in her drugged trance, rocking slowly, seeing nothing but the pretty dreams inside her head.

Ramsey went to the trundle bed and touched the boy's cheek. He rocked the head gently and spoke his name. Adam's lids flickered, but he didn't open his eyes. He murmured something and curled himself into a ball. The smoke from the opium pipe had obviously deepened his sleep. Ramsey slipped a tiny capsule far back on Adam's tongue, then rubbed his throat gently until the child swallowed. Then he carefully wrapped the fleecy blanket around the boy and scooped him up into his arms.

A thick fog was beginning to roll in from the ocean as Ramsey carried Adam to the buggy and tucked him into the corner of the seat. He closed the side flaps and the front isinglass wind-screen and started the horse on a fast clip toward the bay.

The original plan had been to take the child directly to Lorna, but Ramsey thought himself too shrewd to give away all his cards before the game was finished. With Lorna in possession of Adam, Ramsey knew he had nothing with which to trump any ace she might be holding.

No, he'd keep the boy until he could compromise Lorna and what better temporary nursemaid for the child than Sylvia. She wanted company—a child—to keep her occupied in her isolated house in Sausalito. He'd conjure up some cock-and-bull story she'd believe and again lure her with promises of their going to Hawaii. By the time the ferry docked at the Sausalito pier, Ramsey had his story down pat.

"A client," he told Sylvia as he carried Adam over the threshold. "One of my last clients, in fact. The boy's name is Adam; that's all you need to know. Now, don't get too attached to the lad. He'll be here only a day or two."

Sylvia gushed over the sleeping child as she took him in her arms. She was only half listening to what Ramsey was saying. "How could a client give up her child?" she asked as she made a place for him on the bed.

"She didn't exactly give him up. The father took him. It's a custody case. The husband feels he's as much entitled to the boy as the ex-wife, so he had me take him. I'm to hide him for a few days until the legalities can be straightened out."

"Oh, I wish we could keep him," Sylvia said as she stroked his curly head. "He's such a handsome little thing. He has your eyes, Ramsey. Had you noticed?"

Ramsey smiled to himself. *Yes, Sylvia would*

watch out for the kid, he told himself. This was the perfect hideout.

"Now I must be off," he said. "Get whatever you need for the boy, but make absolutely certain he doesn't wander off. Keep him indoors at all times. He's not a particularly strong lad, so keep him away from the damp."

With Adam sleeping soundly in the bed Sylvia made no protests at all when Ramsey left. "Little darling lad," she cooed. All she thought about was how wonderful it would be when he woke up.

Leon and Mei Fei settled themselves at the small table in the Chinatown restaurant. Leon ordered a late supper of crabmeat dumplings, buns with roast pork filling, and flower rolls.

"Did you enjoy the musical revue?" he asked as Mei Fei laid her ivory hand gently on the table.

"Western music is so strange to the ear." She paused and gave him a stern look. "It is not music we should be speaking of, Li Ahn. You must go to your father. He is impatient, I know, and you have delayed long enough."

"I don't think I will go, Mei Fei." He heard her intake of breath. "I know, I know. You think it is my sacred obligation. Well, I have been here too long to believe in the old traditions. America is a free country where a man can do as he wishes."

"There is no tradition in America? No family obligations?"

"That's just it. My obligation, I feel, is toward my American mother, not to Prince Ke Loo."

"Prince Ke Loo!" she said, scorning him. "You speak of your father as a stranger."

"He is a stranger."

There was a sudden commotion in one of the adjacent private rooms. They heard loud voices, the smashing of glass and china, and then a scuffle.

When things quieted down after a moment Leon started to try and explain how he felt about his father without damaging her own innocent belief in all she'd been taught. But the proprietor, a man Leon knew well, hurried toward him. "I am sorry, Leon. It is your friend," he said, motioning to where the commotion had been.

"Friend?" Leon asked, frowning.

"Young Mr. MacNair. He is very drunk, I'm afraid. He's passed out. Could I trouble you to see that he is taken home? It would be unwise for one of us to be found on Nob Hill at this hour."

"Efrem?" Leon got quickly to his feet.

"This way, please."

"Wait here, Mei Fei. I'll be back in a moment. Watch out for her, Wong," he said to the proprietor.

Efrem was lying on the floor of one of the small dining rooms. Three fierce-looking Chinamen stood over him. Leon recognized them as members of the Tong Society. Though he mixed freely with people of Chinatown and was accepted, he was never considered one of them, nor did *he* consider himself as one.

"Get him out of here," one of the Tongs ordered. "Or they will find him in the alley with a hatchet in his back." He spat on Efrem. "You had better tell your friend, Li Ahn, that he is fortunate you were here."

"Fetch a carriage," Leon said sharply. "And bring the girl who was with me. I will take care of whatever damages he incurred." He shook Efrem gently, but he was knocked out cold.

Between them, he and Mei Fei managed to get Efrem into the carriage. When they reached Nob Hill, Efrem still showed no signs of consciousness.

Leon said to Mei Fei, "I'll take you home. It is very late and Mother will be worried. Tell her I am driving my friend around until he is sober enough to be taken home."

"Your friend," Mei Fei scoffed. "Who is this Western man?"

"Never mind. Just go to bed and tell my mother not to worry about me. The lights are on, so she is still up," Leon said, motioning to the lighted windows of the Moonsong mansion.

Before Mei Fei got out of the carriage she shook a finger at Leon. "While you are driving about with your drunken friend, you had best give careful thought to the duty you owe to our father. And think also on this," she added, holding up her ivory hand. "The revolution must not fail. The Empress must be pulled down from her golden throne and trampled into the dust."

Leon let out a long sigh and told the cabbie to drive down along the waterfront. Perhaps the cold salt air would revive Efrem. As they rode, Leon thought of what Mei Fei had said. He would never go to stand at his father's side, he told himself. He could understand why Mei Fei felt obliged to pressure him, but what puzzled him was why April, too, was so anxious for him to go, yet so reluctant to go herself.

333

Efrem stirred. Slowly he lifted his hand and gingerly touched the lump at the back of his skull. He grimaced and let out a low groan of pain.

Leon said nothing. He waited until he saw Efrem open his eyes and look around.

"Hello," Leon said, smiling. "Feeling rotten?"

Efrem tried to focus, not sure if he was still unconscious and dreaming or if Leon was really sitting here close beside him. "Leon?" It hurt to speak.

"You really were celebrating tonight. What's the occasion?"

"Go away," Efrem said, burying his face in his hands. "Just leave me alone, Leon."

When Leon put his hand on Efrem's shoulder, Efrem could control his misery no longer. He cried unashamedly into his hands.

"It's all right, Ef," Leon said slipping his arm innocently about his friend's shoulders.

"Oh, God," Efrem moaned as he buried his face against Leon's chest.

"Hey, come on, Ef. Whatever it is that's been eating you up lately, I'll help handle it. You've purposely been avoiding me and I don't know why. I thought I was your best friend."

"Don't, Leon. Leave me be. Don't have anything to do with me."

"I am your friend," Leon reminded him.

"I have no friends." He pushed himself away, leaning against the side of the cab.

To try and make light of Efrem's obvious agony, Leon said, "Well it was fortunate for you your *nonfriend* was in Wong's tonight. His boys would just as easily have killed you as not."

"I wasn't there by chance," Efrem said. "I followed you and that Chinese girl."

His voice was so bitter it caused Leon's brow to crease. "Mei Fei? She is my half-sister. She has come on behalf of my father who wants me to return to him."

"Go."

"Efrem? What in the devil is the matter? Something's dreadfully wrong. Tell me."

"Leave me alone."

Leon put his hand on Efrem's arm. "This is me, Leon, your friend, whether you want me as one or not."

He felt Efrem physically melt under his touch.

"Oh, Leon, good God," Efrem groaned as he let the tears roll unchecked down his cheeks. He rolled his head from side to side, ignoring the throbbing pain.

"You said you followed me to Wong's tonight. Why?"

Efrem closed his eyes and didn't answer.

"You had to have a reason." He squeezed Efrem's arm encouragingly. "Please, Ef. Tell me what's wrong. If you are in any kind of trouble you know I'll help you out of it. I thought we were a good team, you and I. I can't understand why you've shut me out all of a sudden."

How could he make him understand, Efrem asked himself? How could he keep Leon uninvolved if he told him about Ramsey and the opium smuggling he'd been blackmailed into? Knowing Leon, he'd plunge into the mess headlong, not knowing the horrible consequences, the fact that they would both wind up in prison, branded as perverts.

335

No, Efrem told himself as he let himself be rocked by the slow-moving carriage. Leon had to be kept out of all of it and there was only one thing Efrem could think of to do that would accomplish that. He had to frighten Leon away.

Slowly Efrem steeled himself and then opened his eyes and turned toward Leon. He raised his hand to Leon's cheek and stroked it, watching closely the look of discomfort, the uneasiness that came over Leon's face.

Efrem waited until Leon took the hand away. "Don't, Ef," Leon said with an embarrassed little smile.

"I love you, Leon." Efrem kept his voice low and even. "God help me; I can't help myself. I love you." He threw himself into Leon's arms.

"No!" Leon shoved him roughly away. "Efrem, for God's sake, you don't know what you're saying."

"Don't I?" Efrem put on a mask of pure lust. "What happened that night in the whorehouse—I wanted that to happen and I want it to happen again and again and again."

"Efrem!" Leon shouted as again Efrem tried to throw himself into Leon's arms. "Stop it! You're drunk! You don't know what you're saying. It's wrong, Efrem. You're talking madness."

"You're all I want, Leon."

"Don't say such a thing. I'm taking you home to sleep it off," Leon said desperately as he rapped on the trap door and gave the cabbie the MacNair mansion address.

Efrem buried his face in his hands again and began to cry. He'd have no trouble with Leon persisting in trying to be friends after tonight, he told himself. He'd succeeded. He'd never see Leon Moonsong again, he knew. The pain in his head was nothing to the terrible pain in his heart. Nothing at all.

Efrem got out of the hansom before it came to a complete stop. He stumbled and fell on the cobblestones, bruising his knees. He heard Leon call his name, but didn't wait to find out if Leon was getting out of the carriage to help him. Efrem scrambled to his feet and raced madly up the drive.

Leon watched him go. The turmoil inside him was churning like an angry sea of indecision. He had been right in discouraging Efrem's insane outburst. Yet. . . .

He stopped the cab in front of his home and paid off the driver. As he opened the gate and walked toward the mansion he looked up and saw the lamp still burning in Mei Fei's room. With slow, dragging steps he knew what he must do, both for Efrem's sake as well as his own.

"All right, little sister," Leon said as he went up the steps and fitted his key into the lock. "We'll go to Prince Ke Loo, our father."

He felt a terrible throbbing inside his breast and did not bother to wipe away the tears as they ran from his eyes.

Chapter 7

Lorna awoke when she heard Efrem stumble up the stairway and down the hall to his room. She glanced at the connecting door to Peter's bedroom. There was no light showing under it, so she assumed he had long since come home and gone to bed. Or, perhaps he was still out carousing someplace. Lately, neither interfered much in the activities of the other. She still loved him deeply; yet in the knowledge that he wanted to divorce her, her love often became confused with hate.

Adjusting the pillows, Lorna turned on her side and closed her eyes, reminding herself to speak to Peter about Efrem. She didn't want him to turn into a profligate like his father, regardless of how much Peter chose to ignore and excuse Efrem's drinking.

She'd stood helplessly to one side and saw how Peter had ruined David; he would not do the same with Efrem, she vowed. She'd insist on Efrem leaving that odious job that he obviously despised. His taking to drink and late hours proved that, she told herself, as she tried to clear away her worries and let sleep return.

A moment later there was a terrible hammering on the front door. Lorna sat bolt upright in bed as the banging and muffled shouts continued. It sounded like some hysterical female. Lorna slipped into her quilted robe and velvet slippers.

Peter's door was closed, as was Efrem's, but Susan was in the corridor, staring toward the stairs. "Who do you think it is?" Susan asked, as her mother joined her on the landing, watching as the butler shuffled across the marble foyer, lamp in hand.

"I have no idea, dear," Lorna said.

The minute the bolt was released, the heavy front door flew open, knocking the butler aside. April Moonsong burst into the house.

"Where is he?" she shouted at the top of her lungs, looking wildly around at the strangeness of the place.

"Please, miss," the butler said, "the family is abed."

Lorna held the lamp high and started down the long, curved staircase. "I'll handle this, Jeffers. Go back to bed."

April ran to the bottom of the staircase. She clung to the newel post, her eyes blazing, her face white with rage. "What have you done with him?" she demanded.

In the glow of the lamp, Lorna saw the girl's hysteria as she got nearer. "You are creating a disturbance," Lorna said evenly. "Kindly leave my house or I will summon the authorities."

"I'm not leaving here without my son," April yelled.

A tight gasp caught in Lorna's throat. When she

recovered herself she said, "I know nothing about your son, Miss Moonsong."

"Then ask your husband." She hung onto the newel post as though it supported her life.

Lorna watched her through narrowed eyes. Her suspicions began to fall into place as she thought of Ramsey and their plot. If Ramsey had taken the boy, why hadn't he brought the child here, she wondered? And what had Peter to do with the child's being missing?

Turning to Susan, Lorna said, "Fetch your father." She looked back at April. "Your family may be accustomed to uncivilized ravings, but such behavior is not welcome here."

"Go to hell!" April shouted, throwing back the hood of her cape. "I want my son!"

Susan came back to the head of the stairs. "Father isn't in his room."

"No," Peter said as he came through the open door, "I'm here. What's going on?" He saw April and glowered at her as he took off his hat. "What trouble are you stirring up now?"

"Adam," she snarled, turning on Peter. "What have you done with him?"

"I haven't the faintest idea what you are talking about."

"You're lying. When you stormed out of Mother's house earlier, you went back to my flat and took Adam."

"You're insane," Peter said as he pulled off his gloves and laid them beside his hat on the console. He put his night stick in the cane stand.

Lorna stood holding the lamp, her eyes moving from April to Peter, her mouth slightly open. Every word was registering on her brain.

340

"You are the one who is insane," April charged. "If you think you can get even with me by stealing my son, you had better think again, Peter. Adam has been kidnapped. If you do not return him to me this instant, I will go directly to the police. I will put you all behind bars," she threatened.

Peter stood unruffled. "Do whatever you think you must, April, but you have my word, I know nothing about Adam, nor does anyone else in my house." He glanced at Lorna.

Lorna gave a self-conscious shrug. "Peter, please get her out of here," she said. She turned and regally ascended the staircase.

"I swear I will go to the police," April shouted after her.

Again Peter said, "Do whatever you think you must. Now, kindly leave. You've disturbed my family, which I highly resent. Please leave."

April seethed with hate and frustration. "I'll pull your precious house down around your corrupt head." She shook her fist in his face, then dashed out, her long cloak flowing behind her.

Lorna was standing in the doorway to her bedroom when Peter came up. Susan's door was closed.

"What do you know of this, Lorna?"

"I was about to ask the same of you."

Their eyes locked for a few seconds. There was something in Lorna's eyes Peter did not trust.

He said, "I thought for a moment you'd done something stupid, like snatching the boy."

"I didn't, but I feel I have every right to do so. The mother is totally irresponsible."

"The courts will handle it. Right now I'm con-

341

cerned about the boy. It may well be that April knows we have proof that Adam is our grandson. She may be up to some trick. She's a crafty devil," he said half to himself as he knit his brows together. He started for his room.

"If anyone should know, you should," Lorna said as she went into her room and closed the door.

The following morning Peter read the glaring headline: CHILD KIDNAPPED! It was a rather brief account and dealt with nothing but the facts the police had given the newspaper reporters. Whatever scathing accusations April had made, none were in print, nor would they be, he knew, until proven to be true. The article showed a sketch of Adam and stated that he'd been taken from his bed sometime between ten and midnight. The nurse had been drugged. There were no clues to the identity of the kidnapper and the public was asked to be on the lookout for the boy. A detailed description was given, including the poppy-cluster "birthmark" on the child's thigh.

"She was telling the truth, it seems," Peter said, handing Lorna the morning paper. "Still," he said rubbing his chin, "it could well be some elaborate hoax she's concocted."

"I'm concerned," Lorna said. She'd tossed most of the night wondering if Ramsey had taken the boy. "The girl may be irrational but surely she wouldn't kidnap her own child."

Peter was almost tempted to argue. After that horrible scene at Lydia's, he knew April was capable of anything. Instead he said, "Remember, Lorna, she has Oriental blood."

Lorna reread the account and laid the paper aside. Nervously, she buttered her toast and sipped her coffee, anxious for Peter to finish and leave for his Sunday morning golf game.

The second he was out the door Lorna asked that the carriage be brought around. Then she changed her mind. "No," she told the butler, "hail a cab for me. I may be gone quite some time."

She found Ramsey puffing on a cigar, his feet propped up, his jacket off. When Lorna charged into his office-study he smiled and slowly got up and put on his coat. "You've obviously seen the newspapers."

"Where is my grandchild?"

"Safe."

"Then you did take him. Why didn't you bring him to me as we agreed?"

"Because you and I have some unfinished business that I would like to be kept unfinished." He eyed her with a continuing smile. "I don't know what I see in you, Lorna, but you're in my blood and I want to keep you there."

"I want my grandchild!"

"And you shall have him. But first, I want you to sign a few papers."

"Papers?" She drew back.

"Surely you didn't think I would kidnap a child for you and not want proof that we were in on it together? I'm no fool, even though you may think of me as one. Like me, Lorna, you're as slippery as oil. In order to be rid of me, all you need do is point your finger and raise your high-class eyebrows and nobody would believe what a lowly hired detective had to say on his own behalf."

"I'll sign nothing."

"Then you'll never see your grandson. I'll simply change sides by giving the boy back to his mother. Between April Moonsong and myself we could make your life very uncomfortable, Lorna."

"You're a louse."

"Is that something you didn't know?" He took a document from his desk. "Read this, if you like. I wrote it out myself so no one knows it exists but you and I."

Lorna hesitated. She picked up the paper and read it. It wasn't as incriminating as she'd expected. By signing it she was admitting to the fact that she'd hired a private detective to remove her grandson from the custody of an unfit mother, an irresponsible Oriental who'd left her child with an opium-smoking nurse, who, together with the mother, was teaching the boy to speak Mandarin and bringing him up as a Chinese; that the child was in truth the son of David MacNair, a fact the mother refused to divulge to the MacNair family.

She finished reading and looked up.

"Harmless enough, isn't it?" Ramsey asked.

Lorna said nothing.

"After you sign it I'll arrange to have the boy brought to you and the facts released to the press. I don't think with your connections, April Moonsong will be able to gather any public sympathy. And, of course, we'll emphasize both April's divorce and the fact that her mother married her divorced son-in-law. Just stick with me, Lorna," he said putting his hands on her waist. "I'll have the Moonsongs out of your hair before you can blink an eye."

He handed her the quill pen.

344

Lorna scrawled her name. "When do I get the child?"

"Tomorrow."

"Why not now?"

"Because there are things that must be set up so our story holds water." He reached for her. "Now, how about showing me some appreciation."

She moved into his arms.

The day had grown cold. A heavy mist swept over the little house in Sausalito. Sylvia told herself she should have gone out to get her medicine at the druggist's, but she couldn't leave the child. Her cough was getting worse; she was afraid the boy might catch it.

He didn't seem too hearty, sleeping most of the time as he did. But then Ramsey had said he was a delicate boy. Somehow, however, it didn't seem natural for a little boy to be so drowsy, almost as if he were sedated. How she'd looked forward to today when little Adam would wake up and they'd play games and have fun together.

But he never woke up completely and when he did it was only a short while before he'd nod off to sleep again. He'd slept away the whole day and night, never showing any interest in food or drink whenever he did open his eyes.

She occupied the time stitching up a little sailor suit she'd made by cutting up one of Ramsey's old jackets. It wasn't perfect, but it would be when she'd fitted it properly.

Her loss of sleep had brought on the coughing, but she kept doggedly to her sewing task. The child would need more than the flannel nightshirt Ramsey had brought him in.

Sylvia looked longingly at the empty bottle of cough medicine. If only she could slip out to the druggist's she'd feel so much better.

When Adam stirred, Sylvia rushed toward the bed. She put her hand on his forehead. It felt feverish.

"Adam," she said. She'd always remember his name; it was such a lovely name, a name she herself would have chosen.

His eyes opened. "Mayli?" he said, frowning up at the blurred face.

"No, I'm Sylvia."

Adam rubbed his eyes. "I want Mayli."

"Are you hungry, child? You've been asleep a very long while."

"Where is Mayli?" he asked, his voice thick from the effects of the opiate Ramsey had made him swallow. "Where is my mother? I don't feel well."

Recalling what Ramsey had told her, Sylvia said, "Your father will be here to take you home very soon." She couldn't suppress her coughing. She buried her mouth in the folds of her apron. When she took it away she noticed tiny splotches of blood on the material.

Adam frowned at her. "My father?" He didn't understand. He vaguely remembered something about pretending to have a father. It was a game he and his mother had played when they came over the ocean on the big boat.

"He'll be here soon. Look," she said, holding up the little sailor suit. "Let me try it on you. It's nice and soft and warm." She tried not to cough but couldn't help herself.

His eyes glazed, his thoughts benumbed, he

groggily let the woman lift off his nightshirt. Sylvia studied the strange markings on the inside of his thigh as she fitted him into the trousers. She paid it no mind, concentrating all her attention on the fit of the pants and blouse.

"Marvelous," she said, standing him up on the bed and supporting his weight as she tried to adjust the sleeves. "A nip here, a little shortening of the cuffs, and it will be perfect."

"I want my mother," Adam said again, rubbing his eyes. But he was glad the woman had laid him back on the bed because the room was all fuzzy and it made him dizzy to stand up.

"Soon, dear, soon," she said as she took off the suit and replaced the nightshirt. "I've fixed you some nice porridge. Or I can heat up some soup. Which would you like?"

Adam yawned and closed his eyes to keep the room from spinning. "I want my mother," he said. "I don't feel good."

She felt his forehead again and thought it was decidedly warmer. Some food would obviously help, she told herself as she went to fetch a bowl of porridge. The boy was obviously famished. When she came back to the bed Adam was sound asleep again.

She worked the rest of the morning on finishing the little suit, muffling her coughing as best she could. The rain started about two o'clock, bringing with it a biting chill. Sylvia built up the fire and fought to keep from coughing, which was becoming impossible. She would need to go to the druggist, she told herself. The medicine would help.

Adam moved restlessly, as if having a bad

347

dream, but didn't wake up. Now and again he'd call out for his mother or for Mayli. Then he'd cry. Sylvia would gather him in her arms and rock him gently until he'd fall asleep again. Deep down, she knew that there was something wrong.

As the rain fell heavier, her coughing got worse and Adam became more erratic. Though he never fully became conscious he kicked and screamed and threw himself about as if pursued by demons.

When the afternoon light faded, Sylvia grew more and more concerned, to the point of being afraid. Ramsey had said he'd come, but he hadn't. She needed medicine; she needed someone to see to the boy. Things weren't right.

Fifteen minutes before the druggist closed shop, Sylvia was desperate. She couldn't risk leaving the child, yet she needed her medicine and perhaps some advice from the chemist. The rain was cold and heavy, but she felt she had to chance it. She put the little sailor suit on Adam, wrapped him snug and warm in several blankets, and dressed herself in her warmest cloak. She picked up the still semiconscious child, wrapped a shawl about them both, and started off down the road.

The druggist's was closed. She banged on the door but no one was inside.

"Left early today, missus," the newsseller next door said. "Went to the city with the family. Birthday or something."

Sylvia staggered as a stab of pain cut through her chest.

"Are you all right, missus?"

She waited for the pain to pass. "Yes, I'm fine," she said, trying to think what she should do.

"You and the little one's getting soaked through," the man said. "Step under the overhang for a spell, but it don't look like the rain's letting up any."

He pushed a crate toward her. Sylvia lowered herself, feeling as if a thousand pounds had been lifted off her.

"You shouldn't be trotting about in the rain, especially with a little one."

"I needed the druggist and I couldn't leave the boy alone," she explained.

"No, it don't do no good leaving little ones unattended. Look what happened across the bay just the other night. Snatched right out of his crib, the paper says." He held up a copy of the *Examiner*.

Sylvia stared at the sketch and recognized Adam immediately. Her entire body began to shake as she carefully positioned the shawl over Adam's head, obscuring his face.

"Kidnapped right from his own little bed," the newsseller repeated, holding out the paper to tempt a sale.

Sylvia searched in her pocket and gave him a coin in exchange for the newspaper. She lifted herself, ignoring her pain and trying not to cough. She put the paper under the shawl. "It'll keep the child dry," she said as an excuse, and hurried on home.

The description fit perfectly, even to the birthmark on the child's thigh. This was no simple custody case as Ramsey had explained, she realized. The police were involved and were searching for a kidnapper. She mustn't be found with the boy. She remembered Ramsey telling her of his ene-

349

mies and how he'd once been followed to Sausalito. It was possible that someone saw him the night he came with the child.

A more horrifying thought crossed her mind. Suppose Ramsey had already been identified and had been arrested? He said he would come for the boy but he never did. Perhaps it was because he couldn't.

She had to go to him. She had to find out what was happening.

Chapter 8

Sylvia sat huddled near the wood stove on the ferry, shivering in spite of the thin film of sweat covering her skin. The cold, fresh air and rain seemed to make the boy more aware. His eyes were opened and he asked question after question. Oddly enough, he didn't seem afraid.

"It's a game," Sylvia told him. "Like hide-and-seek. We'll have you home soon now." She kept him amused by the sounds and sights of the ferry boat. He'd never been on a ferry boat before, which to him made it all a new adventure.

He talked about his long trip from China and the beautiful palace he'd lived in, but couldn't be sure if it had all been real or just another of his dreams. When Sylvia occupied his attention by asking questions, Adam found he couldn't remember very much after all.

When they left the ferry, Sylvia stayed in the shadows, leading Adam by the hand. She was relieved not to have to carry him. Her weakness was growing worse and she was glad for the dark comfort of the hansom cab.

She gave the coachman Ramsey's address and

put back her head, answering in monosyllables all of Adam's endless questions. Worried as she had been about his earlier inertia, she now wished he'd stayed asleep.

As they got out of the cab, Sylvia saw the lamps lighted, the curtains drawn closed. She started toward the stone steps and saw a shadow pass across the window. It was a silhouette of a woman, who paused before the second window and removed an elaborate hat.

Sylvia went slowly up the steps, cautioning Adam to keep still, not to make a noise, that they were going to spring a surprise on someone.

"My mother?" he asked as Sylvia tried the door and found it unlocked.

"Hush," she whispered, putting her thin, bony finger against his lips. "Not a sound."

It was unmistakably Ramsey's voice she heard and a woman answering him.

"I don't like it, Ramsey," Lorna said, putting her hat and bag on the table. "Surely you could have made the necessary arrangements by now."

"My contacts aren't in town, love."

Sylvia stiffened. She stepped closer to the door to listen, placing one hand gently across Adam's mouth as a reminder for him to keep still.

"But the police have been asking questions. I told them the Oriental woman was a raving savage and I am certain they believed me. They apologized for troubling Peter and me, but I don't want things to go on too long."

"They won't, believe me, darling."

Sylvia heard the voices move farther away as the pair moved into an adjoining room. She eased open the door and stepped inside, pressing herself into a shadow.

"Come on to bed, Lorna," Ramsey said. "Stop worrying. The boy is fine."

"You say he's with a woman you know. Can you trust her?"

Ramsey laughed. "A smart man never trusts any woman." There was the rustle of clothing. "My God, how I love your breasts, Lorna."

Sylvia bit down on her lip and squeezed shut her eyes. The pain in her chest was worse and she was barely conscious of her hand tightening over Adam's mouth, or of his struggling to breathe.

Ramsey said, "Don't worry about who is taking care of little Adam. I have it all arranged as to how she will be dealt with and you can be sure she'll not make trouble for us."

The bed springs creaked under the weight of their bodies. Sylvia suddenly became aware of Adam's struggling. When she took her hand away he went limp. She almost screamed as he slipped away from her. She caught him before his small body hit the floor. She put her ear to his chest. He was breathing but unconscious.

Her attention was ripped away from the child when she heard Ramsey say, "There is one more condition to our bargain, Lorna."

"Yes?"

There was a long pause and Sylvia could almost hear his mouth on the woman's nipples, her lips, the touch of his hand on her naked flesh. The tears streamed from her eyes. What power held her riveted against the wall she did not know. She couldn't move. She had to hear it all.

"I want you to divorce your husband and marry me."

Sylvia didn't hear the answer. Adam gave a little groan as he regained consciousness. Quickly, Sylvia knelt down and gathered him in her arms, pressing his face against her shoulder, muffling his protests with her shawl.

She ran as fast as she could, her cloak flying behind her like the black wings of some creature in torment. Tears and rain blinded her as she dashed down the street toward the gas lamp at the corner, clutching Adam tightly in her arms, her lungs aching to let loose her agony in a scream.

Leaning against the post she tried to gather her wits about her, but she heard footsteps. It didn't matter to her whose footsteps she heard; every footstep was a danger, she knew.

A hansom came rattling over the cobblestones. She hailed it, but once inside could not think of where she wanted to go.

"Drive around a while. I want the air," she managed, fighting back her hysteria and her wracking cough.

"I fainted," Adam said.

"Hush, child. I'll take you home soon."

He said something she didn't rightly hear and in her distraught state she raised her hand to strike him, shrieking, "Keep still!" Adam cringed to the farthest corner of the seat and sat staring at her. He'd seen his mother when she was angry and knew it was always best not to let her know you were there.

Sylvia could hear Ramsey's voice echoing inside her head. "Marry me. Marry me." If he intended marrying another woman, what did he intend doing about her.

Again his voice came back as she covered her mouth with her shawl to try and quiet her coughing. "I have it all arranged as to how she will be dealt with. She'll not make trouble for us," he'd said.

Somewhere deep inside her head she heard the words: *He means to get rid of you.* Of a sudden she began thinking more rationally. She glanced at Adam. His eyes were wide and staring, shining like a cat's in the dark.

Yes, it was all too clear now, Sylvia decided as she began putting the pieces together. Ramsey would come for the child and give him back to that woman. If he intended marrying her afterward, then the only conclusion Sylvia could reach was that he would have to keep her quiet. And the only way she could think of to accomplish that was to kill her.

All the promises of Hawaii and retiring had been lies. He'd never cared anything for her; she saw that now. What a fool she'd been all these years.

A spasm of coughing reminded her she'd had no other choice but to believe his lies. Where else could she have gone? Who else would have taken care of her?

Her thoughts were running into each other and making no sense. She could go to the police, of course, she reminded herself.

They wouldn't believe her.

The newspaper, she remembered, gave the mother's name. She'd leave him at the doorstep.

She might be seen. Surely the police were keeping a close watch on the house.

Leave him somewhere! Someone will find him.

She was almost tempted to stop the carriage and tell Adam to get out, but he looked so small and frail and so handsome in the little sailor suit she'd made. Despite the hardness that was tightening around her heart she could not bring herself to put the poor tyke out into the downpour to freeze or catch his death of cold before someone found him. Besides, the coachman would remember the heartless woman who'd abandoned her child to the night and to the weather.

The pains began to spread as the cold wet of the night crept over her. She had to get home, get somewhere, anywhere where she could be warm.

She rapped on the trap door. "The Ferry Building," she coughed, thinking of nowhere else to go. The sweat poured out of her. She could think of nothing but the pain, and the need to be in her own bed, warm and safe out of the rain.

It took several seconds before she realized the carriage had stopped and the coachman was speaking to her. Blindly, she paid him his fare. She took Adam by the hand and staggered into the building.

Little Adam was asking questions but she couldn't hear them through the pounding in her head. She gave the gatekeeper a coin and hurried forward, knowing that soon she would be warm again.

Pulling Adam close, not hearing his anxious little voice, she sat near the stove, dazed and barely aware that the ferry was moving, and totally unaware that it was moving in the wrong direction.

She didn't recognize the Oakland Mole at first and when she did, she stifled a scream and tried to get back aboard the ferry.

"Sorry, Madam, it's the last trip for the night," the gatekeeper told her.

Holding tight to Adam, she staggered on, not knowing what to do or where to go. It was providence, she told herself, that kept her away from her home where the police were probably waiting for her.

The police! Fear struck at her with worse force than the pains in her body. Hurrying forward she saw the steam engine belching smoke, the people hurrying toward the string of rail coaches.

Sylvia started for the ticket window, at the same time digging into her drawstring bag. She had her money wadded into a ball with a string around it.

"That train?" she asked the ticket seller. "Where is it going?"

"All the way to New York."

She handed him several large bills. "Will this be enough for me and my child?"

He counted the money. "It'll take you as far as St. Louis."

Sylvia had the sudden presence of mind not to make herself any more conspicuous or suspicious. "Fine," she said, trying to keep her voice natural and hold back her coughing. "That's where I wanted to go. My sister is in St. Louis."

He punched out the tickets and as he handed them to her he cocked his head. "Are you all right?"

"Just a bad cold. I have medicine in my bag."

She clutched Adam's hand again and half-dragged him along toward the waiting train. When she saw the policeman patroling the platform she took Adam up in her arms and covered him with her shawl. "Hush, now, boy," she warned. "We'll be going home soon."

"But . . ."

The policeman was getting nearer. She pushed Adam's face tight against her shoulder and climbed aboard the first car she came to.

There were no seats close to the coal heater in the corner. She had no choice but to content herself with one far down in the center of the car, where an evil draft blew in from under the door and through the cracks in the window frames.

She sat quite still, trying to clear her head and quiet the rasping in her chest. She was careful to keep her face averted from the window and the policeman outside.

When the train finally gave a lurch and started off, she let out her breath and tried to relax. Ten minutes later the conductor took her tickets and as he punched them he saw her pallor.

"Are you feeling all right, Ma'am?" he asked.

"Just very cold," she managed to say, beginning to shiver.

He looked back. "There are no seats near the stove," he said.

"If—if you could just find a warm place for the boy," Sylvia stammered. "I'll manage for myself."

"There's some English swells in a private car," the conductor said. "Rich folks, been slipping me money for little favors ever since they hooked up—might be they'd let the boy come in there for a while. I've heard them talk about kids a lot."

"Please, if you'd ask them," Sylvia said weakly.

When he was gone, she pulled Adam close against her to share their body heat. It seemed to her that he felt cold as ice.

"Where are we going?" Adam asked. He had to ask it several times before the question penetrated Sylvia's fever.

"Going?" she repeated, trying to think. She struggled for an explanation that would satisfy a three-year-old child.

"Your mother is very ill," she said. "She can't take care of you."

"And Mayli?"

"Mayli?"

"My nurse."

"She's gone. There's just you and me."

"Doesn't my mother want me any more?"

"She's very ill," Sylvia said again. "You mustn't get ill too, darling, you must stay strong."

"If my mother doesn't want me any more, where are we going now?"

"To St. Louis," Sylvia managed to say. "Hush, child, that's enough talking for now. Get to sleep."

"I'm hungry."

"Sleep. Then we will have some porridge." She closed her eyes.

Sleep refused to come for her, however, though Adam found it easy enough. No doubt to him it was a big game, like the story he'd told her of crossing the ocean on a big ship.

She longed for the innocence and trust of youth. Still more did she long for sleep and a relief from her terrible pain.

Chapter 9

"By all means, you must bring the young man here," Lady Clarendon told the conductor.

"Do you think that's wise, Millicent?" her husband asked.

"Really, Basil," she said, "you heard him say the boy appeared to be soaked to the skin, and not well. You can't let a little tyke like that die of pneumonia."

Lord Clarendon sighed and told the conductor to bring the boy to their private car. "I suppose you'd better bring the mother with him," he added.

The conductor hesitated, seeing yet another chance to make a few dollars on the side. "I don't know," he said. "I could get into trouble, now that I think of it."

Lord Clarendon took his wallet from his pocket and slipped some bills into the man's hand, a practice he had found made most things move more smoothly here in America.

"You can make up seats for them at the far end of the car there," Lord Clarendon said. "We don't want them too close, in case they've got something catching."

When the conductor had gone, Lord Clarendon noticed that his wife looked unduly excited. It gave him a pang. Immediately he wondered if he had made the right decision after all.

"Are you sure you're all right, dear?" he asked solicitously.

"Yes, of course," she replied. "My nerves are a bit peckish, is all."

"That's quite understandable. You have had a long and a disappointing trip. That Canadian specialist upset you, I know, but have heart, dearest, there are other specialists."

"This last one was reported to be the finest." She let out a deep sigh. "Oh, Basil, I'm so dejected. We've travelled halfway around the world for nothing. I feel we've spent half our lives traveling from one doctor to another, and all for nothing. Perhaps they're right. Perhaps we will never be able to have a child."

"You mustn't talk like that. Someone will be able to help us. I feel it in my bones, someday we'll have a son of our own."

The conductor returned to them, carrying a small boy in his arms, and accompanied by a woman who was barely able to stand. Seeing how ill the woman obviously was, Lord Clarendon forgot his intention of keeping them apart. "Help her to the divan there," he said. "She could use a tot of brandy. There's a bottle over there."

"I'll take the boy," Lady Clarendon said, taking the small figure from the conductor's arms. Her husband felt another twinge of guilt as he saw the way his wife's face lighted up when she held the youngster herself.

Sylvia collapsed into a faint on the divan. With the conductor's help Lord Clarendon tried to force some brandy into her mouth, but she was unable even to swallow.

At length she coughed and struggled to sit up.

"Easy," Lord Clarendon said, trying to keep her still. "Have some of this brandy."

Sylvia's eyes fluttered open. They had the glazed look of one in a delirium.

"The boy?" she asked, looked wildly about her.

"Your son is all right," Lady Clarendon said, rocking little Adam to and fro on her lap.

"You must try to get some rest yourself, or you won't do your son any good," Lord Clarendon said. Sylvia dutifully closed her eyes and at once sank back onto the cushions.

"She's burning up," the Lord told his wife. He looked up at the conductor. "Is there no doctor aboard?"

"I'll see," the conductor said. He paused for a moment, debating with himself whether to try for yet another tip, then decided not to risk seeming too greedy.

He left, and came back a short while later with the report that he was unable to find a doctor. "She'll have to wait till we reach Carson City," he said.

"And when will that be?"

"Not until tomorrow morning, maybe around noontime if the weather doesn't slow us down through the mountains."

Lord Clarendon shook his head. "I'm afraid she'll never make it through the night. My sister died of pneumonia and this poor woman has all the very same symptoms." To his wife he said, "You had better waken your maid, my dear. Tell her to find ice and make cold compresses. It's what I remember they did for Evelyn. Though it proved useless, it seemed to bring her some relief."

The train rumbled on, carrying Sylvia deeper and deeper into a raging delirium. She saw Ramsey and a young, beautiful woman, both naked and locked in each other's arms. She saw herself turn as a heavy hand fell on her shoulder, pulling her away, pushing her toward a dark, cold cell with heavy bars and large gray rats scurrying about the floor. She heard the child screaming as they tore him from her arms and threw him toward a hateful old hag with broken teeth and a switch in her hand.

"No!" Sylvia screamed. "Don't take my son."

"There, there. Lie back, my dear," Lord Clarendon said. He motioned for the maid to replace the cold compress. "Lie back, my dear."

Sylvia stared out through her nightmare. "The boy?" she asked, her words barely audible.

"He's right here on the settee beside you, still fast asleep."

"Dear God, forgive me my sins!"

Basil exchanged glances with his wife. "She's delirious, I'm afraid."

Sylvia clutched the lapels of his dressing gown. "Don't let them take him. Don't let her have the boy. Take care of him. Oh, please take care of my poor boy. He never meant anyone any harm. He's a good lad."

"Please, Madam, you must calm yourself."

Sylvia fell back, the fever wracking her body. "I'm dying," she cried. "God forgive me."

"You aren't dying," Lord Clarendon assured her. "Calm yourself. Your son is safe and well."

"My son," Sylvia said in a fog. "My son. His name is Adam. He has no one but me." She closed her eyes again.

For a long time the nightmares left her in peace. Then of a sudden they were back, more frightening than before. A noose was put about her neck and a black hood was slowly lowered over her head. The last thing she remembered was seeing poor little Adam's thin body being dragged behind a rough wagon driven by the hag with the switch.

"No!" she cried as the tears flowed down her cheeks. "Don't let them take Adam!" She tried to lick her parched lips, but no part of her moved. She felt the cold wetness on her tongue and tried to swallow.

"Ramsey," Sylvia breathed as she opened her eyes. Then her head lolled to one side. Sylvia Ramsey was dead.

As if on cue, Adam opened his eyes and looked around. "Who are you?" he asked Lady Clarendon as she smiled down at him.

Basil got up from beside Sylvia's dead body. "She's gone," he told his wife sadly.

"I'll have her taken out, sir," the conductor said.

"Is she sleeping?" Adam asked, looking at the lifeless form beside him on the settee.

Basil knelt beside him. "Your mother was very ill, my boy."

"I know. She told me."

"I'm afraid she was taken up into heaven."

"You mean I won't see her anymore?" Adam asked in his childish innocence.

"I'm afraid not, child," Lady Clarendon answered, fighting back her tears.

"Will the lady take me to St. Louis like she said."

Lord Clarendon and his Lady exchanged looks. "Is that where you were going?"

"Yes." He looked about. "This is like the palace in China." He saw the tray of fruit on the table. "I'm hungry."

Lord Clarendon lifted Adam out of the buffalo rug in which his wife had wrapped him. "If you're hungry, young man, then you shall eat until your little belly is full to overflowing."

"Can I have pancakes and sugar syrup?"

"You can have whatever you like, my little man."

"You talk funny, like Mr. MacDonald."

"And who is Mr. MacDonald, pray tell?" Basil Clarendon asked. He and his wife moved with the child into the dining alcove.

"He gave big parties when Mother and I were in China."

Lord Clarendon spread jam on a roll and handed it to him. "Here, this will take the edge off until Marie can fix us a good breakfast."

"So you were in China?" Lady Clarendon asked. She tried to ignore the silent movements of the men on the other side of the partition as they carried Sylvia out.

"Oh yes, years and years and years ago when I was very little."

"Your name is Adam, your mother told me."

He gave an exaggerated nod.

"Adam what?"

This time it was an exaggerated shrug.

"If you were in China, then you sailed on a big ship. What did the man call you on the big ship when you came to this country?"

"Wells," Adam said, remembering the game he and his mother had played.

"Adam Wells," Basil repeated.

Millicent laid her hand on his tousled head, an adoring smile curving her lips. He was the most enchanting child she'd ever seen.

Chapter 10

It wasn't until they were nearly at Carson City that Millicent opened the several-days-old San Francisco newspaper she had purchased at the depot. She sat straight up in her chair when she recognized the sketch of Adam and read the brief account of the kidnapping.

She glanced at the boy playing so contentedly in the corner, seemingly unperturbed by the disappearance of the woman he'd been traveling with.

Her husband came back from the lavatory. Millicent shoved the newspaper under the cushion of her seat.

"Almost to Carson City," Basil said, pausing to look at Adam. "I can't help feeling sorry for that poor woman. I suppose she'll end up in one of those unmarked graves."

"I feel sorrier for the boy," Millicent said, "whisked off to some orphanage."

"Millicent," her husband said sternly, "it won't do to get yourself all involved emotionally. No matter how badly we might want a child, he doesn't belong to us."

"Who does he belong to, then?" she asked. "Certainly not to some institution. Look at the poor tyke—you can see that he's starving for love and attention."

"He's already told us his name is Adam Wells," Basil said, "and they were on their way to St. Louis. There're bound to be relatives there who will claim the boy."

"It seems so cold," she said.

"Cold?"

"Yes—handing him over to strangers . . ."

"My dear, they are family. Anyway, we are strangers to him."

"Not any longer. You can see how he's taken to us right off. Besides, we're responsible."

"Just what are you thinking, Millie?" He never used the diminutive of his wife's name except in moments of rare intimacy.

She hesitated, studying her hands. "You know what all of the doctors have told us. We may never have a child of our own, Basil. I thought . . ." She let her voice trail off.

"I see," he said. "And you think we should keep little Adam?"

She stared at the stove for a moment. Somewhere she found the courage to turn and face him. "Yes," she said firmly.

"Well," he said, then hesitated. "I suppose . . ."

"Oh, Basil," Millicent said, kneeling beside him and taking his hands in hers. "It is as if he were sent to us. We could take him to England, give him every possible advantage of position and money, and no one need ever know."

He frowned. "No one need ever know *what*?"

Millicent looked away and got to her feet. "I

368

mean . . ." She searched frantically for some explanation. "I was thinking of his relatives in St. Louis," she said finally. "We need not look them up."

"But of course we must look them up. If the child has relations, then he must be left with his own blood family."

"Suppose there are no relations?" she asked with a sense of urgency.

Basil shrugged. "I really think, my dear, we should face that contingency when it arises—if it arises."

Millicent felt her heart leap. "Then you're saying if we find no relatives in St. Louis, you'll consider adopting the boy?"

"Let's not count our chicks before they're hatched. We're almost certain to find those relatives they were going to."

"I don't think so, dear," Millicent said. She reached beneath the seat cushion for the paper she'd hidden, and handed it to him.

Lord Clarendon's expression grew grim as he read the newspaper account. "Good Lord," he gasped. He glanced up at his wife. "Millicent, dear, have you taken leave of your senses? This child has been kidnapped. How could you think of keeping him?"

"But read the rest of the story," Millicent insisted. "It all sounds so ugly and sordid. The mother blames his grandmother, the grandmother says the mother isn't fit, she's immoral. It says right there the mother abandoned two previous children and a husband to run off with the boy's father, and now the father is dead. Basil, sending the lovely child back to that dreadful commotion

369

would be even worse than sending him to an institution."

"But, Millicent . . ."

"Read the rest of the story, please," Millicent pleaded.

Basil obediently returned to the story. She saw his look turn angry as he read. "Damn barbarians, that's what they sound like," he muttered.

"Don't you see, Basil, I'm not just thinking of myself, I'm thinking of the boy, too. We can't send him back to that."

"We have no right to him," Basil said, "though I agree with you wholeheartedly, it seems a crying shame to do that to such a splendid lad."

"Adam is such a strong, noble name."

"My grandfather's," Basil reminded her.

"So it is. You see, love, it was providence that sent him to us. The child needs us as much as we need him."

For a moment Lord Clarendon beamed with pleasure. He had not seen his wife looking so chipper in years.

Then, abruptly, his face grew sad again. "It's no use, my dear," he said. "We can't just keep the child without all sorts of trouble."

"But who would know?" Millicent said in a lower voice. "The conductor certainly hasn't advertised to the other passengers that the woman has died—all they know is that she and the child went off somewhere. And unless he reports it at Carson City when that unfortunate creature is taken off, no one need know there was even a child on the train with her."

"And what of the conductor himself?"

"He's a very greedy man," Millicent pointed out with a conspiratorial smile.

Basil wrung his hands together in desperation. "I don't know," he said. "It's still a criminal act.

Millicent drew back from him, squared her shoulders, and stood firmly upright, her eyes leveled on her husband's. "It will be no more criminal than what I propose to do with myself."

Basil's eyes widened. "What do you mean?"

"The doctors all agree that a pregnancy will kill me."

"Yes," he said hesitantly.

"Well, I have every intention of trying to become pregnant if Adam is denied me."

"Millicent, you can't be serious."

"I am deadly serious, Basil. It will be either my suicide or a decent chance in life for Adam. It is for you to choose."

"Darling," Basil pleaded. "The doctors may be wrong. We might still be able to have a child of our own."

She shook her head. "For years we've been from doctor to doctor. They all come to the same conclusion. Bearing a child will mean my death. Well, if I am deprived of Adam, then I don't want to live barren and childless. I'm sorry, Basil. I love you very much, but I want a child." She looked out at Adam. "I want THAT child."

Basil visibly crumbled before her eyes when she turned back to him. He sank deep into the chair and hid his face. "You are placing me in a most awkward position, my dear."

She rushed toward him and knelt at his side, putting her head in his lap. "I am placing us both in an awkward position, Basil dearest. Forgive me, I can't help myself. I want to take Adam home to England, away from those horrid Mac-Nairs and Moonsongs and their scandalous lives."

Basil rubbed the tears from his eyes. He sniffed softly, then nodded his head. "Very well, my dear. I'll make the necessary arrangements. You shall have your son."

Now a major motion picture starring
Academy Award-winner
Sissy Spacek

Raggedy Man

by WILLIAM D.
WITTLIFF
& SARA CLARK

Trapped in the backwater eddies
of a small Texas town in the hot summer
of 1943, shadowed by the spectre
of World War II, a young mother and her
two small sons struggle to survive the harsh
realities of hatred…and love. A haunting,
sensitive love story that lingers long
after the last page has been turned.

☐ 41-702-0   RAGGEDY MAN $2.75

Over 1.5 million copies in print!

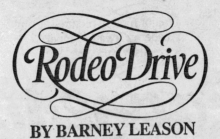

Rodeo Drive

BY BARNEY LEASON

☐ 41-031-X   **416 pages**   **$2.95**

Welcome to the land of silk and money, where the world's most glamorous — and amorous — come to spend their endless nights dancing chic-to-chic under dazzling lights.

Here, against the outrageously decadent background of Beverly Hills — its hopscotch bedrooms and grand estates, posh restaurants and luxurious hotels — is the shocking story of society dame Belle Cooper and her passionate struggle to become a woman of integrity and independent means.

Not since *Scruples* has a novel laid bare the lives — and loves — of people who have everything...and will pay any price for *more*!

Buy them at your local bookstore or use this handy coupon
Clip and mail this page with your order

A Novel Without Scruples

a novel by
Barney Leason

☐ 41-596-6   448 pages $3.50

With consummate insight and shameless candor, Barney Leason, author of *The New York Times* bestseller, *Rodeo Drive*, weaves yet another shocking, sensuous tale of money, power, greed and lust in a glamorous milieu rife with

From the seductive shores of the Isle of Capri to the hopscotch bedrooms of Beverly Hills, London and New York, Leason lays bare the lives and loves of the rich and depraved, their sins and shame, their secrets and